The
Kent Brothers
 Trilogy

NEW YORK TIMES BESTSELLING AUTHOR
JACI BURTON

The Kent Brothers Trilogy

 carina press®

ISBN-13: 978-0-373-42779-6

THE KENT BROTHERS TRILOGY

Printed in U.S.A.

CONTENTS

Dedication

To Charlie. Every day is Christmas because of you. I love you.

ALL SHE WANTS FOR CHRISTMAS

Acknowledgments

To Angela James, a wonderful editor who understands me and knows how to push me to be better. Thanks, Angie!

ONE

"*THIS IS YOUR* home town? This tiny little blip in the middle of nowhere?"

"Yeah, this is it." Riley Jensen tensed as the tour bus pulled down Central Street. In ten years, nothing much had changed. The post office was still there and so was the hardware store, the clothing shop that was probably still owned by busybody Charlene Talmage, and the diner on the corner where her foster mother used to drag her on Saturdays so she could gossip with all her friends. The five and dime still stood in the center of all the chaos.

"And you said people wouldn't come." Riley's publicist stretched her long, lithe body across the leather seats and peered out the darkened privacy glass. "The streets are lined with people." Joann turned to Riley. "See? Your town still loves you."

Riley sniffed. "My town just wants to be on television and they know I come with photographers and a TV crew."

Joann tsked. "So cynical for one so young."

"I'm almost thirty, Jo. I'm hardly young anymore."

Jo swiveled and gave her an eye roll. "You're twenty-eight, not anywhere close to thirty, and you're hardly headed for the rocking chair, so knock it off, put on your biggest smile and get ready to greet your hometown fans. It's show time."

Show time. Hometown. She hadn't been home since she'd bought a bus ticket ten years ago and ran like hell from Deer Lake. And she'd never once looked back, come back or wanted to, until Joann and her agent, Suzie, convinced her—no, forced her—to make this trek in order to film part of the biography special in her hometown.

That they wanted to do it during the Christmas holidays was ridiculous, but whatever. Not that she had any plans anyway.

Why Deer Lake agreed to it considering she hadn't once stepped foot in this place in the ten years she'd been gone wasn't because they loved their long lost home town gal. They should hate her for turning her back on them, for never coming back, for never once giving back to the town that had raised her.

Yet here they were, lined up on the streets as if she were Santa in the annual Christmas parade. And she knew why. All the smiles and waves and banners and screams outside the bus were for one thing and one thing only—exposure for the town that sat on the outskirts of the Ozarks. Deer Lake had its quirky charm and a few interesting attractions. The lake for one thing, which was a hotspot in the summer. Tourism would benefit from the exposure, and so would the town.

Jo held Riley's jacket in front of her. "You ready?"

"Ready as I'll ever be." She slid into the warm suede and took another look at the woman in the mirror. She was so different from the girl she'd been when she'd left ten years ago. Back then she'd been scared out of her mind when she'd bought the one-way ticket to Nashville with nothing but a few clothes in her suitcase, her guitar and the money she'd saved working at both the movie theater and the restaurant.

"They're proud of their hometown girl, Riley. Grammy Awards, ACMs, CMAs. You name it, you've won them all. They know that and they want to celebrate you."

"They know that and they want to capitalize on me."

Jo cocked her head to the side, her dark hair pulled back in a loose ponytail, her lips painted a deep, dark red Riley could have never pulled off. "Girl, you are so mistrustful of your town. Get a grip."

Riley swallowed past the lump in her throat. She was never nervous on stage. She lived for the spotlight. But facing down a few hundred townsfolk—people she'd known since she was a kid—yeah, that got her knees shaking.

At least she could take comfort in the fact there was a less than zero chance Ethan Kent and Amanda Richfield would be out there. She was positive neither of them would want to see her any more than she'd want to see them.

"Let's just get this meet and greet over with, okay?"

She took a step toward the door, but Jo put up her hand. "As soon as all the cameras are in place."

Ugh. She liked doing concerts just fine, loved playing for her fans. But this television stuff was a whole lotta nonsense. And a biography already? Riley thought you had to be old to get a biography. That way you actually *had* a life story to tell.

Apparently not. One of those true story television shows wanted her biography, claimed she had a rich life history and people wanted to know about it. They'd already filmed some concert footage as well as face time with her at her home in Nashville. She thought the whole thing was ridiculous. She was still single, had no kids, hadn't been on drugs or been to prison, didn't hang out at the clubs and party, and spent most of the year on the road. When she wasn't touring she was in the studio writing and recording music.

Which would make for a pretty boring biography, in her opinion.

But the producers and Jo and Suzie thought where she came from was interesting. Sure, her daddy had died when she was a baby and her momma had run off not long after that, leaving her in the custody of foster care, but that wasn't much different than what a lot of kids went through. Didn't make her special. She'd had nice foster parents. No one beat her or abused her. She'd had an okay childhood, and she'd been a damn lucky adult so far, which still in her mind didn't make for interesting television.

Whatever. They knew better about that kind of stuff than she did.

"Cameras are in place, now, Riley. Ready to rock and roll?"

No. "Sure."

The bus doors opened and the sounds of screams and applause rose up, filling the bus. Crowd noise typically made her smile and jazzed her up, because that meant performance time.

But today she'd be giving a different kind of performance. Today she'd have to pretend she was happy to be back home again.

Jo went first and moved out of the way and Riley stepped forward, her heart pounding so fast all she could hear was the buzzing of a thousand bees in her head. She gripped the side rail, dizziness making her feel lightheaded.

If she passed out would she still have to do this? Maybe if she fainted they'd drag her back onto the bus and she could go home. The bio producers would rethink this whole thing. They'd call her a silly diva, not worth their time.

Excellent.

Jo gave her an expectant, move-your-ass-off-the-bus look.

You can do this. These people don't know you anymore. All she had to do was play to the crowd like it was a concert in any city.

She lifted her head, took in a deep breath, and stepped down, becoming Riley Jensen, superstar of country music. She lifted her hand over her head and waved, and the crowd went crazy.

Okay, maybe she could do this as long as she didn't make eye contact with anyone. She looked over the crowd, not at them.

She was invisible. She wasn't really here. She was at home watching reruns of *Bewitched*.

"Riley! Riley! Riley! Can you see me?" Reality intruded and she couldn't help but hear the high-pitched squeals in front of her. She focused her gaze on the little girl in the front row. Wow, there was a tiny explosion of pink. Bundled up in her pink down coat with her pink hat and pink gloves and matching pink boots, her dark pigtails contrasting against the cotton candy color of her coat, the little girl looked like a tiny fan girl maniac. Riley grinned.

She was such a sucker for kids. She nodded at security, who let the little girl come through. Riley squatted down as the kid catapulted herself into her arms.

"Hi, Riley Jensen! I love your music, Riley Jensen! My daddy and me waited all day for you." She pulled back and gave Riley a big, brown-eyed grin. "Gosh you're pretty. I got my nails painted just for today." The little girl pulled off her glove. "Aren't they pretty, Riley Jensen?"

And that's why Riley loved kids. She examined the child's fingers. "Wow, those are awesome. Pink's my favorite color, you know."

"That's what my daddy says. He knows you. Says you two went to school together."

"Is that right?" She scanned the crowd and settled her gaze on a man standing just beyond the little girl, her heart jerking in response.

This—this was why she hadn't wanted to come back.

Or rather *he* was why she hadn't wanted to come back.

He was why she'd run ten years ago. She straightened and

looked into the deep amber eyes of the one man she'd never hoped to see again.

Ethan Kent, the first guy to break her heart. Okay, the only guy to break her heart, and the only guy she'd ever loved.

She felt the tug on her coat and looked down at the little girl, who grinned up at her. "Riley Jensen, that's my daddy."

Oh, hell.

TWO

ETHAN SHOULD REALLY learn to say no to his daughter. If he had, he wouldn't be standing in front of what was essentially the entire town of Deer Lake while facing down the woman who'd left him ten years ago in what had been the biggest scandal of the town. Because Riley had found him in bed with her then best friend, Amanda, who he'd subsequently married, and who had become the mother of the adorable but precocious little minx who'd managed to wriggle her way to the front of the line this morning in order to get the best view of country singing superstar Riley Jensen.

Yeah, hadn't that been a fun time in his life ten years ago? Scandal, drama and tears, and he'd brought it all on himself.

Despite screwing it all up, though, he'd gotten Zoey out of it, and she was definitely the right thing. He'd never regret her.

But facing Riley again? That he hadn't planned on. When she got her record deal and hadn't come home to celebrate it, he figured he'd dodged the big bullet. He'd long ago given up hope of ever seeing her again.

'Til now. And staring at her until she turned tail and ran again probably wasn't gonna happen, so it was time to man up and say something.

"Riley."

She managed a bright smile that he knew was totally for the cameras. "Ethan. So great to see you again. This is your daughter?"

"This is Zoey, yes."

"How…awesome." She looked down and grinned at Zoey, and he was happy she didn't plaster on a fake smile for his daughter, because Zoey had a bullshit meter that was good for about ten miles. "Nice to officially meet you, Zoey."

Zoey slid her hand in Riley's and shook it up and down. "Nice to meet you too, Riley Jensen. I have all your music on my iPod. I'm seven years old. My favorite song is the one you did for the cartoon movie, *The Princess Bee*." She looked around Riley to meet Ethan's gaze. "Daddy, what's the name of that song?"

How about a nice earthquake to swallow him whole? No? Gee, thanks. "The Girl of My Dreams."

"Yeah. That one. Daddy likes that one, too. He sings it around the house all the time, don't you, Daddy?"

It was a damned shame it was December and a tornado couldn't come sweep him away right now. "Sometimes."

"He sings it in the shower. Really loud. I can hear him with the door closed."

Riley arched a curious brow but he was saved by his daughter, who never let a moment go silent.

"Mayor Shims said you're gonna give a concert, Riley Jensen. Are you gonna give a concert?"

"Shims is the mayor now?" Riley's gaze shot to Ethan. His lips lifted at the look of horror on her face.

Stanley Shims had been the worst chemistry teacher at Deer Lake High School, and neither Ethan nor Riley had been particularly fond of him. The feeling had been mutual and their grades had reflected it.

"Yeah. As a matter of fact, he's making his way to you right now."

"Good God." She pivoted just as the mayor arrived. "Mr. Shims! Or should I say, Mayor Shims. Congratulations."

"Well, thank you, Riley. And congratulations to you

on your success. I guess we both reached the pinnacle, didn't we?"

Ethan was certain being mayor of Deer Lake didn't compare to being a Grammy Award-winning musician, but Shims apparently couldn't seem to make the distinction.

The mayor dragged Riley away to officially re-welcome her to Deer Lake and do some pontificating, which Shims did so well. Ethan grasped his daughter's hand and gently tugged her back toward the crowd. Now they could blend back into obscurity, where he'd have been the entire time, if not for the fact Zoey didn't have a shy bone in her entire body.

"Come on, muffin. You got to meet Riley, and she's busy with other people now, so it's time to go to Grandma's. I need to get to work."

"Okay."

They started back toward the crowd but someone caught him by the sleeve of his jacket.

"Excuse me. Are you Ethan Kent?"

He turned around to face a gorgeous redhead with the longest false eyelashes he'd ever seen. She had on skin-tight pants and was wrapped in a thick coat and gloves as if she were expecting this to be North Dakota or something. It might be December in Missouri, but it wasn't that cold.

"Yeah, I'm Ethan Kent."

"And this is your lovely daughter, who obviously made quite the impression on Riley."

Zoey smiled up at her. "You have pretty hair."

"Thanks, honey." She held out her hand to Ethan. "I'm Suzie Mitchell, Riley's agent."

"Nice to meet you."

She handed Ethan a couple tickets. "Backstage passes to the concert tomorrow night."

Zoey's squeal damn near burst Ethan's eardrums. Her eyes

widened as she stared at Suzie like she was her fairy god-mother. "Reallllly?"

"Yes, honey. Really. Riley wanted you to have these."

"Can we go, Daddy? We're going, right?"

Ethan pondered that learning-to-say-no-to-his-daughter thing, then nodded. "Sure."

Which resulted in more ear splitting squealing from Zoey and a wide smile from Riley's agent.

"Wonderful. We'll see you tomorrow."

"Great. Thanks."

Ethan wandered away, wishing he'd never come today. Seeing Riley again had been bad enough. She looked beautiful. She'd always been beautiful, but she'd grown up, lost the roundness of her teen years. Now she sparkled like a woman, curved in all the right places. Her hair waved around her face and shoulders, still that honey-wheat blond. He was surprised she didn't color it since she was famous now. Didn't all women change their hair seemingly every month or so? Hers was still the same color he'd always loved.

Her blue eyes still mesmerized and tongue-tied him. She didn't have on too much makeup like those rock stars and television people wore. She still looked like Riley, she'd just grown into herself more.

And a minute with her had brought back a lifetime of painful memories.

Now they'd have to go to her concert, where he'd have to listen to her sing all the songs she'd written about him.

Live. Where he couldn't turn her off and walk away.

Great. Just freakin' great.

He took the shortcut through the drugstore's back door, knowing Missy and Bob wouldn't mind. They were all busy ogling Riley and nobody locked anything up around here anyway. Zoey's hand in his, he cut through the side streets and walked up the concrete steps of his parents' house.

They had decided not to pay homage to Riley Jensen, mainly because his dad's knee was giving him trouble today and his mom said she had some pies she wanted to bake. Ethan figured the real reason was they thought it would hurt him if they went to see her.

He pushed open the front door. The living room, looking so much like it had when he was a kid, was empty. "Mom? Dad?"

"Back here," his mom called from the kitchen.

Zoey let go of his hand, her gloves and hat flying as she ran down the hallway. Ethan picked them up, shed his coat, hung it up and put Zoey's gloves and hat on the table near the front door. Where they belonged. By the time he made it into the kitchen, Zoey was sitting at the table with a cup of hot chocolate in her hand and a wide grin on her cherry-tinged face.

"And then Riley gave us tickets to her concert, didn't she, Daddy?"

Ethan knew Zoey would give his parents a rapid-fire summary of her meeting with Riley.

"She sure did."

Ethan's mother raised a brow. "Is that right? Well, isn't that nice?"

"It sure is," Zoey said. "And we get to go behind the stage and see her dressing room and hang out there the whole show. Don't we, Daddy?"

"Uh huh."

He got a sympathetic look from his dad on that one.

"Hey, muffin, how about you come down in the basement with me and help me work on Grandma's dryer? You can hand me the tools."

"Okay, Papa." Zoey scooted off the stool and followed Ethan's dad down into the basement, leaving him alone with his mom, who poured herself a cup of coffee and took a seat at the kitchen table.

"Why in the world would you take Zoey to meet Riley?"

He shrugged. "She wanted to go."

"And you obviously haven't learned to say no to that child yet."

"I say no on some things." Like when she wanted to dart out in the middle of the street into oncoming traffic or play with razor blades.

"Spoiling her isn't going to bring her mother back, Ethan. She needs boundaries. She needs to know that you care enough about her to give her limits."

"She's not exactly a brat, Mom. She's a great kid."

"That she is. But giving her everything in the world still isn't going to bring Amanda back from the dead. And speaking of that, does Riley know?"

"About Amanda? No. We barely spoke a word to each other before the mayor dragged her away."

His mother hmphed, then rose and put her cup in the sink so she could resume stirring whatever smelled really good in the pot on the stove. "Not surprising that Shims would want to get his face in front of the camera. Better him than you and Zoey, anyway. Are you going to take her to the concert?"

"I guess. Zoey does love her music."

His mother stirred. And stirred mentally, too. Ethan could tell because she went quiet like she always did when she was thinking.

"What?"

She half turned. "Huh?"

"What are you thinking?"

"I'm wondering what all this means."

"What what means?"

"Riley coming back to town."

His mother always had a point. Ethan just had no idea what it was yet. "She's here to film some stuff about a biography. She'll be gone soon."

"Uh huh. Everything happens for a reason, Ethan."

"Her being here means nothing, Mom." He rose and rinsed his cup. "I gotta get to work. I'll be by to pick up Zoey later."

"Okay. Be careful."

"Always."

He dashed downstairs to say goodbye to Zoey and his dad, then climbed into his truck and drove to his office, the pride puffing up his chest the minute he saw the Kent Construction sign on the brick building. The building housing the office wasn't huge, but it was theirs. The real work was done on the job site. His oldest brother, Wyatt, was already at work studying blueprints.

"Morning," he said to his brother.

"If you say so."

"Rough night?"

He got a grunt in response, but since Wyatt had chosen the extra large cup for his coffee this morning, Ethan assumed he'd been down at Stokey's bar the night before, no doubt continuing his quest to forget he'd ever been married.

From the looks of his brother, that still wasn't going well.

He'd always loved working with his brothers, even though sometimes they were a giant pain in the ass. But they'd rallied around him after Amanda died, just like they'd all rallied around Wyatt after his divorce.

Not that Wyatt wanted any rallying. He just wanted to be left alone and had thrown himself into the business during the day and making a great attempt at partying his ass off at night, which Ethan supposed was a way to shut out the pain. Ethan hadn't had the luxury of that. He had Zoey to deal with. With no kids, Wyatt could handle his pain however he wanted. And he handled it with work, work and more work. And then play, play and more play, which Ethan knew was just a smokescreen.

Wyatt wasn't really having any fun.

Frankly, Ethan thought it might be a good idea if Wyatt actually had a conversation with Cassandra. They'd divorced two years ago and gone their separate ways. She lived on the north side of the lake now and as far as Ethan knew they hadn't spoken a word to each other since the lawyers haggled out the settlement.

Closure was a good thing, or so he'd heard. Ethan had even tried talking to Wyatt about it. Wyatt had told him where to stick that suggestion.

Then again, now that Riley was back in town, Ethan finally realized that whole closure thing? Probably not a good idea after all.

"Where's Brody?" Ethan asked.

"On a job site." Wyatt didn't bother lifting his head from the prints. That would require engaging someone in face-to-face conversation.

"Which one?" Ethan took off his coat and pulled the permits he needed to take to a site today.

"The MacKenzie one. Foreman pitching a fit about a couple of the hands, so Brody went to unruffle some feathers."

"Okay. Tori coming in today?"

"Any minute now."

Ethan had just booted the system up. "I need to look at the books."

"You got a death wish, man? You know how she gets if

someone messes with the system. You want to be on the receiving end of one of her tirades?"

"Good point." Ethan kicked the chair away from the laptop and went for the printout instead. The last thing he wanted was to get on Tori's bad side. She might be no more than twenty or whatever, but she had a head for numbers and a temper that made good on the old Irish and redhead adage. The only one who ever went toe to toe with her was Brody, mainly because he liked to rile her up. Ethan and Wyatt tiptoed around her.

Just as he got the paperwork out Tori walked in, always a tornado in the making, both arms loaded down with bags, popping her gum, her wild red hair spilling down her back.

Tori could have worked for the FBI. She could tell in a half a second when something on her desk had been disturbed. Her green eyes flashed in Ethan's direction.

"You touch my laptop?"

"Do I look like I fear death?"

She snickered. "How about you, Wyatt?"

"Not on your life, sweet pea."

"Where's your idiot brother?"

"Job site."

"Good." She cracked her knuckles and sat down at the desk.

Never a dull moment at the office.

"Heard Riley's back in town," Tori said.

Word spread fast around here. Ethan looked up to see Wyatt's distinct lack of interest as he buried his face in his work.

"Yeah."

"You see her yet?"

"Zoey and I ran into her this morning."

That got his brother's attention. And a frown. "Don't even go there, Ethan."

"I'm not going anywhere with her. Except to her concert."

Wyatt rolled his eyes. Tori grinned and said, "That's interesting."

"Not interesting at all. Zoey's a fan."

"Uh huh."

"Really. That's it. Riley and me are in the past."

Wyatt shook his head and Tori snickered.

It was a good thing he had work to do out of the office today.

It was past ten p.m. when he finally got back from a job site in northern Arkansas, so he called his mom who said Zoey could stay over. She often stayed at his parents anyway, whether she was in school or not. And since she was out for holiday break it worked out well for her to hang out with his mom and dad.

He took the long way home, driving through Center Street, with its quaint old storefronts and the town square, the kind of small town people saw in movies and thought wasn't real.

It was real, and it was home to him. As he left the old town and pulled onto the main highway, he passed one of the hotels and saw Riley's tour bus parked at the new bed and breakfast.

Kent Construction had refurbished the old Victorian for Bill and Macy Grant three years ago. A rambling, beautiful three story, Bill and Macy had retired and bought the house with the intent of going into the hospitality business during their golden years.

Guess that's where Riley and her entourage had decided to stay. Good for Bill and Macy. He hoped Riley was paying them a lot of money. She probably had plenty to spend.

Not that he cared how much money she had, or anything about Riley. He just hoped her visit was short so he could stop thinking about her at all.

THREE

YESTERDAY HAD BEEN brutal. After interviews with the mayor, a few former teachers, and then one-on-one's with the biography host where she asked Riley probing questions about her childhood, teen years and home town, Riley had had enough and needed a break. They'd dragged her all over town so they could get shots of her in front of all the major places in her life from the playground to one of her foster parents' homes to the high school.

Ugh. Nightmarish. Joann had had to kick her once when she rolled her eyes, but really? Maybe no one would be interested enough in her life so far to even watch.

If she was lucky.

She told them no interviews today. She told Joann she needed some free time before the concert tonight, so she made up some flimsy excuse about heading into town to reconnect with her roots, to gain some fresh perspective so she could give some good interviews to the bio team. Joann thought that was an awesome idea.

Ha. Fooled her.

There were no roots to connect with, no people she'd stayed in touch with, and not a single person was interested in seeing her. Correction—they might be interested in hanging with her if there was a camera crew nearby, but no one would want to sit and talk to her.

She had no friends here.

She climbed into old, worn jeans, her boots and a warm coat, and put on a hat because damn it was cold outside.

When she parked one of the rental cars on Central and got out, she peered up at the gray skies. Dismal clouds gathered and hung low, threatening bad weather later and obliterating whatever sun might have warmed the day.

Wind was coming in from the north.

Snow was coming.

When was the last time she got to sit outside and judge the upcoming weather? When she was home in Nashville she was secluded inside from the prying eyes of the paparazzi so she habitually stayed indoors. She might go out back once in a while early in the morning, but mostly when she got a chance to go home she slept, exhausted from being on the road. So she missed a lot of mornings. And when she was done sleeping, she buried herself in her work at the studio.

Despite the bitter cold today, it felt good to be outside, to be breathing actual air, to be able to lift her head and study the shifting clouds and think about coming storms. She remembered hanging out with Ethan and Amanda and her other friends, trying to guess when the first winter snow would hit.

Soon, it looked like. Judging from the cheerful expressions of everyone out on the street, they seemed to be happy about it. Then again, maybe they were always happy. She had no idea. She no longer knew these people. She dragged the cap over her ears and slunk into her coat. She'd braided her hair today and worn no makeup. They'd expect Riley the star, not Riley the schlub.

No one would notice her.

"Morning, Riley. Nice to see you out and about today."

She stopped dead in her tracks and turned, her gaze following the heavyset woman with short black hair who'd just greeted her. Who the hell was that?

"Mornin', Miss Riley. Can I direct you somewhere?"

She pivoted and faced a tall, lanky man in his forties or early fifties. He looked familiar. Who was he? She tried to place him.

He had a friendly smile. "You probably don't remember me. I'm Trevor Troutman. My wife, Karen, and I lived next door to the Landaus, one of your sets of foster parents."

That's how she knew him. "Oh, right. Nice to see you again, Mr. Troutman."

"You lookin' for some place in particular?"

"No, sir. Just out for a walk."

"Good for you. Maybe gonna snow today, so enjoy the nice weather while we have it."

"Yes, sir. I'll do that."

"My Karen, she likes your music an awful lot. So do I, as a matter of fact. We'll be coming to your concert this evening." He looked up at the sky. "Weather permitting, of course."

If she was lucky there'd be a blizzard and she could hide at the bed and breakfast tonight. "Of course. Thank you. I'll see you tonight."

So much for trying to hide out unnoticed. She should have known better. Trevor moved on, so Riley did, too.

Other than a new coat of paint or maybe a different awning, there hadn't been too many changes on Central. It was exactly the same as it had been when she'd left. She browsed the store windows, checking out the fashion that had changed at the clothing stores. Thank God for that. At least they kept up with some trends. She smiled at the red and white striped awning of Clusters Candy Store.

Wow. It had been years since she'd thought about Clusters.

Unable to resist going inside, she hoped to see the smiling face of Paul Hazelton working the counter, his thick mane of white hair perfectly coiffed under the red and white hat he always wore.

Instead, a texting-on-her-phone, gum-popping teenager didn't even notice Riley had come in, despite the bell ringing over the door.

Huh. Riley stepped up to the counter, her sweet tooth sparking to life at the colorful candies and chocolates beneath the glass counter.

Gum popping continued. Buttons were being pushed, both behind and in front of the counter. Deciding what she wanted, Riley looked up at the girl, who had a pile of strawberryish purplish hair pulled up in a twist on top of her head. No cute red and white hat.

Riley continued to wait, hoping she'd be noticed. She wasn't.

Finally, she cleared her throat and the girl sighed as if Riley was the worst inconvenience ever. "Can I help you?"

Good God. Riley could see the color of the girl's gum. She wanted to tell her to close her mouth.

When had Riley gotten old?

"Where's Mr. Hazelton?"

"Who?"

"Paul Hazelton."

"Oh. The old guy?"

Riley supposed bopping the girl in the nose would be uncalled for. "Yes. The man who owns the store."

"He died two years ago. His wife sold the store to Ray Morrow, who happens to be my dad," she said in a snooty, I'm-the-owner's-daughter tone of voice.

"Paul Hazelton is dead?" Riley's stomach pitched. "Oh, poor Pattie. What's she doing now?"

The girl gave a shrug. "Last I heard she's in Florida with one of her kids. So do you want some candy?"

Riley forced back tears. Mr. Hazelton had always had a smile for her when she came into the store. He told jokes.

Bad, corny jokes, but he'd always made her laugh. The candy store had been one of her best memories of this town, and now this smartass teenager didn't give a damn about whether kids were happy when they left the store or not.

"So do you want candy or not?"

She sniffled and nodded, gave the girl her order and walked out, swiping tears out of her eyes as she made an abrupt turn and smacked right into an unmoving brick wall chest, dropping her bag of candy.

Dammit.

She squatted to the ground to pick up the scattered candy.

"You always were a sucker for gum drops and licorice."

Her gaze shot up and there was Ethan, warm eyes considering her. Wasn't this just perfect?

She lifted her gaze to his. "Paul Hazelton died, some snotty teenager who doesn't give a damn works in there now, and I dropped my candy."

Tears filled her eyes. She wasn't weak, she didn't cry. She scrambled to pick up the pieces, both literally and figuratively.

"Let me help."

She shooed his hands away. "I've got it. I'm just clumsy."

He was smiling at her, his sexy, sensual smile that had always made her feel all gooey inside. The smile that probably made Amanda feel all gooey inside now.

If he was even still with Amanda. She had no idea who Zoey's mother was. His little girl looked just like him. Dark hair, whiskey-colored eyes, a dimple on the left side of the cheek. She'd noticed Zoey's dimple, too. It was so cute.

"Riley?"

"No, I'm fine. Sorry. I was distracted."

"I'll go inside and replace your candy."

"Don't. I don't need it anyway."

He laughed at that and was already up and in the shop before she could object. She followed him inside.

"You back for more already?" the girl asked.

"She's a candy fiend," Ethan said. "Always was."

"Har har."

"Actually, she dropped her bag outside, Tiff, so replace whatever it was she had, and add two bricks of rocky road and a quarter pound of Now and Laters for me."

Despite not wanting to be in here—again—she couldn't help but smile at Ethan's selection. "I see your candy choices haven't changed, either."

"I need the energy for work."

"Yeah? What work is that?"

"Wyatt, Brody and I own the construction company now that Dad is retired."

"That must keep you busy."

"Very."

She took the bag from gum-chewing girl. Ethan paid. "I can pay for my own candy."

He slanted her a look. "And I can afford a couple bucks for it."

They walked outside. "Thank you."

"You're welcome."

Ethan started walking, so Riley went with him. "So... you working in town today?"

"Yeah, over there." He pointed across town where a steel frame could be seen. "New performing arts center. Gotta have culture here. If you'd waited a year you could be putting on your concert there."

"Oh. I guess I'll have to suck it up at the high school gym."

He reached into the bag and pulled out a handful of candy. "I imagine that's one hell of a step down for you."

No way was she taking the bait. Time to turn the tables.

"Where's Zoey today?"

"At my parents."

"Not home with her mother?"

"No."

Maybe Zoey's mother worked. And wasn't Ethan being evasive? She'd bet she knew why. Might as well find out and get it over with. "So…did you end up marrying Amanda?"

He stilled and Riley bit her cheek, wishing she'd kept her mouth shut. Why couldn't she have talked about the weather or something?

"Yeah, about that."

"Hey, none of my business. Sorry."

"I did marry Amanda. In answer to your next question, yes, she's Zoey's mother."

"Okay. Look, Ethan, I'm sorry. I shouldn't have—"

"Amanda died four years ago."

The sidewalk spun out from under her. She stopped, turned and stared at him. "What?"

Ethan dragged his fingers through his hair. "Shit. Not the way I wanted to tell you this. I should have told you sooner, but didn't want to in front of Zoey. It's not something you blurt out when you first see someone after ten years."

She hadn't heard anything he'd said, his earlier words still spinning around in her head. "She died?"

"Yes."

Riley knew she was staring, but she had no idea what to say. Shock left her speechless. She'd had so many things she'd wanted to say to Ethan and Amanda, so many of them self-righteous, so many of them scathing and damning. She'd even had a speech all planned out, full of indignation and finger pointing, everything she'd wanted to say ten years ago and couldn't because she'd run. And all her anger and hurt had just disappeared into the ether. Her chest tightened. She reached up and rubbed the aching spot on her breastbone.

Had everyone she cared about died while she was gone? It suddenly seemed that way. Tears sprang fresh again and she finally made eye contact with Ethan and saw the pain in his eyes. "Oh God. Oh, Ethan, I'm sorry. I didn't know."

There was kindness in his face, sympathy for her she knew she didn't deserve.

"I know you didn't."

She had no idea what to say, could only gawk at him as she stood rooted to the spot, frozen in time as she was propelled back ten years ago, before she found Ethan in bed with her best friend. Back when Amanda and she were tight, were best buds. When they used to laugh with each other, share all their secrets. They'd been inseparable then, had vowed to never be apart.

They were supposed to be best friends forever.

And then one night had shattered all that and she'd never spoken to Amanda again.

Now she'd never be able to.

"Riley?"

Pulling herself from the past, she looked around at the crowds, at the people who slowed down to stare, and finally dragged her gaze to Ethan.

What must he think of her? He was the one who'd lost everything. He'd lost his wife, the woman he'd obviously loved. Zoey had lost her mother.

"What happened? You don't want to talk about this, do you? It's none of my business. I'm sorry. I should move on instead of asking questions you don't want to answer."

Ethan knew the time would come when he'd have to tell Riley about Amanda. He just hadn't figured it would be right now. Then again, would there ever be a right time?

Judging from her shocked and pale face, probably not.

"Come on." He took her arm and led her through the library and out the back door, waving at Barb, the head librarian, as they hurried past. On the other side of the street was the construction trailer. He opened the door for her and she stepped inside.

Fortunately, they were alone.

"Have a seat. Want something to drink?"

"No, thanks. Really, you don't have to—"

"It was leukemia, and it was bad. She didn't make it a year after the diagnosis. We tried everything. Chemo, radiation, alternative treatments, but it was aggressive. There was nothing we could do."

Riley stared up at him. "That's too young. She was, what? Twenty-four or so?"

"Yeah."

"I'm…not in touch with people here. I didn't know."

He shrugged and leaned against the desk. "No reason for you to know."

She inhaled and shuddered out a sigh. "So many people I knew. My whole life was here and I just walked away from it. From everyone." She lifted her gaze to his. "It's not like I didn't care. I did."

"I know." And he did. He understood why. He was the reason. He and Amanda.

"I never hated you. I never hated her."

He gave her a faint smile. "Yes you did."

Her eyes filled with tears. She let them slide down her cheeks. He hated being the cause of her pain again.

"Dammit, Ethan. She's dead. I never wanted that. I was angry and hurt, but I never wished harm to Amanda."

He pushed off the desk and came to her, kneeled in front of her. "Don't cry. I know you didn't. Amanda dying isn't on you. It was a circumstance."

She sniffed, shoved the heel of one hand under her chin. "I'm just so sorry for you and for Zoey. It's a horrible thing."

"Zoey's resilient. She misses her mom, but she has me, her uncles, and my parents."

"What about Amanda's parents?"

Ethan shook his head. "They took her death hard. Really hard. They withdrew and couldn't cope, not even with Zoey."

Her eyes widened. "Good God. How could they miss connecting with Zoey?"

Ethan stood, shrugged. "Don't ask me. I tried to reach out to them, but they wanted no part of me or Zoey after Amanda died. They left town a year later, said they couldn't handle the memories."

Riley shook her head. "That makes no sense, Ethan. Zoey was their connection to her."

"Don't ask me to explain them. I can't."

"I'm sorry for them, but not surprised. They were always so wrapped up in Amanda. She *was* their life."

"Losing her broke them. They were so angry, bitter, blamed me for it."

"How could they blame you for a disease? You didn't give her leukemia."

"I shouldered it because they needed to blame someone for the senseless loss of their little girl. How else do you explain why a twenty-four-year-old healthy woman dies?"

Riley bent her head to her chest for a few minutes and Ethan let her grieve. When she lifted her head, she wiped her eyes and straightened her shoulders. But the pain in her eyes—that shredded him. It brought back the loss as if it had just happened yesterday.

If she hadn't left, she would have been here when Amanda died.

That was on him. He had to bear some of the responsibility for that.

"It's good that you've been there for Zoey. She needs you."

He relaxed, thought about Zoey. "She's everything to me. I've made a lot of mistakes in my life. She's the only thing I've ever done right."

Riley wanted to ask him what his mistakes were, but she saw the raw hurt in his eyes, and the pride when he talked about his daughter. She wouldn't push any further, not after what he'd told her about Amanda.

Amanda had been her best friend once. There'd been a lot of water under the bridge since she'd left, a lot of betrayal and hurt, but for a very long time Amanda had been the closest thing to a sister Riley would ever have.

If she'd stayed in touch with the town, with Amanda, if she'd learned forgiveness sooner, she'd have known. She could have been here for her best friend during the last year of her life.

"I'm sorry I wasn't here for her."

"You didn't need to be, but if it's any comfort to you, Amanda felt awful about what happened. She said if I ever saw you again I was supposed to tell you that."

Riley's eyes widened. "I don't want to hear that."

Ethan frowned. "Why not?"

"Because now I can't tell her that I'm sorry, too. I said some terrible things to her before I left. I hurt her."

She'd hurt them both, but she couldn't make it right with Amanda now. She'd called Amanda a slut and Ethan a cheating bastard, and then left them both in the dust and never looked back.

Ethan hooked his thumbs in his jeans, the action so familiar to her it caused an ache in her throat.

"From what I remember she did the same to you."

"And now you tell me she said she was sorry. I'll never get the chance to tell her."

"You did."

"What?"

"You did already. In your music. She listened to every song. She knew, Riley. She heard your apology."

"You know my music. What Zoey said yesterday…"

"Yeah, I listen. I heard it all."

The condemnation, the hurt, the raw agony of those first years. She'd always written her own music. Her first album had been her catharsis, pouring her heart out over losing Ethan to Amanda. It had been the grief of young love lost, about betrayal and anger. She'd sung about what it was like to open your eyes to what was around you so you'd never feel stupid again. The album had gone triple platinum, and she felt like she'd grown up and walked away from all of this, determined to never look back.

But she had looked back, because later on she had written about forgiveness, about becoming wise and learning from your mistakes. She had written about people doing what they thought was right, and everything not revolving around you and what you wanted, and she'd sung about letting go. After time and distance her anger had dissipated, and she had said she was sorry in her music, because she had bared her soul in her lyrics, and so much of her hurt had been directed at Ethan and Amanda. She'd made sure the whole world knew it.

She'd gotten famous off her pain, but she'd finally realized that she had caused other people pain, too. Maybe no one else knew who she'd been writing about, but Deer Lake had known.

"I'm sorry, Ethan. For the lyrics, for the hurt I must have caused you and Amanda."

"Why are you sorry? You didn't do anything wrong. I did. Amanda did. I said it that night all those years ago, and I don't think I'll ever be able to say it enough. But you? You don't ever have to be sorry, Riley. You did what you knew how to do. You made music and you wrote your heart out. Don't apologize for that."

She shuddered out a sigh. They'd needed to have this talk, but there was so much more she wanted to say, and so many things that should probably be left unsaid. For so many years she'd wanted to undo the past.

But the past was etched in stone and there was no going back and changing it now.

Yet no matter how many years went by, she'd always want to know why.

Why he'd told her he loved her, then chose Amanda over her.

She doubted she'd ever have the nerve to ask the question. The answer didn't matter anymore anyway.

"I should let you get back to work." She stood, grabbed her coat and put it on. She reached for the door handle, then turned. "You and Zoey coming to the concert tonight?"

He gave her a puzzled look. "Yeah. You had your agent gives us backstage passes, remember?"

Damn that Suzie. "Oh. Right. Of course. Won't that be great? See you then."

As she headed back toward her car, she felt empty inside.

And everything hurt more now than it ever had before.

FOUR

ZOEY WAS ON a high no sugar could match. Backstage in the gym, the sounds and lights and traffic of people buzzed past them as Riley's concert team readied the stage, transforming the gym into something unrecognizable with lights and speakers and screens befitting Riley's status. Zoey bounced up and down on her light-up tennis shoes, unable to stand still as the roadies prepped for the event and Ethan tried to keep his daughter from climbing right out of her hair.

The concert wasn't going to start until nine o'clock, which was his daughter's bedtime. She hadn't napped today, either, despite his mother's attempt to get her to rest.

His kid was going to be toast by the time the concert was over. Or she'd be on excitement overload and up all night.

Ethan prayed for toast.

"Is it time yet, Daddy? Have you seen Riley Jensen yet? I haven't seen her. Can we go to her dressing room now?"

Zoey tugged on his hand for the millionth time. "I'm sure Riley's busy getting ready for her concert. How about we just try to stay out of the way and be patient."

Patient. A word not in a seven-year-old's vocabulary.

"But why can't we go see her? I bet she won't mind. She likes me."

"How about we wait until after the concert when she isn't so busy?"

"But, Daddy, I want to see her nowwwww."

Whining. Sure sign of a tired kid. Ethan kneeled down and looked his beautiful daughter in the eyes. "Zoey, we're not going to Riley's dressing room. The concert people were nice enough to give us backstage passes, which means you need to be on your best behavior. I know you're excited, but you still have to be good. And that means doing what I tell you to do, okay?"

Her bottom lip trembled. Man, was this kid good or what? He should get her an agent. He was usually a sucker for the quivering lip, but not tonight. He didn't want to be here. He'd already seen way more of Riley than he'd intended to during her visit, so his daughter was just going to have to suck it up.

As soon as Zoey saw that her drama routine wasn't working, she lifted her shoulders practically to her earlobes, then dropped them, accompanied by a loud, dramatic sigh. "Okay, Daddy. I'll be good."

And now he had guilt. Of course, when *didn't* he have guilt?

Fortunately, Riley came out of her dressing room, zeroed in on Zoey and Zoey sure zeroed in on Riley.

"Riley Jensen! I've been waiting alllll night for you!"

Riley grinned and scooped Zoey up in her arms. "You have? Why didn't you come to my dressing room?"

Zoey shot Ethan a scathing look. "Daddy said we couldn't."

Riley put her down and Zoey slipped her hand in Riley's.

"Oh. Well you could have come in. I just relax a little before I go on."

"Believe me, if Zoey would have been in there with you, there would have been no relaxing."

She laughed. "It's no big deal." She looked down at Riley. "From now on you're welcome to be wherever I am."

"See, Daddy? I told you she liked me."

"You'll be sorry you said that. You won't even be able to go to the bathroom alone."

Riley arched a brow. "She's a kid, Ethan."

"She's seven. And demanding. Trust me on this."

Riley looked down at Zoey. "You ready for the concert?"

"Yup."

Suzie came over. "I have a spot all picked out for you two side stage with a great view. Why don't you come with me so Riley can get set up?"

Ethan took Zoey's hand. "Let's go, Zoey."

"See you two later," Riley said, and moved off, a few people following after her.

Suzie set them in a chair at the side curtain where they had a perfect view of the stage. Ethan hoisted Zoey in his lap and waited while Riley set up with her band.

She looked beautiful in tight jeans and cowboy boots, a flowing turquoise top, her hair spilling in soft waves over her shoulders and long earrings that sparkled in the light. She wore bangles on both wrists that shimmered in the overhead lights, too. She looked magical. She looked like a star. Hell, she *was* a star.

The announcer came out and the packed-to-capacity crowd went crazy. Ethan had never seen so many people in the high school gym. Once word had gotten out that Riley had come home, people from the surrounding cities came in droves. The gym was at capacity, given that it was a free concert. Ethan heard Riley's crew had set up a big screen and speakers outside for the overflow of people who couldn't get inside, especially since the fire marshal was keeping a close count on the number of people in the gym.

After the announcer left, the crowd started clapping, their raucous cries and stomping feet commanding her to come out, demanding the curtains to part. But when the lights went out and the stage went black, a hush fell over the crowd.

The curtains opened to a darkened stage and the spotlight fell on Riley sitting on a stool with her guitar.

Riley began to play, the song so familiar Ethan could hum it in his sleep. One of the songs from her first album, a song of loss and pain so deep it brought a stab of pain to him as she sang the words that had torn him apart the first time he'd heard them.

"Turns out forever meant different things to us after all.
Loving you was gonna hurt me after all
After it all, after it all, all the tears and all the pain
I still loved you, after all."

Her voice struck him deep in his heart. When she was younger, he'd loved to listen to her whenever she picked up her guitar. But then it had just been her and her guitar in his basement or in his room or his parents' living room or wherever they were gathered with their friends. And later, when he'd bought her CD, he'd been struck by the sheer magic of how incredible she sounded.

But the maturity of her voice and listening to her live was so much better than what he remembered from ten years ago, and light years from plugging in his iPod. This was the voice of an angel, and she sang only to him, about him, and even when she damned him for the sins he'd committed it was pure heaven.

Even Zoey was enraptured, her blue eyes wide, her normally chirpy voice silent as she leaned against his chest and stared at Riley as she went through the strains of song after song. Whether fast and upbeat and singing about cutting loose and dancing, or the slow and haunting strains as she sang of love gone wrong, she wrapped her music around Ethan and his daughter, further reminding him of what he'd given up all those years ago.

Every note further sealed for him that he'd made the right

choice in letting her go, in not trying harder to find her after she'd left. This is what Riley had been meant to do, and if he'd had to fall into Amanda's trap and lose Riley for this to happen for her, then it had been all worth it.

The concert lasted an hour and a half, and when she ended on the soft melody of a country lullaby, his baby girl fell asleep in his arms. Not even the thunderous standing ovation the crowd gave Riley could wake Zoey. He sat there while Riley did an encore, not wanting to miss a moment of the last song she sang. When she came off the stage, she stopped, paused and stared, and tears sparkled in her eyes as she stared down at Zoey.

"I don't think I've ever seen anything more beautiful," she said, her gaze meeting his.

He was about to say the same thing to her about her music.

"Do you need to go home?"

"Probably."

"Okay."

He sensed her hesitation, that she wanted to talk. What he really wanted to do was get the hell out of here. His head and his heart were filled with her and her music and the memories of the two of them. Big mistake to linger. He needed to shake the dust off the past and get his mind firmly in the present, where Riley didn't exist.

"Stay. Please."

Damn. "Okay. I just need to lay Zoey down."

She nodded. "Bring her on back to my dressing room."

Ethan lifted Zoey, followed Riley and laid her down on the sofa in the makeshift dressing room they'd set up for her in the high school drama department's changing room. He covered Zoey with his jacket and took the bottle of water one of Riley's staffers offered him, then sat on the arm of the sofa while Riley shooed everyone who wanted to crowd in out of the room. She shut the door behind her and turned to him.

"That was a beautiful performance tonight."

She grinned. "You think so? Thanks."

"I always loved your singing. Your voice is amazing."

Her lashes tilted closed as she turned away. He couldn't believe she was unaccustomed to praise. She probably got it all the time.

"I'm glad you came tonight."

"Me, too. Zoey loved it, too. She fell asleep on the last song."

Riley pulled up a chair next to the sofa. "Late night for her."

"Long day for her. She was excited about this. I can't tell you how much I appreciate the invitation."

She crooked a smile. "For Zoey, of course."

"For both of us. I enjoyed the concert, too."

It hovered on the tip of her tongue, the *why not me* question she wanted to ask. But Zoey lay sleeping like an angel on the sofa a foot away from Ethan. Now wasn't the time.

It would never be the right time to ask a question for which there wasn't ever going to be a good enough answer.

Because he'd preferred Amanda, and she'd never seen it coming. She'd spent years going over it in her head—all the times the three of them had been together. Why hadn't she seen it?

Enough. She wasn't eighteen years old anymore. Amanda was dead, and there was no point in rehashing old hurts.

But the question still burned inside of her, desperate to be asked.

She hoped she could get out of this town and soon before the question spilled out.

"Great crowd tonight," he finally said, no doubt to fill the silence in the room.

"Yeah, it was. Who knew everyone would come?"

He tilted his head to the side. "Riley, everyone here is proud of you."

"I didn't think anyone here liked me anymore. I hadn't been back since I left."

"People don't hold grudges like that. You know how this town is."

"I guess I forgot how forgiving folks could be." She'd forgotten a lot of things. Like how to *be* forgiving.

She lifted her gaze to Ethan, remembered the past, only this time the good parts instead of the bad.

He looked good tonight in his dark jeans and long-sleeved dark blue button-down shirt, his muscles filling out every square inch. He used to be on the skinny side, but strong. Judging from the way he fit the shirt, she could only imagine the muscles now.

He studied her and she wondered what he saw.

Country diva who couldn't be bothered to come home once she'd left.

Ex-girlfriend who'd run and never returned.

Bad friend who hadn't been here when her best friend had needed her most.

What else must he think of her?

Then again, she hadn't created this mess alone, had she? She hadn't been the one to climb into bed with Amanda and ruin what she and Ethan had.

And again, the question burned on the tip of her tongue, begging to be asked.

Why?

Ethan shifted, dragging the smoke of the past away and reminding her that she was a lousy hostess.

"Yeah, well, I should get Zoey home and into bed."

Great job, Riley. "Sure."

He put on his coat and turned to her. "Thank you again for the backstage passes."

She wanted to tell him she hadn't even known about the passes, that it had been Suzie's doing. But what point would that serve, other than self protection?

"You're welcome. Glad you came."

"How much longer are you staying in town?"

She cocked a brow. "Anxious to get rid of me?"

His lips lifted. "No. No, that wasn't it at all. I was just wondering if there was someplace you needed to be, with the holidays and all."

She shoved her hands in the pockets of her jeans. "No. I have to hang out here with a few of my people until this… thing is over with."

"Thing?"

"Biography thing."

"Oh. Yeah, right."

She shrugged. "Not my idea. Honest. I'm a little young for a bio."

"The television people seem to think otherwise."

He was delaying leaving. She wondered why. "They said I've lived a lifetime in twenty-eight years, or some nonsense to that effect."

"Haven't you? You've gone through a lot to get where you are now."

Was it her imagination, or was he drawing closer?

"Not really. I just got lucky."

She found herself focusing on his lips, which was such a bad idea, because it got her thinking of how great a kisser he was, and how long it had been since she'd kissed him. And then she licked her lips, and his gaze traveled to her mouth and settled there.

"Luck had nothing to do with your success. Pure talent."

She really wished he'd look somewhere other than her mouth, because now her throat went dry, and she had to swallow. And lick her lips again. She suddenly wanted to kiss him more than she wanted to breathe.

He took a step closer and reached for her.

"Daddy, I have to go potty."

Riley took two steps back and so did Ethan, both of them turning to focus on a very sleepy-eyed Zoey, who sat up and rubbed her eyes.

"Sure, muffin."

"Where are we, Daddy?"

"In Riley's dressing room."

Zoey blinked, yawned and grinned at Riley. "Hi, Riley Jensen. You sing good."

Riley laughed. "Thanks, sweetie."

He took Zoey's hand and she slid off the sofa.

"We'd better go find a bathroom, and then head home. I'll see you later."

"Okay. Bye, Zoey."

Zoey waved. "Bye, Riley Jensen."

Only after Ethan closed the door to the dressing room did Riley sink onto the sofa and exhale.

Ethan had almost kissed her. Even worse, Riley had really wanted him to.

She had to get the hell out of this town, and fast.

FIVE

"HAVE YOU SEEN the contract for the Lincoln project?" Tori asked him the next day.

"No."

"It's your project, Ethan. You were out yesterday having the contract signed."

"I don't know where it is. Maybe my truck." He kept his focus on the blueprint he was studying, trying to tune out anything else but work.

"Well, do you think you could go get it so I could enter it into the system?"

"Later. I'm busy."

He heard an audible sigh.

"Ethan, only Wyatt has the market cornered on brooding asshole."

"Hey. I *am* here," Wyatt grumbled from the corner of the office.

"So?" Tori replied. "It's not like your attitude is a big secret. And Brody is a close second in the annoying-me-until-I-want-to-scream department."

"I do my best," Brody said, having made an appearance this morning.

"Shut up, Brody." She turned her attention back to Ethan. "Ethan, you're supposed to be the nice guy of the three brothers. If you turn cranky or irritating like these two, I might just have to start cracking some heads around here."

He lifted his head and stared across the office at Tori. She tapped her pencil against the corner of her desk and gave him one of her trademark don't-screw-with-me looks.

"You wouldn't like her when she's angry," Brody teased.

"Shut. Up. Brody." Tori's jaw was clenched. It was clear she was reaching the boiling point.

"Sorry. Have a lot on my mind." Ethan fished his keys out of his pocket and tossed them to her. "I'm pretty sure the contract is laying in the seat."

She caught the keys and stood. "Thanks. And what made you so bitchy today?"

"Nothing. I don't know. Not much sleep last night."

"Oh, a date?" She stopped at his desk and leaned against it, obviously eager for some good gossip.

Too bad he had none for her. "No."

The place went silent. Good. Until he felt eyes on him. He lifted his gaze and Tori was still there, leaning over his desk to give him her X-ray vision, as if she could see into his brain.

"What?"

"You know that's not good enough."

"And you're not my mother."

"And you know I'm going to continue to stare at you until you tell me where you were last night."

Jesus, she was like a dog with a bone. "Why?"

"Because it obviously has something to do with your less-than-stellar mood today."

"No, it doesn't."

"Then you should have no problem telling us where you were last night."

Shit.

"She's got you now, Ethan," Brody said, propping his feet up on his desk and no doubt grateful he wasn't the one under Tori's microscope this morning.

It was clear she wasn't going to give up. "I went to Riley's concert."

Tori made a face and stood. "Glutton for punishment, aren't you?"

"Huh?"

But Tori was already out the door.

Brody stood and came over to his desk, leaned against it and folded his arms. "What the hell possessed you to go to Riley's concert?"

Ethan was already nose down in blueprints again. "Zoey likes her."

"Uh huh. And you sat in the back row and sucked it up?"

"No. We had backstage passes."

"Oh. Extra-strength pain and humiliation."

"It wasn't bad. It's been ten years. She doesn't hold a grudge."

Wyatt snorted. "Bullshit. All women hold a grudge."

"Yeah, and you don't?" His brother held a deep grudge against his ex-wife, and it was affecting everything about his life.

Wyatt shrugged and took up his pencil again, effectively tuning them out.

Brody, unfortunately, didn't. "Seriously, man, what's up with you seeing Riley?"

"I'm not 'seeing' Riley. I took Zoey to her concert. Then I came home. Now I'm at work. Trying to work." He motioned his head toward the blueprints.

"But you can't deny there's some serious history between you two. And unfinished business."

"Brody's right." Tori came back in and shut the door to the office, laying the folder she'd retrieved on her desk. "You should settle it or you'll end up a grumpy old man like Wyatt."

"Again, I'm *in* the room," Wyatt grumbled.

"Oh, like you care what we say about you, Wyatt," Tori said as she took her seat and opened the folder. "You ignore us all anyway like you've been doing for the past two years. Go back to brooding. I'll pick on you another day."

Wyatt had no comment.

Maybe Ethan needed to try the silent approach in the future, because arguing with them was getting him nowhere. There was no business to finish with Riley.

"So they want to interview Ethan."

Riley's head shot up from the page where she'd been jotting down notes for a song and gaped at Joann.

"No. Absolutely not."

"He's part of your past, Riley. A big part. You've written like twenty-five songs about him."

"And no one knows that but you and Suzie and the band, and you're all sworn to secrecy. You promised."

How had they found out about Ethan?

"The producers don't know about the connection between Ethan and the songs. They just know he was your teenage boyfriend, which makes him a part of your past, a part they feel should be explored."

"No. We talked about this. No Ethan." She'd made it clear Amanda wouldn't be interviewed, either, but of course that would never happen now. "I don't want him or Zoey involved in this."

Jo took a seat in the living room across from the roaring fire. The temperature had dropped and the skies were an ugly gray outside. Riley snuggled up in her sweats, Henley shirt and thick socks in front of the fire, intent on sipping hot cocoa and working on the song she'd started on the bus ride here. She'd spent part of the day lost in her music, happy to be alone and away from the production of the biography.

When she wrote she could shut out everything, including what had almost happened between her and Ethan last night.

Except her songwriting had drifted into thoughts of first love and first kisses, and that's not at all where she'd intended to go.

Instead, her idyllic moments of peace had been shattered by this. No way was she going to allow it.

"The thing is, Rye, Ethan has agreed to it."

She laid her guitar to the side, letting it rest against the chair. "What?"

"They called him this afternoon and he agreed to the interview tomorrow as long as they promised to keep his daughter out of it, not mention her and make sure she stays off camera."

"Oh, no. That's not going to work at all." She stood. "He absolutely cannot do the interview."

Jo nodded. "I'll get a staff member to contact the biographer, and then Ethan."

"No. I don't want this staffed out. I need to talk to Ethan myself." She went into the kitchen and looked around. "Surely there has to be a phone book around here somewhere."

One of her staff members grabbed it from the counter and handed it to her.

"Thanks."

She flipped through the book and found Ethan's name, dug in her purse for her cell and dialed Ethan's home phone number.

"No answer." Damn. "I'll try his parents. They might know how I can reach him."

She dialed his parents' number, and his mother picked up. It had been years since she'd spoken to Mrs. Kent. A lump the size of her tour bus lodged in her throat.

"Mrs. Kent?"

"Yes?"

"It's Riley Jensen."

She waited for silence, for condemnation, for something other than the enthusiastic response she got.

"Riley, honey! I'm so glad to hear from you. Why haven't you been by to see us yet? I'm so sorry we didn't make it to greet you when you arrived the other day, but Roger's knee is bad and I knew Ethan would be dropping Zoey off. And look at me talking your ear off and you haven't had a chance to say a word yet."

Riley breathed a sigh of relief. "It's so wonderful to hear your voice, Mrs. Kent."

"Please, call me Stacy. You're a big girl now."

"Thank you, Stacy. I was wondering if you knew where Ethan was. It's kind of important I talk to him."

"He's over here tonight. Everyone came over for dinner and game night. Why don't you swing by? I know everyone would love to see you."

Oh, right. She'd just bet his brothers would "love" to see her. "Oh, I don't know about that. If I could just talk to Ethan…"

"Well, he's in the middle of a rather rousing game of Yahtzee at the moment, so you'd better come on over. Though I realize you're a big and important star and probably busy doing something, so I understand if you can't."

It hadn't been said with malice. Stacy Kent thought Riley's dance card was full. Ha. "I'm not big and important, and I'll be right over. Thank you for the invitation."

"Great, honey. See you soon."

She hung up and wondered why she'd agreed to step foot into the lion's den.

As she stood outside Ethan's parents' house and stared up

at the brightly blinking Christmas lights lining the roof as well as the smiling, waving mechanical Santa and snowman parked on the front lawn, Riley took a deep lungful of bitter cold air and wondered what she was doing here. She should have just asked Ethan's mother to have him call her when he was free.

But it had been a long time since she'd seen his parents, and they'd always been so nice to her.

Still, his brothers were here and she'd just bet they weren't members of her fan club.

Her knees knocked against each other and her heart slammed against her chest as she rang the doorbell.

One would think she'd never get nervous, but since she'd come back to Deer Lake, she'd had a ton of leg-shaking moments.

Ethan's dad swung the door open. He'd changed a little in ten years, gotten a little grayer and a lot heavier, but his generous smile was still the same.

"Riley Jensen. Aren't you just all grown up and more beautiful than ever? Come on in."

"Thank you, Mr. Kent."

He shut the door behind her, then took her coat. "Everyone's in the family room. He limped next to her. "You have your choice of Yahtzee, Uno or Scrabble."

She remembered family game night, a required weekly event she'd always loved, and a tradition that obviously still continued.

Family traditions. She'd never had them because she'd jumped around from family to family. That's why she'd loved the Kents. They'd been her stability, her normalcy in a childhood that wasn't.

The house hadn't changed much. As she surveyed the Christmas tree and the decorations she remembered so well, she was struck with a pang of homesickness she hadn't felt since the day she'd grabbed a bus out of town and hadn't looked back.

The Kent home had been as much a home for her as it had been for Ethan. When she and Ethan had started dating her freshman year of high school, they'd been inseparable, which meant she'd spent much of her time at his house because she tended to bounce around here and there at foster homes. And even when she was stable, she didn't want to burden her foster family with yet another kid.

The Kents had been like parents to her—kind, welcoming, treating her like their own daughter.

She'd loved them.

And like so many others in Deer Lake, she'd left them behind without explanation and without saying goodbye.

She hadn't realized how much she'd missed them until she saw the stuffed Christmas moose on the table in the foyer, or the strings of lighted garland winding up the stairs, or the smiling snowmen who decorated Stacy's mantel. She heard the whistling of the train under the tree, remembering sitting in the living room and staring at that train for hours, marveling at the magic of a family holiday.

All of these were part of her memories of Christmases past.

Not everything in the past hurt.

She'd had good memories too.

Fighting back tears, she put on a smile as Roger led her into the oversized family room.

"Guess who I found at the front door?"

Several pairs of eyes turned and the raucous noise in the room quieted down.

The guys all stood.

The Kent brothers had certainly all grown up. Between Ethan, Wyatt and Brody, the three of them were devastating in the looks department. All of them with thick dark hair, tall and well muscled. Wyatt had dangerous good looks and a firm jaw, Brody looked like one of those sexy calendar models, all lean and lethal, but it was Ethan who caught her eye the most. It was in his eyes, the way he looked at her when she entered the room. Maybe because she'd been in love with him for half her life.

Ethan came over to her.

"Riley. What are you doing here?"

"I called your house but you weren't there so I called your mother. She asked me to come over."

Stacy greeted her with a hug and held it for a minute. "More like demanded she come join us. So wonderful to see you again, Riley."

The hug was so warm and welcoming, Riley never wanted to let go. "It's nice to see you again, too."

"Now, what would you like to drink? Hot chocolate?"

Riley nodded. "That would be great. Thanks."

"Good. I'll be right back."

"I'll go work your Scrabble words while you're gone," Roger said.

Stacy shot him a glare. "You even so much as peek anywhere near my side of the table and I'll hobble your other leg."

Roger narrowed his gaze. "You're cutthroat, woman." He turned and gave Riley a wink. "She thinks I cheat."

Ethan rolled his eyes. "Duh, Dad. You do cheat."

Roger lifted his chin. "Do not. I just can't spell good so your mother takes that advantage and uses it against me."

"Are we going to play here or what?" Brody asked. "I'm ahead of you and Wyatt and I intend to kick your butts."

"I need to talk to Riley."

"Well make it fast. And hi, Riley. Nice to see you around

here again. Try to visit more than once every ten years, will ya?"

"Thanks, Brody. Nice to see you again too. And I'll try. And hi, Wyatt."

"Uh huh." Wyatt offered up a half-assed wave, then lifted a bottle of beer to his lips.

Ethan led her out of the room and into the formal living room. They took seats on the sofa. "Ignore Wyatt. He's got a major chip on his shoulder. It's not you, trust me. He treats everyone with the exact same amount of disdain."

"Really? Why?"

"It's his divorce a couple years ago. He's still carrying a grudge and isn't fond of women in general."

"Oh. Ouch. I'm sorry."

Ethan shrugged. "That's his problem to deal with."

"Where's Zoey?"

"Spending the night at a friend's house."

"Oh. I'm sorry I missed her."

He smiled. "She likes you too. And she had fun at the concert, even though she passed out at the end."

Riley laughed. "It's no problem. It was late. I'm glad she had a good time."

She was stalling. She should tell him why she was here.

"Here's your hot chocolate." Stacy handed her a steaming mug, then hovered while Riley sipped.

She moaned. "It's just how I remembered. Thick, with an overabundance of marshmallows. It's wonderful."

Stacy beamed. "I'm glad you like it."

Ethan looked up at his mother. "Uh, Mom?"

"Oh. Oh, of course. If you'll excuse me, I'd better go get back to Scrabble before Roger steals all my tiles."

She left the room, and Riley turned to Ethan. "It's about the interview you're doing tomorrow."

He frowned. "The one with the biography people?"

"Yes. Please don't do it."

"Why not?"

Did she have to spell it out? "You know why not. I can't believe you even agreed to it. The history between us, what happened between you and Amanda. Do you really want all of that broadcast?"

He gave her the kind of indulgent smile he probably gave his daughter when she was overtired and acting out. "Do you really think I'm going to give them details? How dumb do you think I am, Riley? All they want to talk about is us dating in high school. I figure I'll toss them a few crumbs and they'll be on their way."

"I'd like to keep that part of my life off limits."

He laughed. "Right. It wasn't off limits in your music, was it?"

Irritation skittered across her pulse, driving up her heartbeat. "No one knew it was you."

"Wrong. Everyone knew it was me. Everyone who counted to me. Maybe none of the millions of your fans, but every single person in this town heard your lyrics and felt sorry for you and turned their eyes to Amanda and me. We couldn't walk down the street together for a long time when your first album came out."

She stood and stared down at him. "Is that why you agreed to the interview? You're looking for a little payback?"

He stood, too. "What do you think I'm going to say to them, Riley? You were the victim in all of this. Nothing I say to them could paint you in a bad light. I did sleep with your best friend, and that's why you couldn't get out of Deer Lake fast enough. Hell, you'll come out of it looking even better, so I don't know why you're worried. You should be pushing me to talk to the media. Think of all the new songs you'll get out of this."

A stab to her heart couldn't have hurt more than his words did. "Is that what you think of me? After all we've been through, is that all you think of me? You believe that I'm back here to eke out some more heartache and song lyrics, Ethan, that I looked forward to reliving the nightmare of ten years ago so I could grab a few songs for my next album? After all, the well might be dry now so maybe you and I could relive old times, or maybe even drum up something new and painful and I could go platinum again. It's all about using each other, isn't it? Because that's what you really think of me, isn't it? That it's all about the fame and the money."

He didn't answer, which was, she supposed, his answer.

She flicked her gaze to the doorway and there stood his mother, his father and his brothers.

Great. Did they all believe the same thing about her?

The walls seemed to close in on her. She couldn't breathe. She had to get out of here. Now.

SIX

RILEY DID WHAT she'd always done best. She ran.

She turned and escaped from the room, grabbed the door handle and fled out the front door, realizing as soon as she did that she'd forgotten her coat and that's where she'd slipped the keys to the rental car.

No way was she going back inside that house. Instead, she sprinted past the car and down the street, not even noticing the temps outside until she slowed down to a brisk walk. She hadn't even felt the tears streaming down her cheeks until she was struck by how cold her face was. Her sweater and jeans were no match for the frigid evening temperature, and once her flushed anger ebbed, she realized she was freezing.

She stopped, automatically shoved her hand into her jeans, then rolled her eyes. She'd slipped her cell phone in her coat pocket, too.

She had no one to blame for this fiasco but herself.

She'd acted like a child in there, tossing accusations and arguing with Ethan just like she had with him before she'd run out of town ten years ago. She had a right to be angry at Ethan. The things he'd said to her were unforgiveable. What she should have done was stand her ground and tell him exactly what she thought of him. But no. She'd had to play the victim and run out of the room all hurt.

The running part she was really good at.

Old hurts and angers. Some things didn't change, and some hurts could never be repaired. If she was smart, she'd turn around, go back to Ethan's house and suck up the embarrassment, grab her coat and keys and drive home. It was over a mile walk back to the bed and breakfast and she was not dressed for that.

But dammit, he'd hurt her, and she would not go crawling back there. She had her pride and she refused to humiliate herself any further. It wasn't like she was going to die in a mile. Uncomfortable, yes. Dead, no. She'd send someone over for the car and her coat tomorrow.

Shivering, it didn't take a block and a half before her ears began to sting and she was certain her toes were going to end up with frostbite.

What was the temperature outside anyway?

Okay, maybe a mile in this cold was a little far.

When the first snowflakes started to fall, she laughed.

Perfect.

Dumb, Riley, really. Next time you decide to storm off in a huff, grab your coat first.

She saw headlights and wondered if it was someone she knew. She was so cold she'd offer up an autographed guitar to whoever drove her back to the bed and breakfast.

The car slowed and pulled to the curb. She stilled when the window rolled down.

It was Ethan.

"Riley, get in."

She thought for all of a quarter of a second about telling him to stick it, but she wasn't that stupid. She was freezing and she was certain she'd lost a few brain cells. She shuffled her frozen body to the car and slid inside.

Thankfully he had the heater blasting, and her coat was on the seat next to her. She pulled it over her. And then he scooted over toward her.

She shot him a look. "Wha...what are you doing?"

"Warming you." He pulled her against him. "Are you out

of your mind running out of the house without a coat? It's five degrees outside."

No wonder she thought she was going to die out there.

She wanted to argue with him, but he'd opened his coat and drew her against his chest and he was so damn warm all she could think about was the heat of his body. She was shivering uncontrollably now and couldn't seem to stop her teeth from chattering.

"I'll be f...f...fine in a minute. Then you c...can let me go."

He rubbed her back and hair, his voice gentle. "I know. I will."

The snow came down harder now, obliterating her vision of the outside. The heater and their breath fogged the windshield and windows, reminding her of what they used to do in his car to steam up the windows. It had a lot to do with body heat, but not because she'd been stupid and walked outside in the cold. Those thoughts and memories coupled with being in his arms again warmed her more than the heater.

"I...I'm..."

"Shhh. Just relax, Riley. Your body is so cold. I'm not going to move this car until you're warm, so you can just listen to me."

She was still shaking, so he was probably right.

"I'm sorry. Really sorry. I was out of line. Seems like I'm always hurting you and I never meant to. The things I said were unforgiveable. It was a knee-jerk reaction."

"More like a jerk reaction."

He laughed, the sound deep and vibrating against his chest.

"You're right there. I was a total jerk. For some reason you bring out the worst in me."

"Gee, thanks."

"Not what I meant. God, Riley, I just make a mess of things when I'm around you, don't I?"

"You seem to." She wasn't going to let him off easy. Not this time.

"If you don't want me to talk to the television people, I won't."

She listened to his heart beating against his chest, so strong and sure. She had always believed in Ethan. From the time she was fourteen years old he'd been her rock, her lifeline, and everything she'd loved.

Until Amanda.

She'd been running away from the answer for so long. It was time to stop and just ask the damn question.

"Tell me about Amanda."

She felt his heart speed up.

"What do you want to know?"

She lifted her head and met his curious, wary gaze. "Why did you choose her over me? I didn't even know you were interested in her."

He offered up a half smile. "I wasn't. She wanted me."

Riley frowned. "No she didn't."

"Honey, she had a thing for me for years. She wanted me as much as she wanted the career you ended up with."

She shook her head. "That's not true. I mean, yes, she was a singer, too. A great singer. Of course that's the career she was after."

Riley and Amanda had met in choir freshman year. Amanda had a beautiful voice, clear and strong. Her parents had spent a fortune on private lessons. Amanda intended to go to college and study music. Fame was in her future, she'd told Riley. She wanted to front a rock band, or become a pop star.

She had the chops for it. Riley had been mesmerized by

Amanda's voice. They'd spend hours together at Amanda's house, harmonizing on songs.

They'd become friends and had been inseparable in all things.

Except Amanda had never had a boyfriend. She said she was too busy with her singing lessons to worry about boys. But she'd never begrudged Riley's relationship with Ethan, because Riley had always included her. She'd never shut Amanda out, had always tried to fix her up with guys so they could double date. Amanda went, though it was half hearted. Nothing ever came of those dates. Amanda never seemed intrigued enough by any of the guys to end up with a boyfriend, though she was beautiful, with mink brown hair, emerald green eyes and her captivating voice.

"She never told me she was interested in you. She never even dated anyone long term in high school. I didn't know."

Ethan nodded. "She didn't want you to know. She was so jealous of you, Riley. Of your voice, your relationship with me. You had everything she wanted."

"No. That's not true. That's not the Amanda I knew."

Ethan sighed. "There were parts of her you never knew about. Hell, I didn't even know about them until after you were gone."

"Like what?" She couldn't believe the things he was telling her about Amanda.

"Like her fear that you were more talented than she was, that her voice would never measure up to yours."

"How can that be? I'd never had training, and she'd been taking voice lessons her whole life. Her singing was beautiful."

He swept her hair away from her face. "You've been in the business long enough to know that all the lessons in the world can't compete with raw ability. That's what you had,

Riley. You might not have had all the training she had, but you had natural talent, and no training can compare to that. And when it was clear your talent would outshine her, that you were destined for big things, she decided to take the one thing from you she knew she could."

Riley almost couldn't say the word out loud, but knew she had to know the truth. "You."

He nodded.

"How?"

"You sure you want to know all of it?"

"Yes." Because she refused to believe that Ethan loved her one day and just decided to switch to Amanda the next. Though she had believed it, hadn't she? She'd spent the past ten years believing it. Maybe it was time she let Ethan tell her what really happened.

"She called me one night in tears. It was right after graduation and she said she'd been turned down for a scholarship to Julliard, the one and only place she really wanted to go."

"But she'd gotten so many scholarships to so many different schools. She could have chosen from...what? Five or six?"

He shrugged. "I didn't really know what she was talking about, but you know we'd all gotten close. She was always where you were, so I considered her a friend. I trusted her. I don't remember where you were. She said she couldn't get hold of you and there was no one else to talk to, so I went over there to give her some comfort because she was pretty freaked out. We were drinking beer, then whiskey. Her parents were gone, and you know Amanda always had a lot of freedom and access to whatever she wanted. And then we were drinking a lot. I was trying to make her feel better. It was stupid. We were talking and talking and I thought I had relaxed her by making her laugh. Hell, I was drunk as hell. Next thing I know it's morning. I wake up in bed with Amanda naked next to me, and you're standing there."

"Did you have sex with her?"

He shrugged. "No. At least I don't think I did, but maybe I did. I don't even remember what happened that night. Does it matter? I shouldn't have put myself in the position to be alone with her. I should have called you right away. I shouldn't have been there drinking with her. It was stupid and I let her manipulate me, but I had to take responsibility for being there, even if nothing happened. I knew from the look in your eyes you believed what you saw."

She had believed it. She and Amanda had plans that morning. Plans Amanda had organized. She'd walked into Amanda's room and found the boy she loved naked in bed with her best friend.

She'd believed right away what she saw, put two and two together and figured Ethan had slept with Amanda, that Ethan had seduced her best friend. She'd assumed she hadn't been enough for him, that he'd wanted what Amanda could offer him.

And she'd never spoken to either of them again. Hurt and rage had taken over, and she'd left town the next day without asking for explanations, without seeing Ethan again.

It had been a knee-jerk reaction, a youthful reaction.

"So she manipulated us both."

"I guess."

"Why did you marry her?"

"She was pregnant. And it was mine. Or so she told me."

"You got proof?"

"She showed me the pregnancy test. I had no choice but to believe her. You said it yourself. She was never around other guys."

Her eyes widened. "You mean she got pregnant after that night?"

"Yeah, I guess, because I didn't sleep with her again after that."

"So you did have sex with her."

He laughed. "I have no idea. I don't think I did. If I did, I sure as hell don't remember it, but I wasn't one hundred percent confident, so I was kind of stuck. I couldn't deny I was in bed with her that morning."

"What about her scholarship? Did she really lose it?"

"Doubtful. I think she was just afraid she'd never be as good as you. And she'd taken me away from you, so that was her triumph. So I married her. And then she miscarried a couple months later."

"I'm sorry, Ethan."

He dragged his fingers through his hair and laughed. "You know what? So was I at the time. As hurt and angry as I was with her, I was still upset when she lost the baby. I didn't love her, but I wanted the kid."

"You didn't love her?"

"No. I never loved her. I did what was right and took responsibility. I screwed up and I paid the price for making a mess of my life. But I was in love with you, not her."

Riley's heart squeezed. She so wanted to believe that. "But you stayed married to her."

He let out a short laugh. "Yeah. I did."

"Why?"

He lifted his gaze to hers, the pain in his eyes so raw she wanted to run from it. "Because when I commit to someone, I honor that commitment. I said I was going to be with her until death do us part. That meant something to me."

Riley blinked back the tears. That was Ethan. Once he had committed to her, he'd stuck by her side. Until she'd left him, hadn't allowed him to explain what happened that night with Amanda.

"Did you ever love her?"

"I'd like to say yes. You knew her. She might have been a little spoiled, but she had her moments. She was fun and a little wild and crazy. And she could be so sweet and loving. And then we had Zoey."

Riley smiled. "Zoey is amazing."

"She is. I'll always be grateful to Amanda for giving me Zoey. She's the best part of my life. And Amanda was a wonderful mother. She seemed to settle after we had Zoey. It was almost as if she'd found what she was searching for."

"And then she got sick."

He nodded. "It devastated her, knowing she was going to leave Zoey behind. She felt as if that was somehow a punishment for all the lying and hurt she'd caused."

Riley's throat constricted. "Oh, God. That's not fair."

"She didn't think it was, either. Neither did I. But we weren't in charge. And Zoey lost her mother."

Riley felt sick inside. "I'm so sorry, Ethan. For you, for Amanda and for Zoey."

"I'm the one who's sorry. There are so many things I could have done differently that night. When Amanda called, I should have called you to see what was up. I could have tried to find you to make you come over there with me. I didn't do that. I just assumed what Amanda said, that you weren't home. And when you ran off that morning after finding us together, I went after you. God, I spent days trying to find you."

Riley's heart stuttered. "You did?"

"Of course I did. I searched everywhere. I didn't know where you went. I was crazy worried about you. But then I thought...you know what? Maybe you're better off without me. Maybe this is for the best. I was such a fucking coward letting you go. I should have tried harder to find you."

"Oh, Ethan, I didn't know you came looking for me."

He shrugged. "It wasn't enough. I should have tried harder. But look at you now, look at what you've done with your life. If I had found you, you might never have all you have now. I can't regret that for you, you know? Sometimes destiny plays a big part in things. Maybe I was supposed to screw this all up so you could become famous."

She tilted her head. "Is that some kind of twisted logic?"

"Maybe. It's not an excuse though. All of this is my fault. And I'll never be able to say I'm sorry enough times to make it stop hurting you. I know that. But I'm still sorry. I'm sorry for hurting you, and for what happened with Amanda."

She saw him in a new light. "That's a load of heavy burdens you're carrying."

His lips curled. "I have wide shoulders."

Her eyes filled with tears. "We both lost so much. Time, friends, people we loved."

"But you can't change the past. It is what it is and I have to live with it."

She shuddered, realizing that no matter how much she wanted to go back, Ethan was right.

She threw her arms around him and hugged him, needing to give him comfort, and forgiveness. And maybe she needed to give herself a little comfort too for all she'd lost.

Ethan wrapped his arms around Riley while she cried, held her while she grieved for the friend she'd had and lost. He'd long ago cried all he could for losing Amanda. He might not have loved her like a husband should love his wife, but he'd been a good husband to her, a good friend, and he'd never felt guilty for still being in love with Riley after all these years, because while he'd been married to Amanda, she'd been the only woman in his life.

Their lives might not have been perfect, but he'd given her all of himself for the time they had together.

And the two of them had given Zoey the best life they could.

After Riley cried it out, he reached into the glove compartment and handed her a box of tissues. She wiped her eyes, blew her nose and tossed the coat aside. "Now I'm hot."

He laughed. "Feeling better now?"

She nodded. "I'm sorry. I'm not usually this dramatic. You probably think I'm some Nashville diva who throws fits and storms out of houses and, oh, God." She lifted tear-filled eyes to his. "What your family must think of me."

"Actually, they thought I was an asshole."

"They did? Why?"

"Because I was the one who came at you and said all the wrong things. My mother gave me the look."

"Yikes. Not the look."

"Yeah. I realized I'd stuck my foot in my mouth right away, but you'd already run out. By the time I ran after you, you were gone. Damn, woman, you're fast."

She laughed. "I run for exercise."

"I went inside to grab my coat and that's when I saw yours, so I got my keys and came looking for you. So no, my family isn't mad at you, they're mad as hell at me. Trust me, I'm in no hurry to go back there."

She settled back against the seat only to find his arm draped back there. She was plenty warm now and he could have shifted back over to his side of the car, but he hadn't yet.

Not that she was complaining. She felt like they'd finally gotten past the huge chasm that had stood between them for all these years, at least the one she'd put there.

She tilted her head back and looked into his eyes. God, she could get lost there. She'd spent all of the past ten years on her work, hadn't had time for serious romance. She hadn't taken time to look for a man in her life, because first she'd been heartbroken over Ethan, and then she'd put all her energies into building her career. There just never seemed to be light left at the end of the day for love. Writing about it, singing about it, yes. Finding it, no. And maybe she'd been afraid to fall in love, because love could hurt.

With the paparazzi dogging her every move, her life was under a microscope. She couldn't imagine trying to have her love life scrutinized the same way her career had been. Men in her life had been brief, never anything long term.

But here in Deer Lake, time had seemed to slow down the past few days. No one followed her probably because they knew she was kind of boring. And really, what would they see? It wasn't like she was in Los Angeles or even Nashville where the possibility of her hooking up with another country music star or even a movie or television star meant a photo op that could generate some buzz. Here there was nothing happening.

At least to the film and print media. But for Riley as she leaned against Ethan's arm and stared into his eyes, there was plenty happening. A shift in her entire perspective had occurred within a matter of days and hours.

Now what was she supposed to think? Everything she'd believed to be true had been a lie. Old grudges had slipped away, her protective armor torn off, leaving her naked and raw and not sure what to do about feelings she'd kept buried for all these years. They'd suddenly roared to life again, but it was ten years later. Surely she couldn't still feel the same.

Ethan didn't feel the same. He'd lived a whole different life while she was gone. He had a child now, different responsibilities. They'd both grown up and grown apart.

But as he swept his hand across her cheek and cupped her neck, his touch sent skittering sensation throughout her body. Her skin flushed with heat.

It might not be love, but the spark was still there, and she needed to explore it. She raised her hand and brushed her fingers across the beard stubble on his jaw, shuddering at the raw desire that filled every part of her from the simple touch of her fingers to his face.

Ethan brushed his lips to hers, a tentative kiss meant to test and explore. The shock of meeting his lips curled her toes. It was an explosion from within and there was nothing tentative about her reaction. She grabbed his jacket and pulled him to her, letting him know that soft and gentle wasn't at all what she needed. Not when she had ten years of pent-up passion to release. She tangled her fingers in his hair and pressed her lips to his, deepening the kiss, taking control and letting him know she wanted more.

Suddenly she was on her back on the seat, Ethan looming over her, all his guy parts lined up against all her girl parts and it felt so damn good to be this close to a man again.

Not just any man. Ethan. The first boy she'd loved. Only he wasn't a boy now, evidenced by the thickness of his muscles, the wide chest and the oh-so-hard evidence of what kissing him and touching him was doing to him.

She could write a song about how good this felt, but she doubted it would ever see airtime. Instead, she concentrated on how he held her, his hand slipping underneath her to cup her butt and lift her against that omigod part of him that reminded her they weren't kids anymore making out in the front—or back—seat of his car. This was adult stuff and she was ready to act like an adult with him. She'd been robbed of that back then because she hadn't been ready yet, but she was sure as hell ready to consummate now.

Right now, in fact, parked along the curb in front of who-knew-whose house. Frankly, she didn't care, because Ethan had one hand tangled in her hair and the other was rubbing her backside while his mouth was doing delicious things to hers and she was afraid she might just have an orgasm right there before any clothes got undone.

And then he vibrated.

Whoa. He was really talented, and if she shifted just a little to the left, those vibrations...

"Dammit," he said, lifting his head. "My phone's ringing."

He shifted, climbing off her and for the first time in a while she felt cold.

"Seriously? Can't you ignore it?"

He gave her a regretful smile. "It could be about Zoey. Sorry. Give me just a second. He checked the display. "Shit."

He pressed a button and put the phone to his ear. "Hi, Mom."

Wow. It was ten years ago.

Ethan rolled his eyes. "No, I found her. She's fine. We're just sitting here...talking." While he listened, he gave her a look that sent her up in flames again. "Yeah, I'm going to bring her back shortly. Okay."

He pressed the button and tossed the phone on the dash, then dragged his fingers through his hair. "Sorry. Kind of lost myself there for a minute."

Riley shuddered out a sigh, realizing whatever had been about to happen, or might have happened, wasn't going to. Not here, not tonight. "It's okay. I did, too."

"I'll drive you back to my parents."

The only good thing was, Ethan looked as frustrated and regretful as she did.

He hit the defrosters and the windshield wipers and by the time everything cleared, Riley realized how much snow had fallen already.

They took a slow drive back to the house, giving Riley a chance to fix her hair and put on some lip gloss so she didn't look quite so...ravaged by the time Ethan pulled into the driveway. They made a mad dash to the house where Ethan's mom was waiting with the door open.

"It's horrible outside. I was so worried about you." She enveloped Riley in a hug. "I already sent Brody and Wyatt home, which is where you both need to go before this gets any worse."

"Yes, Mom," Ethan said, with a roll of his eyes, then a laugh and a kiss.

"I'm sorry we didn't get to spend more time together. I blame my son for that." She glared at Ethan.

"Already discussed and apologized, Mom. Topic's closed."

"Okay, okay. You two get on the road."

"I've driven in snow before. I have a four wheel drive, Mom."

"And I'm still your mother and I'm going to worry. You should drive Riley back to her place."

"I have an SUV, too, Mrs. Kent," and at her look, corrected it to, "Stacy. I'm sure I'll be fine, but thank you."

"I'll follow her," Ethan said. "To make sure she makes it there safe."

"That'll make me feel better." She hugged Riley and Ethan and they were out the door.

Snow pelted her on the face as the wind picked up. "Wow. It's really coming down."

"Really, do you need me to drive you back to the B and B?"

"No, it's not that far. I can make it."

"Okay."

He seemed as reluctant to let her go as she was to be let go of. But since Ethan's mother was peeking through the blinds, she opened her car door. "I'll see you later."

"Yeah. Later."

She started the car up. She hadn't thought about gloves because she was a moron, so gripping the icy cold steering wheel was torture, but she managed to back out of the driveway and made the trek back to the bed and breakfast. She had to admit it gave her some comfort to see Ethan's SUV behind her the whole way. When she pulled into the parking lot and turned off the car, he waited in the street until she opened the front door and went inside. Only then did he drive off.

Leaving her aching and frustrated. And alone.

She sighed and turned off the lights.

SEVEN

THERE WAS A holiday celebration at town square tonight, with Christmas carolers, ice skating on the makeshift rink, a parade and, of course, Santa. It was one of Zoey's favorite parts of the holiday, though Ethan wasn't sure if it was because of all the events that took place at town square or because she knew that meant Christmas was only a couple days away. Either way, he loved watching the joy in her eyes. He fed off her excitement and this was the event that always got him in the mood for Christmas.

Because it had snowed, the whole town had a holiday look to it, which made everything perfect. Wreaths hung on every street light, banners and lights decorated every store front, and with the seven inches of snow they'd gotten the entire town looked like something out of a Christmas movie.

Zoey had spent the past couple days building snowmen in the yard, complete with black button eyes, tattered scarves, carrot noses and red gumdrops for the mouths. It had stayed cold enough that Mr. and Mrs. Snowpeople were still standing, which thrilled Zoey even more and thankfully had given her something to do so she hadn't bugged him nonstop about when Christmas was.

The only drawback to this extravaganza was that Riley would be singing.

Not that there was anything wrong with her singing. It was just that he'd been kind of avoiding her since two nights ago in the car when he'd totally lost his mind and climbed all over her. Fortunately she'd been busy wrapping up all her biography stuff since then and he hadn't run into her.

Today was supposed to be her last event, a filmed thing where she would sing a medley of Christmas songs from her last holiday CD. Everyone from town would be there, Riley would sing after the parade, and then she and her entire crew would pack up and go, along with all the media.

So really, what had been the point of refiring the past between them, except to remind him that the two of them were worlds apart and he still couldn't have her?

He didn't deserve to have her.

Besides, there was Zoey to think about. Her life was here in Deer Lake where his family was. Where Zoey's family was. Riley's life was somewhere else, probably always on the road on that big tour bus of hers.

And even though he'd driven home the long way to get his riotous libido under control that night, and he'd been thinking about Riley nonstop ever since, especially about that hot interlude in the car and how it had felt to remap her body with his hands, it was pointless.

She was going her way soon, and he was staying here.

With his daughter.

So despite wanting to call her the next day, or go over to the bed and breakfast to see her, he hadn't. Because his life was reality, not fantasy.

And since Riley had left, the icy cold hand of reality had firmly clenched him in its grip.

"Daddy, I want to go ice skating."

He looked down at his adorable daughter who looked like a puffy pink marshmallow in her pink coat, pink hat and pink mittens. He'd done her hair in pigtail braids this morning and she'd insisted on puffy pink bands to hold them. She even wore pink boots.

The girl liked her some pink.

"We'll go ice skating later. The parade's about to start. You don't want to miss it, do you?"

Her eyes got big and wide. "Oh. No. Let's go, Daddy."

She tugged on his hand and dragged him toward the center island of town where the parade ended. They were lucky and found a bench to sit on, a perfect viewing area for the parade. They were joined shortly by his mom and dad and brothers.

"It's cold as a well digger's—"

"Brody," his mother warned, casting her glance to Zoey.

"Shovel," Brody finished with a tweak of Zoey's nose.

Zoey giggled.

Wyatt shoved his hands in his pockets, turned up the collar of his coat and looked about as happy to be there as he would be if he was having a root canal.

But missing the annual town Christmas event would somehow be a direct insult to their mother, and even Wyatt wouldn't do that, no matter how much he hated the world these days.

When you lived in a small town, parades weren't exactly like the Macy's Thanksgiving Day parade in New York City. They didn't go on for hours. You had the cops because they could run their sirens and all the kids liked that. And the fire department, too. Then there were the middle school and high school bands, a few local clubs like Rotary and Knights of Columbus, some private organizations and businesses who put some holiday floats together, and that was pretty much it.

And then came Santa on his big float at the end, waving from on top of his makeshift chimney. Dave Bowman was doing a fine job as Santa this year, and Ethan suspected Dave's rosy cheeks were due to the shot or two of whiskey Ethan had seen him downing at McGuffey's Tavern prior to the start of the parade.

The Santa float was always the biggest hit with the kids, since Santa's "elves" tossed candy. There was Tori dressed as an elf in her green stockings and short skirt, her flaming red hair a perfect compliment to the whole elf gig.

"Damn," Brody whispered. "Her skirt is short enough that every time she bends over, you can see—"

Brody whistled instead. Tori shot him an evil glare and threw candy at his head.

"Maybe you shouldn't look." Ethan suggested.

"And maybe I should." Brody unwrapped the candy, popped it in his mouth and walked away.

The parade over, the crowds milled around for a while. Zoey amused herself by playing a few games, ice skating and, of course, eating. Chairs were being set up at the town center gazebo area for Riley's concert. The television crews were in hot turnout today, no doubt because it was the weekend and that meant people from surrounding areas would come, increasing attendance.

Great. Good for the town, Ethan supposed, but it just meant more crowds.

"Riley Jensen is going to sing today, Daddy."

He smiled indulgently at his daughter. "I know."

"There's no backstage today, because she's gonna sing on a stage that has no back." Zoey giggled.

"So I noticed. We'll just hang out here and listen, okay?"

"Do you think Riley Jensen will see us all the way back here? It's kinda far."

"I think she'll probably be a little busy, but maybe she'll be looking for you. You can stand on your chair and wave to her while she's singing. But no talking, because that would be rude."

"Okay, Daddy."

When it looked like people were starting to claim seats,

Ethan moved in with his parents and brothers. Tori had joined them, too, along with one of her friends. They made it about three quarters of the way back since it was pretty well packed in. Damn there were a lot of people here.

"Daddy, I can't see," Zoey whined.

His kid needed a nap. As soon as Riley finished singing, they were outta here.

"It's the best we can do, muffin," he said, tugging on one of her pigtails. "Sorry."

Then his phone buzzed, an unfamiliar number.

"Hey, Ethan, it's Joann, Riley's publicist. Are you here at the festival?"

"Uh, yeah."

"Riley has the front row saved for you and your family if you want to watch the concert."

"Oh. We're already seated, kind of in the back."

"Then come on up front. I'll be waiting here to seat you."

"Okay."

He hung up and turned to his mom. "That was Riley's publicist. She has the front row saved for us."

"Oh, isn't that nice," his mom said, then herded the family up and out of their chairs and toward the front row.

Zoey, of course, was thrilled. And the view was much better up here in the front row. What he didn't care for was having to endure knowing looks, encouraging nods and smirks from everyone as they made their way up there.

Great.

"Hey, didn't know you and Riley were back together." Mark Roberts patted him on the back. "Nice going, man."

"We're just so thrilled for you and Riley, Ethan," Callie Roberts said.

Ethan half turned. "It's not like that. She likes Zoey and

wanted to make sure she could see. Plus she's known my parents for a long time."

Callie gave him a sly grin. "Sure, honey. Whatever you say."

Ugh. Zoey was bouncing in her seat waiting for the concert to begin and telling everyone around her that she was Riley Jensen's new best friend. Even his own mother had gotten into the act, sharing that he and Riley had "gone out" alone together the other night.

Maybe Ethan could just slip out and go home.

But then Riley and her band came out, and damn if his libido didn't tie him to the chair, because she looked gorgeous in tight blue jeans, sinfully sexy thigh high boots, a wide-open suede jacket and a shirt that clung to her curves. She'd worn her hair down. It swept her shoulders in loose waves and all he could think about was how good she'd smelled the other night when he'd held her close and kissed her and touched her. And oh, man, he was sitting next to his mother and thinking about having sex with Riley.

He was probably going straight to hell for that.

At least this time she wasn't singing about him. It was all Christmas songs, and Zoey couldn't help but sing along, despite his mother's best attempts to admonish her to stay quiet. But Riley smiled down at Zoey, since his daughter wasn't exactly a quiet singer. Fortunately, she did have a great voice and Riley finally motioned to her to join her on stage. And since his daughter didn't have a shy bone in her entire body, she got to stand with the choir and sing her little heart out along with Riley and the choir.

His mother took approximately ten thousand pictures. Plus video.

Ethan had to admit he was pretty excited about it, too, though it wasn't like he thought of Riley as a celebrity. She was just Riley. But he was always thrilled to see his daughter happy, and Zoey was grinning from ear to ear, especially when one of the choir angels put her halo on Zoey head.

Zoey probably wouldn't touch ground from her happy place for at least twenty-four hours.

After the concert, Zoey jumped into his arms. "Did you see me, Daddy? I got to sing on the stage."

"I saw you. You were awesome."

"Did you hear me? I sang really loud."

He laughed as Riley joined them. "I had no problem hearing you."

Riley rubbed Zoey's back. "This young lady has a beautiful voice, just like her mama did."

Zoey frowned. "Did you know my mama, Riley Jensen?"

Riley lifted her chin and Ethan could tell she fought tears. "I did. She was my best friend in high school."

"Wow." Zoey turned to Ethan. "I didn't know that, Daddy. Did you know that?"

"I did." He put Zoey down and lifted his gaze to Riley. "You did a nice job out there tonight."

"Thanks. I'm just glad all *this* is over with." She swept her gaze over the camera crews who were packing up.

"Everyone leaving?"

"They are."

He frowned. "You're not?"

She shrugged. "I've sprung my people loose. Figured I'd hang out here until after the holidays and write some music."

"By yourself?" his mother asked.

Riley smiled. "Yes. Everyone has their families to go home to. I plan to stay and enjoy the solitude. I do my best songwriting that way. No one to hover over me and no place I have to be."

What she hadn't said, Ethan noted, was that Riley had no family to go home to for Christmas.

"You'll come to our house for Christmas," his mother said, taking the words right out of his mouth.

Riley's eyes widened and she shook her head. "Oh, no. I couldn't. I wasn't trying to wrangle an invitation. I really do intend to just spend a couple weeks alone and write."

"That's just fine, dear. You do that. On Christmas Eve you'll come over for dinner and games. Christmas morning we have pancakes for breakfast, turkey for dinner. You won't be spending Christmas alone."

Riley slanted a helpless gaze his way.

"No use arguing with her. You know how she is. If you don't come over she'll just send one of us to fetch you."

She inhaled and let out a sigh, then smiled. "Of course. Thank you, Stacy. I'd love to come over for Christmas."

Ethan wondered how many holidays Riley had spent alone the past ten years. She'd never come home before so he had no idea where she'd spent her Thanksgivings and Christmases.

It would be…interesting spending Christmas with her. And okay, maybe he was thinking about carving out some time to be alone with her.

They might not have a future together, but they had right now.

He looked down at Zoey, who leaned against his mother and yawned. "Mom, why don't you and Dad take Zoey home? She looks tired. I'd like to hang out with Riley for a bit."

He knew his mother would jump all over that one. "Of course. Come on, little miss. Time for bed for you."

Ethan picked up Zoey and gave her a kiss.

"Night, Daddy."

"Night, muffin."

She turned sleepy eyes on Riley. "Night, Riley Jensen. I love you."

Riley's eyes sparkled with tears as she pulled Zoey into her arms. "Good night, Zoey. I love you, too."

As they walked away, Riley lifted her eyes to Ethan. "She's an amazing child. You're very lucky."

"Thanks. I think so."

"And she really does have a beautiful voice. So clear and perfectly on key."

"She gets that from Amanda because if you recall I can't sing for shit."

Riley laughed. "Your singing is great." At his dubious look, she said, "Hey, at least you sing on key."

"Okay, maybe that, but Nashville isn't going to come calling to offer me a record deal anytime soon, so I'm grateful Zoey got her singing genes from her mom."

"Me too."

He looked around and realized it had gotten dark. The crowds had thinned.

"Was there something you wanted to talk to me about?" she asked.

"No." He took her hand. "I want to take you ice skating."

Her brows lifted and she grinned. "Really?"

"Yeah."

"I haven't been ice skating in years."

"Good."

The rink had been poured in the middle of town on one of the grassy fields behind the high school. Ethan had a hand in prepping and building it, and God knows it was plenty cold enough to sustain it. Proceeds from the sale of admissions and concessions would be split between the women's shelter and the new field stands at the high school.

"I'm not sure I even remember how to skate," Riley said as she finished lacing up.

"Oh come on. You never forget. You were always good at it."

"Ha. I think it's something you definitely forget. Plus I'm a lot older now."

He rolled his eyes and took her hand as they headed over to the ice entrance. "You're still plenty young and you bounce around on that stage like you're fifteen, so don't give me any of that 'older now' crap. Let's skate."

He rolled out onto the ice and turned to face her. She gave him an arched brow, hanging onto the entrance. "I don't bounce."

He laughed and held out his hand. "Yeah, you do. Like you have springs on your feet. If you don't believe me, check out concert footage. Now come on."

She took his hand and tentatively slid out onto the rink. She was a little wobbly at first as she fought for balance, but he held onto her, his hand around her waist. Not that he minded holding her close.

"Do you remember ice skating at the park on Friday nights?"

She grinned up at him, slipped and her eyes widened.

"I've got you. I won't let you fall."

She stared up at him and her eyes, so clear and full of trust, were like a punch to his gut.

They glided along and she finally got her balance. "Yes, I remember skating nights in the winter. You, me, Amanda— all our friends. Even on the coldest nights we'd skate, then have hot chocolate and pretzels."

He laughed, remembering it. "You and Amanda would try to lead the whip and fail miserably."

She pulled out of his grasp, finally confident enough to

skate on her own, though she stayed close enough to grab onto his arm whenever she started to wobble. "Hey, we were good at the whip."

"You sucked at it and made everyone crash into the wall."

"We did not. You have a faulty memory. When you led you deliberately crashed us into the wall."

"Now who has the faulty memory? I whipped you all around until you squealed like...girls."

She giggled. "Those were fun times."

Ethan turned and skated backwards, facing her.

"Show off."

"Zoey can do it, too."

"Oh, sure, make me feel bad."

"We skate at the park a lot."

She lifted her gaze to his, her hand on his arm. Did she even realize she leaned on him? Probably not.

"The rink is still open?"

"Yeah. Zoey loves to skate. She and Amanda..."

"It's okay, Ethan. You can talk about her."

"She and Amanda loved to skate together on the weekends." His chest felt tight.

Riley moved to the side wall and held on. Ethan followed.

"Does it hurt you to talk about her?"

"Not really. The pain has mostly passed now. I just don't want to hurt you."

She shook her head. "I want to know about her, about the two of you and your life with Zoey. There's so much I missed out on."

He tucked an errant hair into her hat. "I think that would just be uncomfortable for you."

She shrugged. "We can't pretend it didn't happen. The best thing to do is get it all out in the open and talk about it. Then there won't be any more secrets between us."

And then what, he wanted to ask, but didn't.

Because there would be no "then what?" Riley was looking for closure, and nothing more. He owed her that much.

"What do you want to know?"

"Tell me about your life with Amanda."

He shrugged. "Not much to tell. We got married. Struggled at first. We had to get jobs, work full time and I was trying to take classes, too. Then it was hard after she miscarried. There was a lot of mistrust. I didn't believe she was pregnant in the first place and she knew it, but once she showed me proof of her pregnancy I was committed, so we worked at the marriage, day by day."

"Did you believe the baby was yours?"

"No. I asked her for a DNA test. We were going to do the test but she had to be farther along. Then she miscarried before we could make it happen. So I'll never know if the baby was mine or not. If there was a baby."

"That must have been difficult for both of you. Hard to have a relationship without trust."

"It is. But eventually she mellowed, wasn't as high strung as she'd been when you knew her."

Riley nodded. "A lot of that came from her parents pushing her so hard. They wanted everything for her."

He smiled. "That didn't stop. They were so pissed about the whole pregnancy and marriage thing, accused me of seducing her and trapping her here. They hated me."

Riley stepped off the ice and Ethan followed. They took off their skates and turned them in. "Let's order a pizza and head back to the B and B to continue this talk. Unless you have to be somewhere else? Do you have to pick up Zoey?"

"No. She's fine at my mom's. I'll just call her and have her keep Zoey for the night."

"Okay."

Once they got the pizza, they went to the bed and break-fast. Since Riley had rented the place out and all her people had left, she was alone.

"Aren't Bill and Macy here?"

"No. They're vacationing for the holidays in Colorado with their kids. We took over the whole house from them."

"So you're entirely alone in this big place?"

She grinned and grabbed plates from the kitchen cabinet, then laid out slices of pizza. "All by myself. You have no idea how awesome that is. I'm never alone."

"Huh. Never thought about that. You probably have peo-ple around you all the time."

She dug into a slice and moaned. "You have no idea. Oh, this is good."

"Catarina's is a new place. Opened up about a year ago. Cat's family is from Italy and let me tell you, every pizza they make is amazing."

Riley looked as if she'd died and gone to heaven. She dug into the pizza as if she hadn't eaten in a week. They each had a beer and didn't talk much while they enjoyed their food.

"Okay," she said as she wiped her mouth with a napkin. "So Amanda's parents hated you because they thought you trapped their daughter into marriage."

He took a long pull off the bottle of beer, then set it down. "Yeah. Amanda tried to tell them it wasn't my fault, but you know how they were."

"Yeah, I know. They weren't fond of me, either. Thought I wasn't the right kind of friend for their daughter."

"They always thought they were more upper crust than they actually were. I mean this is Deer Lake, not Boston or New York. And yeah, her father came from money, but he was no industry giant, either."

She shrugged. "Amanda was never influenced by it. A

little spoiled, but she and I had always been great friends. I still can't believe she was jealous of me."

"She was. She had a great voice, but it could never match yours. She was envious. And when you went off and became famous, she was so jealous. She wanted your life in a way that I don't think she ever got over."

Riley pushed her beer aside then lifted her gaze to his. "But she had you. So which one of us was the real winner?"

Ethan stared at her. He had no words, no answer, for what she'd just said. "Riley."

What he saw in her eyes was truth. And forgiveness, which was what he needed more than anything, but didn't deserve.

He reached out and took her hand, swirling his thumb over the softness of her skin. In his line of work he dealt with steel and wood and only the roughest raw materials. But the raw material that was Riley was nothing short of perfection. She was silk and gloss, her skin a creamy glow. Not even the harsh fluorescent lights of the kitchen could spoil her beauty, the way her eyes caught and reflected so much of who she was. He saw such innocence there, and such strength. She'd been through so much, had forged her destiny on her own with no one backing her or pushing her to succeed.

Satin over steel.

"Ethan," she whispered, and he saw need and desire, no longer the girl she once was, but a woman.

A woman he wanted.

He stood, pulling her into his arms, his mouth covering hers, drawing in her gasp, then her moan.

All he'd been thinking about since that night in the car was kissing her again, touching her again, feeling her body pressed against his. She slid her hands in his hair and tugged, igniting his passion like dry timber catching fire.

All the careful consideration he'd given about keeping his

distance went up in a puff of smoke as soon as their lips met. They crashed together, her hands went under his shirt and the logical part of his mind went blank. All thought fled south and the thinking part of his brain settled firmly in his pants.

He wanted Riley. Hell, he'd always wanted her.

And now he was going to have her. They had the house to themselves, the night to themselves, and nothing was going to stop this now.

A bombardment of sensations made Riley's breath catch. Ethan's scent—fresh soap mingled with the crisp outdoors, the satiny steel of his chest as she held onto him for support, his groan as he kissed her. She buried her face in his chest as he pushed her up against the kitchen wall.

Oh, my. This was hard passion, a need that had gone too long without being met. Their mouths and tongues tangled while they fumbled with clothing. Boots were kicked off in a hurry and she grabbed for the button of his jeans while he reached for hers, the only sounds in the quiet house their own harsh breaths as they fought to get each other undressed.

Ethan fumbled for the buttons on her flannel shirt, then ripped them, the sound of buttons flying across the wood floor only adding fuel to her steadily rising fire. She raised his shirt over his head, taking a few seconds to marvel at the sculpted abs, the wide expanse of his shoulders and chest. That's all he'd give her before he kissed her again, hard, shoving her back against the wall and lifting her legs. She wrapped them around him, hard meeting soft.

He ripped her panties and she delighted in the feral hunger he had for her. She tangled her fingers in his hair and tugged as he entered her, making her cry out with the sheer delight of feeling him inside her. This was what she'd wanted her whole life, what she'd needed. This connection, this fire.

Ethan.

She came almost immediately, and rode the wave while he pushed her to the edge again and again, his mouth on her lips, her throat, his tongue blazing a trail of hot sensation she could barely endure but never wanted to end. And when she climbed to the edge and fell over again, he fell with her, this time his mouth taking hers in a searing kiss that left them both shaky and breathless.

And still, he held her, the corded muscles of his arms able to take her weight as he balanced her against the wall.

When she could find her voice again, all she could manage was, "Wow."

"Sorry. Not a finessed moment."

She swept his hair off his brow. "It was a wow moment. It was perfect."

He grinned, kissed her and set her down. Riley fixed them something to drink, then they gathered their clothes and went upstairs to the bedroom.

Ethan seemed comfortable wandering the house naked. Then again, why not? It was just the two of them and oh, man, he was magnificent. She could tell he worked his body hard, and he had the best ass she'd ever seen.

Riley remembered their makeout sessions used to be all hands and mouths and couldn't get enough of each other, but they'd never made love. Maybe that's what had hurt so much about finding him in Amanda's bed that morning. Amanda had had him, and she hadn't.

She forced thoughts of Amanda out of her head, refusing to let the past intrude on the present. She couldn't go back and change what was. Now was what she was interested in, and right now Ethan was hers.

Only hers.

They climbed onto the bed together and Ethan dragged her against him.

"Let's try to slow things down this time," he said.

"I thought last time was pretty good."

"It was, but I want to touch all of you this time, linger over you."

She shuddered out a sigh when he brushed his lips across hers, then drew her in for a hungry kiss that melted her to the sheets.

As he slid his fingers up her ribcage, she was afraid she was going to slide right off the bed from the sheer pleasure of it. He pulled his lips away and she felt consumed by the raw hunger in his eyes, the need she saw reflected there.

She'd missed so much with Ethan, had hesitated all those years ago and she'd lost him. And she might not really have him now, but she was going to have him tonight, even if she didn't tomorrow. She wanted this one night with him no matter what happened after that.

And now it was her chance to explore, too, to lay her palms over his chest and let them wander over the rock-hard steel of his abdomen. The solid, muscular feel of him was so different than when he'd been a boy. This was a man's body, the sculpted angles and planes telling her what he did for a living.

And below his belly, she wound her fingers around him, rewarded with a slow hiss of his breath.

This was a new side to their relationship, the adult side, something they'd never had before. When she was younger she'd been tentative, innocent, not knowing what to ask for.

Now she knew exactly what she wanted.

All of him.

He rolled her onto her back and climbed on top of her, kissing the spot between her neck and shoulder that drove her crazy, before lazily mapping her body with his lips, from her collarbone to her breasts. And when he reached her breasts he took his damn sweet time, torturing her with nips and kisses and bites that had her arching her back and crying out for more.

Bastard. She loved every second of what he did to her, was damp and ready for him again in seconds. She raised her arms out for him, but he only chuckled and laid them on the bed, holding them there while he kissed her ribs, her belly, working his way between her legs, nudging them apart with his shoulders, then putting his mouth on her sex to pleasure her until her mind no longer worked, until her back bowed and she muttered unintelligible words as she cried out with a shattering climax that left her shaking all over.

And when his face came into view again, he gave her a satisfied smile, rolled her onto her side facing him and lifted her leg over his hip. He entered her and this time it was slow and achingly sweet—at least in the beginning.

She touched his face, her fingertips tracing his lips as he stroked her so gently it almost moved her to tears. Having Ethan inside her, being one with him, was what she'd always wanted. They were meant to be together like this.

Passion rose in a hurry, and soon she was scraping her nails down his arm, and he gripped her hips and drew her hard against his thrusts. It seemed there could be no light and easy between them, because they had held off for too long, and the desire they felt had to be satisfied in the most primal of ways.

She demanded, and he gave, and when they both shattered, it was wrapped around each other, bodies, mouths and souls.

They played all night long, stopping only to eat a snack in the pre dawn hours.

They went to sleep tangled together like two people who'd been apart for so long they never wanted to lose sight of each other.

Riley wondered briefly what the next day would bring, then decided she just didn't care, because they'd had tonight, and that's all that mattered.

EIGHT

ETHAN SPENT CHRISTMAS EVE morning at the office, something that didn't make his mother too happy.

But he needed to get a few loose ends tied up, plus he just wanted some time alone with his thoughts since for some reason his mother had let everyone know he'd spent the night with Riley. Which meant nudges and winks from Brody and smiles from his Dad. Wyatt just shook his head and called him a dumbass.

He didn't want any of it, just some peace and quiet to think about what it all meant.

After a couple hours of mulling it over, he realized it meant nothing. Because after Christmas Riley would be going back to Nashville, where she had a life and a blockbuster career. He'd be staying in Deer Lake where he had a job, a family and a daughter to raise.

The fact he was still in love with her didn't enter the picture of her world at all, nor should it.

He knew he should have kept his distance. In fact, it would have been better if he hadn't seen her at all. Then all the old feelings he'd had for her wouldn't have come rushing back.

It was payback for hurting her. Because when she left, it was going to hurt like hell and it was going to be just like ten years ago all over again. The heartbreak he'd experienced when he'd gone out searching and couldn't find her, couldn't explain to her what had happened. The loss, the anguish, the wish that he could find her and bring her back home.

But this wasn't her home anymore and never would be again.

What would she do in a tiny town like Deer Lake? What did Ethan have to offer her now that she was rich and famous? She already had everything.

There was nothing he had to give her that she didn't already have.

He dug into his paperwork and shut down the dumbass thoughts in his head.

Riley had spent entirely too much time primping for Christmas Eve. A ridiculous amount of time considering when she wasn't on tour she never fussed with her appearance. She loved downtime because it meant no hairdressers or makeup artists hovering around putting false eyelashes on her and doing her hair "up to there."

So when she had time off, it meant straight hair and no makeup. No high-heeled boots, no glitter, and absolutely nothing with sequins.

Absent the glitter, sequins and high-heeled boots, she had styled her hair and put on makeup. She'd put on her favorite pair of black jeans, a tight sweater and a pair of fancy boots.

She twirled in the mirror and thought about changing clothes, then realized she wasn't going on a date, she was going to Ethan's parents' house to spend Christmas Eve with his entire family.

But her heart still fluttered with excitement when the doorbell rang.

She ran downstairs, flung the door open and saw Ethan's smiling face.

"Hey," he said.

"Hey, yourself."

Despite all they'd shared last night—and again this morning before he'd left—she still didn't know where they stood.

Until he stepped inside and dragged her into his arms for a body-melting kiss that left her dizzy.

"Nice to see you too," she said when he let her go. "I missed you today."

"I worked for a while at the office, then had the obligatory help-the-parents-get-ready-for-Christmas Eve thing. How was your day?"

She loved that he asked as she went to grab her coat. "I did a little writing. It was a productive day."

He helped her put her coat on and they walked outside. It was cold and the skies were dark, no sign of stars. Maybe it would snow for Christmas, which would be delightful.

"Glad it was a good day for you."

She slid into the car and waited for him to get inside. "I don't think it could have been anything but a perfect day after last night."

The smile he directed at her was dazzling. And promising. "I'm glad."

Still, they hadn't talked about last night or what it had meant or where they'd go from here. Riley tried not to make more of it than what it was—really great sex between two people who'd known each other for a very long time.

And maybe it had seemed like more at the time—more of a soul-type connection. But she was both a woman and a songwriter, a lethal combination. Women were emotional by nature, and artists tended to throw their hearts and souls into everything they did, whereas Ethan had probably just wanted to get laid.

So she should probably stop turning last night into the holy grail of lovemaking experiences, when to Ethan it had likely just been a night of decent sex.

"You're kind of quiet over there," he said as they pulled into his parents' driveway.

"Oh, just thinking of some lyrics. Hard to turn off the job sometimes."

He laughed. "I know how that is."

They went inside and Riley was assaulted by a three-foot whirlwind with dark hair in a ponytail. "Riley Jensen! You're here!"

Ethan took her coat with an apologetic look and leaned in to whisper. "Sorry. You'll get no peace tonight. She kind of adores you."

She grinned and whispered back. "It's okay. The feeling is mutual."

"Miss Zoey. How are you tonight?"

"Did you know Santa is coming tonight? You have to go to bed early or he won't come to your house. Where is your house, Riley Jensen?"

"I'm staying at the bed and breakfast over on Conner Street. Do you think Santa will be able to find me?" Riley said as she and Zoey wandered into the living room.

"Santa can always find you."

Everyone was there already. Wyatt and his scowling face, Brody and his amused one, and Ethan's parents, who grinned and enveloped her in a huge hug.

They had dinner, then spent the evening playing board games and cards, then watching *How The Grinch Stole Christmas*, both the half-hour cartoon version and the movie version because Zoey loved both. And so did Riley. She and Zoey snuggled together on the sofa, laughing at the Grinch, then feeling bad because he was misunderstood.

As Zoey scooted closer and held Riley's hand, it occurred to her how much she'd missed out on, and how much she craved a family of her own someday.

Or now.

Family. She fell into it and welcomed it for as long as she had it.

This wasn't her family. Zoey wasn't her daughter, and Ethan wasn't hers to keep. After Christmas she had to head back to Nashville, and Ethan and Zoey's lives were here.

She couldn't have everything.

There were no television cameras, no photographers, and as Ethan watched Riley snuggled up on the sofa with his daughter, his heart clenched. Riley had scooped her hair up into a ponytail, kicked off her boots and thrown a blanket over her and Zoey, both of them yawning as they watched television.

She'd wriggled into his family as if she belonged there, as if she'd never left. She threw Brody's zingers right back at him, ignored Wyatt's bad moods, and helped out with cooking and serving dinner and then the dishes, never once acting as if she were a superstar or a diva.

And then she'd sat on the floor cross-legged and played with his daughter. For hours. Not out of any sense of obligation, but as if she'd truly enjoyed playing with a seven-year-old. They'd done puzzles, sang together, read together, played dolls and even make-believe fairies. Riley hadn't once acted as if it were a chore to play with his kid. She'd seemed to be having a great time with Zoey.

Now they curled up together on the sofa watching a movie. Riley stroked Zoey's hair as his daughter's eyes drifted closed, and so did Riley's. They looked comfortable together, right together, as if they belonged to each other.

Shit.

He was making something out of nothing. Riley was being polite, was being herself. And Zoey had a monster case of hero worship. Though she didn't take to women all that well. Ethan had tried dating a few times, had included Zoey once or twice, and while Zoey was friendly, she didn't have mad love for the women like she did with Riley. And despite Riley's star status, he didn't think Zoey would be snuggled up against her like this if she didn't have feelings for her, considering Zoey's bullshit meter and all, which was outstanding. The kid just knew whether someone genuinely cared or not.

Which was just making the fact Riley would leave them both even harder. He should separate them before his daughter got hurt. He could handle it. Zoey wouldn't understand it.

Coward that he was, he went into the kitchen and grabbed a cup of coffee, and found his mother pulling down plates from the cabinet.

"Let me help you."

He reached the top cabinet and pulled the plates down.

"Thank you. And why aren't you in there watching television with Riley and Zoey?"

"They're both asleep. Or almost asleep."

"Aww, how sweet. Zoey really likes her."

"Too much, I think."

His mother frowned. "What does that mean?"

"It means when Riley leaves town it's going to hurt her. I need to put a stop to the two of them getting any closer."

She put her hands on her hips. "Don't you dare, Ethan Kent. I never thought of you as a coward before."

He backed up a step. "What do you expect me to do, Mom? Riley will be leaving after the holidays. And by then Zoey will think she can keep her."

"Oh, I see." She pushed the plates to the side and pulled out a chair, then pointed to another. Ethan sat. "We're not really talking about Zoey now, are we?"

"Yes, we are."

"Okay, we're not talking only about Zoey. You're afraid for your own heart, too."

He shrugged. "I'm a big boy. I can take it. She's just a kid. She won't understand."

"You still love her."

"I've always loved her. I never stopped."

She laid her hand over his. "It's okay to feel that way. Have you told Riley how you feel?"

"What good would that do? She still has to leave."

"But you never told her before. Maybe it's time you do. Maybe it'll make a difference."

He laughed. "No, it won't."

"See, that's always been your problem, Ethan."

"What's my problem?"

"Guilt. It's been your best friend for so long you don't know how to live without it."

"I don't know what you're talking about."

"Don't you? First it was guilt over the whole Amanda thing. It kept you from seriously trying to find Riley. Then it was Amanda's pregnancy, so you ended up staying married to her when maybe you shouldn't have."

"If I hadn't stayed married to Amanda, I wouldn't have Zoey."

"That's true, and we're all grateful for Zoey. But what about what you want, Ethan?"

"I have everything I want."

"No, you don't, and you're once again going to let guilt decide for you. You feel guilty for letting Riley down. You're still feeling guilty about it, and it'll keep you from thinking you're good enough to ask her to stay."

"It's not the same thing at all this time, Mom."

"Isn't it? You're going to let her go without letting her know how you feel. To me it's the same thing."

"I need to take her home."

His mother nodded, then stood and came over to him,

wrapped his face in her hands. "I have faith in you, Ethan. I think it's time you had faith in yourself and what you have to offer."

"I can't compete with what she already has."

Her eyes twinkled as she smiled. "Can't you?"

She kissed his cheek and let him go.

When he walked in to the living room, his heart turned over at the sight of Riley's head lying on top of Zoey's, both of them sound asleep.

And then he thought about what his mother said.

Riley was going to spend the holidays alone. She had no family. How many Thanksgivings and Christmases did she do that? What must that be like for her, to send her crew home to their families, then go home to an empty house for the holidays?

Ethan had his mother, father, brothers, and he had Zoey. He was wrapped up in the warmth and love of family surrounding him, not just at the holidays, but every single day of his life.

As he looked down at Riley and Zoey huddled together, he realized maybe there was something he had to offer.

But would Riley even want that? Maybe she was content with the life she'd created for herself.

He swept his daughter up and took her upstairs to the bedroom where she slept at his mom's. They were going to have Christmas over here in the morning, so she'd spend the night here anyway. He tucked her in, kissed her forehead and swept her hair away from her face.

"I love you, Zoey," he whispered, then turned out the light. She pulled her snuggly bear close to her and he smiled, then closed the door partway.

One beautiful girl down, one to go.

Riley was still out, so he slid on the sofa next to her. "Hey, Sleeping Beauty."

She moaned, then turned on her side.

"Time to wake up."

"Don't wanna."

He laughed, then nuzzled her neck with a kiss. "You want to sleep on the couch tonight? You might get a peek at Santa. Or is it the cookies and milk you're after?"

She giggled. "You've spoiled my master plan." She turned over and tunneled her fingers into his hair, pressing her lips against his.

"If you're going to start something, we should head to your place."

"Why?"

"Because we're at my parents and my mom is in the kitchen."

"Oh. Good point. Okay." She pushed off his chest, yawned and stretched.

With her hair half sticking out of her ponytail and a sleepy look on her face, she was devastating to his senses.

She stumbled into her boots, went into the kitchen to say good-night to his mother, and they climbed into their coats. But instead of heading over to the B and B, he took her to his house.

She turned to look at him when he pulled into the drive-way.

"I wanted you to see my place."

She smiled. "I'd love to."

"It's nothing fancy. Nothing like your house in Nashville."

She reached for his hand. "Ethan. Don't compare Nash-ville and here. It's never about money. It's about home and what makes you happy."

She opened the car door and stepped out, staring at the house. "I wish it was daylight. Did you build the house?"

"Yeah."

"It's lovely. I'm sure Amanda loved it."

"This isn't the house where Amanda and I lived."

She turned to him, frowning. "It's not?"

"No. After she died I wanted a fresh start, didn't want those memories clouding mine and Zoey's life. Plus the house we had was tiny. So I built this place."

He tried to imagine what Riley would think of it. It wasn't oversized. It was a two story, gray and white, with a nice-sized back yard.

"I love all the trees. And the porch. I love porches."

He opened the front door and turned the lights on, let Riley walk in.

"Oh, Ethan, this is nice. The marble tile is beautiful."

"Being in construction has its advantages. I get a lot of stuff at cost, or not much markup. So I got to upgrade a lot."

She was already steps ahead of him. "This kitchen is magnificent! Double oven, granite counters. Ethan, I can't believe you built this. It's every woman's dream."

He smiled at that. "Glad you think so. My mom had some input into what she called a woman's dream kitchen."

Riley turned around and leaned against the counter, folded her arms. "She was right. The island, the pots and pans hanging over it, the sink in the island, the sub-zero freezer. Everything you could want in a kitchen is in here."

He couldn't help but feel pride at the work he'd done on the place. "It's big enough for more than me and Zoey, and the yard is huge." He clicked on the back porch light. "Zoey wants a dog. I've waited until she's old enough to be responsible."

"Oh, the yard is huge. I love the playset. And yes, it's perfect for a dog or two. I love animals, always wished I could have some."

He looked at her. "I remember."

"I used to love playing with Jack, your lab."

"Yeah, he died a few years ago."

Her smile vanished. "I'm sorry. That must have been so hard on everyone."

"He was an old dog, and he lived a great life. We buried him in my parents' backyard by the big oak tree."

"Jack would have liked that. He loved sleeping under that tree."

He took her hand and showed her the living room with its oversized couches and chairs and the giant television.

"Definitely a man's room," she teased.

"Hey, Zoey likes to watch Disney in here."

She snorted.

He led her upstairs. "Only two of the bedrooms are in use. Oh, and there's a full bath and another bedroom or possible office downstairs. Haven't decided yet."

"So five bedrooms, three bathrooms?"

"Yeah."

She stopped in the hallway. "You planning on a couple more kids, maybe?"

"I don't want Zoey to be an only child, so yeah, I'd like to have more kids someday."

Something flickered in her eyes. "That would be nice. Zoey would be a great big sister."

"This is Zoey's room." He opened the door and turned on the light.

Riley laughed. "Somehow I knew it would be pink. Very, very pink. I love her bed. Did you build that yourself?"

"I did."

She put her arm around him. "It's beautiful, Ethan. Every

little girl dreams of a canopy bed, with a pink tulle canopy and fairy sparkles on the ceiling."

"Zoey loves her room, and thanks."

She stepped in and took a look at the Noah's Ark of wooden carved animals on Zoey's dresser. "These are amazing. Where did you get these?"

"I made them."

She swiveled, her mouth agape. "You carved these?"

"Yeah. I started when she was a baby, before she was born. I made the Ark first, then started on the animal pairs. I add to them every birthday."

"Oh, Ethan. They're gorgeous. The intricate workmanship in each piece and the level of detail." She ran her finger over the elephant's trunk. "I hope Zoey treasures them. What a wonderful gift from father to daughter."

He felt his cheeks burn hot, but admittedly enjoyed the praise. "Thank you."

She lingered at the Ark exhibit for a while, then stepped out of the room.

He led her down the hall to his room. "It's kind of sparse. Just a giant bed and a dresser."

She turned to him and smiled. "How utterly perfect."

"Tired?" he asked as he helped her remove her coat.

"I didn't think I was. I think little girls who snuggle against you have some kind of sleeping dust attached to them."

"Yeah, she does it to me, too. It's the cuddle factor."

"Lethal. I was out before I knew what hit me." She held out her hand and he followed her to the bed.

"We didn't get much sleep last night," he reminded her.

Her lips quirked. "Guess what? We aren't going to get much tonight, either."

He pulled her against him, knowing he'd never tire of the feel of her curves pressed to his. "Who needs sleep?"

He took his time undressing her, the frenzy of last night somewhat satisfied. Plus, there was something about taking a woman's clothes off, piece by piece, like unwrapping a gift without tearing the paper.

He lifted her sweater over her head, had her sit on the bed and slipped her boots off, then her socks, before gently pushing her to the bed so he could pull off her pants. When he spied the golden silk and lace panties that matched the bra, he arched a brow.

"Prepared yourself tonight?"

"I wasn't ready for you last night. I am tonight."

"These look expensive," he said, tracing his fingers around the tiny bows at her hips, then snaking his finger up her belly to the matching bow between her breasts. "I'll try not to rip them."

He felt the pounding of her heart beneath his fingers.

"Oh, I don't mind. I have plenty of lingerie."

"Do you?"

"Yeah."

It made him wonder why. He wanted to ask, but it wasn't his business.

"Not that any man's seen my underwear for a very long time," she said in answer to his unspoken question. "I just have a thing for lingerie."

His lips lifted. "No woman's seen mine for a long time either. But the only lingerie I have a thing for is yours."

She sat up and reached for the button of his jeans. "How disappointing. And I was so hoping?"

"Does Calvin count?"

She waited while he kicked his boots off, then drew his zipper down, her gaze meeting his as she shoved his jeans to the floor. "Calvin definitely counts."

When she helped him divest himself of his Calvins, he

pulled his shirt off and climbed onto the bed, way more interested in what she was wearing. He smoothed his hands over the hills and valleys of her bra, paying attention to her breathing, the way her eyes went all glassy when her nipples peaked and hardened. He swept his fingers over the cups, seeing the buds of her nipples arching against the silk.

Leaning over her, he took a taste of her through her bra.

"Ethan," she said, her voice soft and buttery as she slid her fingers into his hair. He drew the cups down to taste her, teasing her with his tongue and his mouth until she arched her hips against him, letting him know she was ready for more.

Pleasuring her was so easy because she was so responsive with her body, and he loved touching her. He moved down her body and slid his hands over the silken softness of her panties, rewarded with a rush of unintelligible words from her lips. Ethan was pretty sure they were all good words as he slid his hand inside her panties and took her to the edge, watching her face as she came apart for him, shuddering out a cry that held his name.

She was undoing him with every minute he spent with her. When she took off her bra and panties and climbed on top of him, taking control, he might have died a little.

And when she leaned over, her breasts sliding against his chest as she took his mouth and claimed him at the same time she took possession of him with her body, he knew for sure she was his, always had been and always would be. And neither time nor distance had ever changed that or ever would.

She held his hands and rocked against him, and he couldn't remember ever being with a woman who surprised him, challenged him, or made him question his priorities more.

And when they came together, both of them holding tight

to each other in the darkness of night, he knew then that no matter what, he was never going to let her go.

Because for the first time in his life he wondered just what he'd be wiling to give up to have Riley in his life forever.

After, they held each other in the dark, both of them quiet for awhile.

"Ethan?" she finally whispered.

"Yeah."

"This time we've had together has been really amazing."

"Yeah, it has." His gut tightened. This might be an "It's been great, but" kind of speech.

"I wish it could last forever."

"Me too, Riley."

He waited, but she didn't say anything else, making him wonder if she hesitated because she didn't want to hurt him, or if she was waiting for him to make the next move.

Hell, he'd never been very good at figuring out what women thought, or what they wanted.

It took awhile before he realized she'd fallen asleep.

While she slept, he got up and wandered the house, wondering how he was going to approach this, how he'd ever ask her to stay with him.

Hour after hour he walked from room to room, realizing he'd be asking her to make all the sacrifices. He'd be giving up nothing, and she'd have to give up everything, or at least make a hell of a lot of adjustments in her life.

Great for him. Not so great for her.

Maybe this wasn't such a good idea after all. Maybe the best thing he could do for her was let her go, instead of presenting her with a no-win scenario, because it was his only option, which meant what he had to offer her was really nothing special.

Really, nothing at all.

NINE

ETHAN WOKE RILEY early the next morning. Like, before dawn kind of early. He said he had to get over to his parents to be there before Zoey woke so they could do the whole gifts and Santa thing. He wanted to take her with him, but Riley thought it would be best if he had Christmas morning alone with his daughter.

Plus, there was something she had to do, so she told him she was going to go back to the B and B, take a shower and change clothes, and then she'd drive over to his parents.

She'd read his hesitancy last night, and at first she was hurt. She'd been hoping for some kind of declaration from him. She thought she knew how he felt, knew for sure how she felt, and was determined not to be the first to say something.

But she realized she held the upper hand now, that the situation wasn't at all the same now as it had been ten years ago.

He wasn't going to ask her to stay. Not now, not when he knew she had so much at stake.

Silly men and their egos. Didn't he realize she was in love with him?

And love always trumped everything, especially money and career. At least it did with her. And when you were in love, the rest of it could be worked out.

Not that she had any intention of walking away from her career. She wasn't stupid.

But she had an idea, so when Ethan dropped her off, she ran upstairs and took a shower and dressed, then grabbed her guitar and got to work. It took a few hours, but she finally had everything figured out. She'd already been working on it for days, she realized.

She loaded the gifts she'd bought into the car and drove over to Ethan's parents' house. Brody opened the door and grabbed her, planting a short but deep kiss on her lips.

"Merry Christmas, Riley!" he said, clearly already deep into the rum punch.

She laughed. "Merry Christmas, Brody."

He carried the gifts into the house for her while she greeted everyone. Zoey ran up and hugged her, waved some kind of fancily dressed doll in front of her face, then dashed off to play with all her new "stuff" as she called it, but extracted a promise from Riley that she'd come see all her presents as soon as she got settled and said hello.

"Coffee, hot chocolate, or rum punch?" Ethan's mother asked.

"Actually, a cup of coffee sounds great, thanks."

"With or without brandy or whiskey in it?" Ethan's dad asked as he came up and hugged her.

"Oh, now you're tempting me. How about a little brandy?"

"There's a girl after my own heart."

"There's a girl who'll be face down on the floor before lunch," Ethan said. "Merry Christmas, Riley." He pulled her into his arms and planted what Riley considered to be one seriously hot kiss on her lips. In front of his parents, and his brothers.

"Daddy, you kissed Riley."

And his daughter.

He broke the kiss and grinned at his daughter. "I did. Is that okay?"

Zoey nodded. "Yup. Will you come take my game out of the package?"

"Sure, honey." He shifted his gaze to Riley. "Sorry, Dad duty calls. Back in a sec."

Apparently, Zoey was utterly unfazed about the kiss between her and Ethan. One hurdle down. And as she surveyed his parents and his brother, Wyatt just shrugged, Ethan's mother beamed a smile, and his father grinned from ear to ear as he poured what Riley considered a face-down-on-the-floor-before-lunch dose of brandy into her coffee.

"You trying to get me drunk, Mr. Kent?"

He laughed and smacked her on the back. "Nah. Figured you're a tough girl and you can take it. Drink up, it'll put hair on your chest."

"Now there's an unattractive visual," Wyatt grumbled, taking the bottle of whiskey and pouring it straight into the glass with a couple ice cubes.

"Too early for that, Wyatt," his mother warned.

Wyatt kissed Mrs. Kent on the cheek. "I'm here. Isn't that enough?"

"I suppose, but that's all the whiskey you get today. Switch off to coffee after that."

Wyatt nodded, but Riley caught the roll of his eyes as he walked away.

"He's had it rough the past couple years," she explained to Riley after he walked out. "But I sure wish he'd get over Cassandra, stop with the bitterness and move on with his life."

"With some people it takes awhile."

"You talking about yourself?"

Riley laughed. "I guess so. I carried a grudge for a long time."

"But now you're over it."

"I did it all wrong, Mrs. Kent. Stacy. I wish I had known then what I know now. I would have done things differently."

Ethan's mother held up her hands. "No way to change the past or predict the future."

"I made a mistake in running. I should have stood my ground and fought for Ethan."

She smiled. "I'm glad to hear you say that. Did you tell him that?"

"Not exactly."

Mrs. Kent rolled her eyes. "Hell's bells. What is it with you kids not telling each other how you feel? You're talking to the wrong person. Go. Go tell my son you love him."

Riley smiled. "I will. Sometime today. I promise."

She gave Ethan's mother a quick hug, then wandered out to find Ethan. He was on the floor with Zoey, who was playing a handheld game while Ethan frowned over instructions.

"It says to reach Level two—"

"I'm already on Level four, Daddy," Zoey said, not looking up from her game.

"Oh." Ethan tossed the instructions in the pile of trash.

Riley laughed. "Technology is for children, you know." She sat down on the floor on the other side of Zoey.

"So I'm beginning to understand."

Riley watched Zoey play the game for a while, then Zoey handed it over to Riley to play.

She figured it out after a few rather embarrassing tries and Zoey showing her how it was done. Then she realized she wanted one of these handheld game devices, especially when Ethan showed her the catalog of software that went with it.

"It has cooking recipes. It tells you step-by-step instructions while you're cooking. And here I thought it was a kid's device."

"It's multifunctional for all ages," Zoey said.

Riley looked at Ethan, then at Zoey. "How old are you again, kid?"

"Seven."

"Are you sure? You're awfully smart for seven."

Zoey giggled. "That's what my daddy says, too."

Riley excused herself to help Mrs. Kent set the table for lunch. They ate an abundance of turkey and dressing with more side dishes than Riley could count. It was the best holiday home-cooked meal she'd had in ages. After they cleared the table and loaded the dishwasher, it was time to sit in the living room and Riley handed out the gifts she'd bought for everyone.

She'd bought Wyatt and Brody new coats, thick down ones that would be great for the job site. She gave Mr. and Mrs. Kent a new television because they'd been complaining their old one was about to give up the ghost. She gave Zoey a guitar and the little girl's eyes widened. Then she squealed.

"Really?"

"You're old enough, but you'll have to take lessons."

"I'll practice every day. I want to play like you do."

"You have a beautiful voice, Zoey. But you only have to play guitar if that's what you want to do. Otherwise it can just sit in your room and you can look at it and think of me."

She grinned. "Cool."

"Now I have a gift for you," Ethan said, interrupting her. "It's not as nice as the gifts you gave my family, but I've been working on it for the past ten years."

She tilted her head to the side. "You have?"

"Yeah. You seeing Zoey's room last night reminded me, so I finished it today."

He handed her a box. She opened it and inside was a carving much like the ones of Zoey's Noah's Ark animals. Only it was a woman sitting on a stool with a guitar.

"It looks just like you, Riley, when you're singing and playing your guitar," Zoey said.

Riley's eyes filled with tears. She lifted her gaze to Ethan. "It does. Thank you. Thank you so much. It's the best gift ever."

Ethan leaned over and brushed his lips over hers. "I love you, Riley. I always have. I always will. I don't have much to offer, but what I have is yours. A home. A family. My family. My love. Forever. I want you with me. I want you to be a part of my life."

Her heart swelled and soared. The words she needed to hear made joy spring from every pore, from every fiber of her body.

She sniffed, fighting back the tears. "I have a gift for you as well, Ethan."

She went to get her guitar. "I thought about what it meant to come back here again. To come back and see you again. But now I realize that seeing you was what I needed, and what I wanted the most. And also what I was most afraid of.

"I ran once, but I want you to know I'm never running again, no matter how hard it gets. I love you, Ethan."

She started the song, the music perfectly clear in her head, soft melody, heart-filled strains of love pouring from her guitar as she sang only to the man she loved. A slow, sweet melody, a pouring out of her heart, her very soul, for Ethan.

"The swing out back where we'd talk for hours
You'd smile, I'd blush, the world was ours
Back then I didn't know all I had
I threw it all away when it all went black

Girlish dreams are glitter and polish
Up in smoke without a backwards glance
You gave me your heart then you let me go
I thought you didn't care. I didn't know

You set me free to give me a chance
I took my heart with me and never looked back
I hurt you then because I didn't see
What it was you did for me

I was blind and foolish on my own
The lights were bright, it was all for show
Lonely nights, years on the road
It's not enough anymore. I want to come home.

The world's a big place with so much to see
I've learned a lot, I soared and was free
But the tie still remains, drawing me here
And now I stand next to you without fear

The soul knows who lights the flame
Of love and desire, I know his name
I don't want to run, I don't want to roam
I want to come home, I want to come home

My wandering ends but our journey begins
All it takes is for you to let me in
Open the door and give me your love
I want to come home, I want to come home
To you."

THE ROOM FELL SILENT, and Mrs. Kent cleared her throat.

"That was lovely, Riley. Now the rest of you can come help me in the kitchen."

"But Grandma, I want to hear Riley sing some more."

"Later, Zoey. Riley and your daddy have some talking to do."

"Riley, do you love my daddy?"

Riley turned a tear-filled gaze to Zoey. "Yes, Zoey, I do love your daddy."

Zoey grinned. "I thought so. That's pretty cool, because he loves you, too, don't you, Daddy?"

Riley turned back to Ethan to see him nodding at his daughter. "Yes, muffin, I do love Riley."

"That's so cool. My daddy loves Riley Jensen."

Riley laughed through her tears.

After everyone left, Ethan came over to her, took her guitar, and laid it against the sofa. He pulled her into his arms and kissed her, a deep kiss filled with all the love she'd always wanted but was afraid she'd never have.

And when he broke the kiss, he said, "I was afraid to ask you to stay. I couldn't ask it of you."

"I'll have to travel. I was afraid to ask that sacrifice of you. I love my career."

"I'd never make you give it up. Zoey and I can travel with you in the summers."

"You'd do that?"

"I'd do anything for you."

She smiled, then laughed, put her hands around his neck. "Anything?"

"Yes."

"Will you give me babies to fill that huge house of yours?"

He arched a brow. "How soon do you want them?"

"Really soon."

"Then I guess I'd better put a ring on your finger and marry you. Really soon."

"I love you, Ethan."

"I love you, too, Riley."

As Ethan kissed her, and then as her family—because they were all her family now—crowded in to offer congratulations, she realized she'd been given all she wanted for Christmas. The man she loved, a beautiful daughter, a family who would always be hers, and love.

The best gift of all was always love.

★ ★ ★ ★ ★

Dedication

For Charlie. I love you.

A RARE GIFT

ONE

WYATT KENT STOOD outside Small Hands Day Care Center, debating whether or not he could actually go inside.

He was no coward, but it wasn't often he was faced with something like this.

He was about to give a bid on a construction job for his ex-wife's younger sister.

How he'd gotten stuck with this he didn't know. That was what he got for not paying attention in meetings. He'd been bulldozed by his two brothers along with Tori, Kent Construction's oh-so-efficient but manipulative office manager.

"No big deal, Wyatt."

"Calliope Andrews is nothing like your ex-wife, Cassandra."

"No one else can do the project, Wyatt. It's either you or the job doesn't get done."

Might as well suck it up and get this over with. The wood-frame house was painted shocking blue and blinding white. The sign out in the front yard was plastered with a bunch of multicolored handprints.

So it was cute. The house needed a new coat of paint. Probably would need a new roof within the next year or two, too. But that wasn't his problem. He stood at the end of the walkway and watched the endless parade of parents driving up to the side of the house. The side door opened, parents dashed in to retrieve kids, then the car drove through to the back alley and the next car pulled up.

Wyatt went up to the front door and rang the bell, then

waited for someone to answer. And waited. And waited. He tried the door, figuring he'd let himself in, but it was locked.

Great.

He went around to the side and was halted by a tall, thick woman with short cropped black hair and likely more muscles than he had. She wore jeans and a T-shirt and looked more like a wrestler than a day care worker.

She frowned, gave him the head-to-toe once-over.

"Who are you?"

"Wyatt Kent. I have an appointment with Calliope Andrews."

She laid her hand on his chest to keep him in place. "Stay here. Miss Calliope, there's a Wyatt Kent here. Says he's supposed to meet with you."

"Oh, that's right. It's okay, Beth. I'm expecting him."

Beth tossed a thumb over her shoulder. "Go on back. You're in my way."

"Go on back where?"

"Straight down the hall, then turn right. All the way to the end."

Wyatt nodded and dodged a bunch of giggling little girls on his way. They were a few years younger than his eight-year-old niece, Zoey, but they were all dressed in pink—Zoey's favorite color.

Most of the kids must have gone home by now. With the exception of a few stragglers dashing by him on his way down the hall, the place had gone quiet. He found the room Beth had directed him to. It was fairly small and completely empty.

A playroom, it was stuffed with overflowing bookshelves and toys and tables and a giant castle.

He stood in the middle of the room, figuring Calliope had stepped out.

Until he heard a rustling in the castle, then a groan. He

turned around and saw one very attractive, jeans-clad butt attempting to back out of the castle opening.

"I swear if my butt gets any bigger I'm not going to be able to clean the toys out of this thing and we'll need to get a bigger castle."

He disagreed. She had a great ass.

She flung toys over her shoulder while Wyatt stood there, feeling sort of inept.

"You need some help there?"

She stilled, her head jerked up and she bumped it against the opening. "Ow. Dammit." She rubbed the wild curls on top of her head, then backed all the way out and sat on the floor, adjusted the tortoise-shell glasses that had ridden down the bridge of her very cute nose.

"Wyatt. I thought you were Beth. You're not Beth."

"No, I'm not."

"Sorry. I was cleaning up in here." She pushed off her knees and stood, adjusting her shirt over some very full breasts and grinned at him. "I'm so glad you're here. Let's go to my office where it's a little less insane."

The last time Wyatt had seen Calliope Andrews, he'd still been married to her older sister Cassandra, and Calliope had been—hell, in college? Maybe nineteen or twenty, at most, was his guess. She'd been chubby, her hair a corkscrew of untamed brown curls, and she'd worn really ugly glasses. In short, she'd been a hot mess.

He followed her down the hall, watching the way her hips moved when she walked.

"Here we are." She opened the door and led him into a small office. Her desk sat next to the window and there were a couple chairs on either side. He took one and she sat across from him instead of at her desk.

She still wore glasses and her hair was still curly and she

was still hot, all right. But she wasn't a mess at all. Calliope had grown up. It had to have been six years or so at least since he'd seen her last. She'd lost the baby fat, was curvy in all the right places, and her glasses made her eyes look like sparkling emeralds.

God, she was gorgeous.

But she wasn't at all like Cassandra, who'd been tall, slender and blonde.

And the devil in disguise.

"Thank you for taking on this project, Wyatt."

"No one else had the time."

She quirked a brow, then grinned again. "So you're stuck with me, then?"

"I didn't say that."

"You didn't have to." She laughed and didn't seem at all offended. "I know this is probably hard for you, seeing as how you've managed to avoid me since I came to town."

"I haven't avoided you."

"Yes, you have. But it's okay. I understand why. You're not very fond of my sister, and you think we're exactly alike." She patted his hand. "But trust me, I'm nothing like Cassie."

He blinked, not sure he understood anything that had happened so far. He figured the two of them would dance around the topic of Cassandra, and here Calliope had said her name, torn open the wounds, making them bleed fresh, like it had happened yester…

"Wyatt. Wyatt." She snapped her fingers. "You okay?"

"I'm fine." He stood. "Let's go see where you want this addition."

"Sure." She stood, too. "Surely you're over her by now, aren't you? I mean it's been three years. She's not worth mourning over for that long."

Calliope opened the door to her office and walked down the same hallway they'd come from.

Her saying it that way made him feel foolish for feeling closed up and angry for three damn years over a woman who'd only cared about herself.

"You are over her, aren't you?"

God, she was persistent. "Yeah. Over her."

"Good. Because I want us to be friends."

He stopped in the middle of the hall. "What?"

She stopped, too, turning and dipping her head back to look into his eyes.

Damn she had pretty eyes. Pretty hair. And she smelled good, too. He couldn't figure out what she smelled like. Something that made him want to swipe his tongue across her neck.

His jeans tightened. It had been a long damn time since that had happened. He didn't trust women, tried to stay away from them.

And he sure as hell planned to stay away from Calliope.

"Wyatt. Are you drunk? Did you stop at the bar after work?"

"What?" He looked down at her. She must have been saying something, because her lips quirked.

"I've been talking. You're not listening. Want to do this another day?"

"No." He didn't want to do it at all. "Show me what you want."

She paused, her cheeks turning pink. "Sure. This way."

They went into the room where the castle was. "I want the addition off this room, to extend the play area so I can separate the kids by age group. Younger kids in here, older kids in the new room."

Finally, something to distract him from Calliope, from

the way she looked, the way she smelled, the things—people—she reminded him of. He took out his tape measure and started making some notes based on what she wanted, which was a room a little larger than the one they stood in, with ample storage space.

Nothing fancy. Doable. Easy enough. He'd bring in some extra labor to help, and he'd be out of there. Calliope stayed quiet while he wrote down materials and labor needed to get the job done. He turned to her. Looked at her. And all the memories came flooding back.

He couldn't do this.

"Wyatt. I know I was kidding you about getting over things and doing this job, but if you're seriously having second thoughts, I know there's this other company I looked up that can handle it. The Johnson Brothers?"

That did it.

Kent Construction was a family-owned business and had been since their father and grandfather had started up the company over fifty years ago. They'd had a stronghold on Deer Lake with very little competition.

The Johnsons were a new outfit who'd been leeching into their territory for the past few years, stealing business away from them. Wyatt didn't mind competition, but he didn't like the Johnson brothers. They weren't local, their workmanship was shoddy, they cut corners and used inferior products. And he hated losing to them.

It was only a single room addition. How long could it take? A month, six weeks at most.

He could suck it up and deal for six weeks. And even if he couldn't, he wasn't about to give a job away—an easy job he could handle.

"I don't know what you're talking about. I'll go back to

the office, write up an estimate and have it delivered to you tomorrow."

She cocked her head to the side. "Won't you bring it by so we can get the contract signed? I'd like to get started on this as soon as possible." She raised her hands out to her sides. "As you can tell we've outgrown the space and really need the extra room here."

He inhaled, let it out. "Fine. I'll deliver it in the morning and bring a contract with me."

There was that grin again. She had dimples. Awfully cute.

No. She wasn't cute. Not at all. Nothing about her was cute. Or sexy.

"I gotta go." He turned and fled the room.

"Okay." She skirted in front of him. "Here, let's go out the front door."

Once again he was forced to trail behind her, giving him a great view of her ass.

Calliope was the first woman he'd noticed—really ogled, as a matter of fact—in a long time.

That sent danger and warning signals flashing in his head. *Say no. Walk away. Don't do this job.*

But he'd be damned if he was going to lose another job to those asshole Johnsons. How much danger could he be in with Calliope Andrews? She owned a day care center. She would be busy all day. So would he. They'd barely run into each other, right?

She opened the door and stood with her hand on the door knob, the other pushing up her glasses.

"Thanks for coming by, Wyatt. I'll see you tomorrow."

"See ya."

He hurried out the front door and hadn't even realized he'd been holding his breath until he reached the sidewalk. He turned back to look at the door.

Calliope was still there. She waved at him.

Like an idiot he waved to her, then snatched his hand back and shoved it in his jacket pocket.

He was not going to be nice. He didn't have to be. All he had to do was his job.

And nothing more.

TWO

Calliope finished cleaning up the playroom, then went into her office to shut down the computer.

That was when she saw Wyatt's clipboard.

Oh, no. He'd need that if he was going to do her estimate. She picked up the phone, intending to call his office, then laid it back down.

She was on her way out the door anyway, and the offices of Kent Construction were a few miles away. She'd drop it off on her way home.

So maybe his office wasn't exactly on her way home, since she only lived a couple blocks from the day care center, but she didn't mind going out of her way to deliver his clipboard.

And maybe she might want to see him again tonight.

And maybe she might still have a crush on him.

But crush or not, this was business, and it had to come first. She needed the addition to the day care center and she needed Wyatt focused on giving her that estimate.

She climbed into her car and headed toward his offices, remembering how it had been all those years ago.

She'd been more than a little bit in love—or at least lust—with Wyatt since she was fifteen years old and her older sister Cassandra had dragged him over to the house to meet their parents. When he'd walked through the door, she'd been sitting at the kitchen table doing her homework. She'd looked up, saw him and her breath had stopped.

Wyatt had been twenty-three back then—and gorgeous. And then Cassie had walked in and slipped her hand in

Wyatt's and all Calliope's hopes were dashed. Cassie had been taken with Wyatt's lean good looks, his dark hair and blue eyes. And why wouldn't she? Every girl in Deer Lake wanted him, and Cassie loved competition—loved to win. She'd won Wyatt, though Calliope had been certain Cassie had never loved Wyatt. She'd only wanted him because every other girl in town had wanted him, too. Once Cassie had him, she paraded him around town like a prize possession.

Cassie was beautiful, with her dark blond hair that fell straight and sleek to her waist, and a killer body that she honed for hours at the gym. And she was so smart, had gone to college and gotten her business degree, then gone to work for one of the top real-estate firms in town, eventually branching out to start her own company. Real estate and construction—Cassie and Wyatt's businesses had even meshed.

They'd really been the perfect couple.

But the two of them hadn't been the perfect couple at all, and it had broken Calliope's heart to see both of them so unhappy. Sometimes things don't work out. They were better apart than together. Cassie had moved on, but for some reason, Wyatt seemed to hold a grudge.

But the past was the past and she'd hoped Wyatt was over it by now. Nobody was worth pining over for three years—not even her sister.

She pulled up to the offices. Wyatt's truck wasn't there.

Huh. She got out anyway and went to the front door, tried to open it, but it was locked up tight. She peered through the glass. It was dark.

Maybe he decided he'd come in early in the morning to do the bid. She shrugged and got back into her car, deciding she'd come back in the morning and bring him the clipboard.

On her way back down Central, she spotted his truck parked in front of Stokey's bar.

Oh. That's where he was. She'd drop off the clipboard to him there. She parked and went inside, blinking to adjust her eyes to the darkness.

She wasn't much of a drinker, so she'd never been in Stokey's before. There wasn't a whole lot of atmosphere to the place. Dim lighting, bottles of alcohol stocked behind a very dark wood bar. There was a pool table off to one side, a dart board on the opposite wall and a couple televisions scattered about showing various sporting events.

There were only a handful of people inside—all men. Then again it was a Tuesday and not even seven-thirty yet. Maybe the big crowds didn't show up until later.

The men who were present stopped what they were doing to give her the once-over as she made her way to the bar.

Wyatt had a beer in hand, his focus on one of the televisions mounted behind the bar. She climbed onto the barstool next to his.

"Hey there."

Nothing. He didn't even acknowledge her. Then again, the television was turned up pretty loud, so maybe he hadn't heard her.

"Wyatt, you forgot your clipboard."

He finally turned his head, then frowned. "Calliope. What are you doing in here?"

She slid the clipboard across the bar to him, then smiled at him. "Your clipboard. You left it at the center. Thought you might need it to work up those numbers for me."

He looked at her like he had no idea who she was. Then he gave her a quick nod. "Yeah, right. Thanks."

He used to be so full of life. He'd laugh and his face would light up when he smiled. Her toes curled remembering what he looked like when he smiled.

"You want something to drink?"

She shifted her gaze to the bartender, a heavyset guy with male pattern baldness.

"Oh. Uh. You know, I don't know." She turned to Wyatt. "What should I have?"

Wyatt stared at her. "How should I know?"

"Well, I don't really drink that often, so I'm not the best judge of what's good. What do you suggest?"

Wyatt raised his bottle to his lips. "Beer."

She nodded and looked at the bartender. "I'll have a beer."

The bartender flipped the top off the bottle and slid it to her. She reached into her purse for the money and paid him, leaving an extra dollar for a tip. Then she slid around on the stool to check out what was going on while she took a long swallow of the beer, shuddering at the taste.

Soda would be better, but this would have to do.

She slipped off the barstool and walked over to the pool table to watch the two guys play. She'd never played pool, either, though there'd been a table at her dorm in college.

The cool people played. She'd never been one of the cool people. Now that she was a single adult, she should learn to do cool things instead of always being wrapped up with work.

One of the guys—a burly, halfway decent-looking type wearing jeans and a plaid shirt, shifted his gaze to hers and grinned at her. "Want to take me on, honey?"

"Oh, I've never played before. Can you teach me?"

He took his shot and straightened, grabbed his beer and came over to stand beside her while his partner took a shot. "Honey, I can teach you anything you want to know."

"Great. Then I'd love to learn how to play."

They finished up their game, and the guy—who introduced himself as Joey Johnson—put the balls in the triangular thing. He called it "racking the balls". Once they were all set, he put the white ball in front of them.

"Now we break," he said, leaning forward with the pool cue.

She watched as he shot the white ball toward all the other balls. They scattered, some falling into the holes around the table.

"We'll play simple eight ball," Joey said. "I'm solid, you're stripes. I shoot until I miss. Then it's your turn to get your ball into the pockets."

"Seems simple enough."

Except Joey didn't miss very often. He put four of his balls in one of the pockets before she had a chance.

Of course that meant she'd gotten to watch his technique. It seemed easy enough. She bent over the table and tried to hold her pool cue the same way he did.

She wasn't very coordinated, though, and couldn't quite remember the hand positioning.

Joey laughed. "Here, let me help you."

He aligned his body next to hers, his pelvis shoving up behind her.

She might be naïve about pool, but she wasn't dumb about men. Joey was hitting on her in the most basic of ways, and wasn't subtle about it at all.

He could teach her to play pool, but she wouldn't be going home with him tonight.

"Just do it so it's comfortable for you." He put the cue in her hands, showed her the proper positioning. And that wasn't the only positioning he showed her.

Really? Sometimes men were so obvious.

Her gaze drifted over to Wyatt, who had swiveled around on his barstool and glared daggers at them.

He looked upset. At her.

She rolled her eyes.

And sometimes men were just plain dumb.

She straightened, smiled at Joey. "I think I've got the hang of it now, and if you shove your—" she looked down at his crotch, "—assets at me again, I'm going to knee you in the balls. Understood?"

His eyes widened, then he grinned. "Loud and clear."

Now that they had that straight, she took her shot. And amazing thing, the ball fell into the pocket. She let out a loud whoop and the guys around her cheered and high-fived her.

She might yet get the hang of this game.

WYATT WATCHED CALLIOPE play pool. She wasn't very good at it, but maybe it was an act to gather an entourage of men who were all too eager to help her out.

Within a half hour there were six guys hanging on her. And who wouldn't? She had a great ass, perfect breasts and the kind of hips a man wanted to grab on to and never let go. She looked you straight in the eye and smiled—a lot. And her laugh—damn, her laugh made his balls tighten. Deep and throaty, and she threw her head back and let it go for all she was worth.

Cassandra had always been subtle. She only had to enter a room and the men would come running. And she loved the attention. She barely noticed Wyatt was in the room once the guys swarmed around her.

He guessed the sisters were alike in that respect.

Except after two games, Calliope put the pool cue down, waved goodbye to the guys she'd collected and headed toward him.

She slid back onto the barstool and signaled the bartender. "Another beer?"

"No, thank you. How about a diet soda?"

She turned to Wyatt. "You don't play pool?"

"I play."

"Why didn't you join us?"

"I don't hang out with the Johnson brothers."

She quirked a brow. "Why not?"

"They're competitors."

She thanked the bartender for the soda and dug into her bag for money.

"I've got this. Add it to my tab, Bill."

"Thanks." She turned back and took a sip from the straw. "So because you and the Johnson brothers compete in business, you can't be friendly?"

"Not with those guys."

"Huh. Why not?"

He turned his head and gave her a look. "Because they're assholes."

She snorted. "Seemed like nice enough guys to me."

"I'm sure you'd think that."

"What does that mean?"

He faced ahead again. "Nothing."

"You're very irritable, Wyatt. Did you have a rough day?"

Calliope—unlike her sister—wasn't subtle at all. "No, I didn't have a rough day. And I'm not irritable. I'd like to be left alone."

"Being alone just makes you lonely. And that's not good for anybody. Is this what you do every night?"

Now he was forced to look at her again. "What?"

"Do you come here every night by yourself?"

Mostly. "Sometimes."

"And do what? Drink alone?"

She had him pegged. He didn't like it. "Why do you care?"

"I've always cared about you. You should get out and have some fun, not sit in this dark place and brood. You're like Heathcliff. Or the Beast from *Beauty and the Beast*." She laid her hand on his thigh. It made him want to groan. He didn't want to think about her being a woman—and a very attractive, sexy woman, at that. He wanted her to go away.

"Who's Heathcliff? And the Beast? Thanks a lot."

"I told you. Brooding. And really? Heathcliff? *Wuthering Heights?* Surely you've read that."

"Heard of the book. Never read it."

She leaned an elbow against the bar and put her lips around the straw, sucking up soda. His brain immediately registered *lips* and *suck* and there went the quivering in his balls again. She had a great mouth—a full bottom lip made to be tugged on.

Dammit.

He pulled out a couple bills and paid his bar tab, then grabbed his clipboard. "I gotta go."

He headed for the door. She followed.

"Yeah, I probably should, too. 6:00 a.m. comes awfully early. Thanks for buying me a drink."

"It was just a soda, Calliope."

It was dark outside. She zipped up her jacket and turned to him, gracing him with her beautiful smile again. "Still, you didn't have to and I really appreciate it."

Cassandra had never thanked him for anything. She'd always expected men to do things for her—buy her things, hold the door open for her, worship her.

He walked Calliope to her car. She grabbed her keys out of her bag, opened the door and quirked her lips up at him.

A man could get lost in a smile like that. There was something so guileless and innocent about it.

She laid her hand on his arm, then surprised the hell out of him by stepping in and wrapping her arms around him to hug him. The warmth of her seeped through his jacket, and every part of him that was a man felt every curve of her body as she pressed against him.

It was a brief hug, likely nothing more than something friendly. She pulled back and said, "I'll see you tomorrow, then. Goodnight, Wyatt."

His breath caught in his throat. "Yeah. Goodnight."

He went to his truck and climbed in, laying the clipboard next to him while he watched Calliope pull out of the parking lot.

He could still feel every part of her body that had touched his, could still smell the faint scent of vanilla.

He shouldn't have taken this job.

THREE

TORI BROUGHT THE bid by the next morning. She explained that Wyatt had to finish up a project on another site. Calliope signed off on the bid and Tori told her they'd start on it right away, but it would likely be a while because they couldn't do anything until they filed the permits and the cement floor was poured.

It took a week for the whole permit and cement thing, and through it all she didn't see Wyatt again. He'd sent a cement crew out to lay the foundation, and then trucks came to drop off materials. Tori had called saying Wyatt would start the project today.

Not that she'd been counting the days until she saw him or anything.

Not that she'd spent any time thinking about that ridiculously impulsive urge to hug him that night a week ago outside the bar.

What had she been thinking? They were about to enter into a business relationship. And she might be a touchy-feely type of person, and maybe she did hug just about every person on the planet, from her kids at the center to their parents and everyone who worked for her, but that didn't mean she had to go and hug Wyatt.

But oh, he'd been a solid wall of muscle, his body a hot furnace of steel that she wanted to climb onto and never let go of, once again reminding her of how incredibly lucky her sister had been.

He hadn't hugged her back—not that she'd given him any

time to. As soon as she realized what a bad move that had been, she'd taken a step back and said good-night. He hadn't looked at her like she'd grown two heads or anything, but he hadn't exactly been swept away and put his arms around her, either.

Then again, she wasn't swayed by rejection. Wyatt had a big gaping hole in his heart from the way his marriage had ended, and it was about time he healed. She figured she was the right person to help him with that. The fact he'd been married to her sister didn't factor in to her way of thinking.

And she'd been doing a lot of thinking about Wyatt, so while she was in her office doing financials, she heard the trucks pull up. She grabbed her jacket and walked outside.

Wyatt was there along with two other guys. She stayed out of sight and watched as he directed his employees.

If she thought he was gorgeous before, seeing him strip off his jacket and strap on a tool belt nearly made her knees buckle. There was something about a man who worked with his hands that was downright devastating to a woman's libido—or at least *her* libido.

She walked over to him, and just seeing him put a giant smile on her face.

It was already noisy, his two laborers setting up the frame with hammer and nails. Wyatt was inside the small trailer he'd brought with him hitched to his truck. She stepped inside, knocking on the open door as she entered.

"Hey."

He straightened, turned to her, frowned. "What are you doing here?"

"Checking in to say hello. How's it going?"

"It's not going at all yet since we're just getting started."

He was good at pushing women away. Tori had told her

he hadn't dated at all since the divorce. It was time to put a stop to that.

"If you or the guys need anything, come on in to the center and the staff or I will fix you right up. There's coffee or soda or—"

"We have everything we need right here."

"Okay. I'll let you get to work."

He didn't say anything, so she stepped out of the trailer and got back to doing her job. Other than listening to drilling and hammering, she mentally tuned him out. Kids were excellent for that. They commanded your attention and didn't let you think of anything but them. By the time the last kid and the last of her employees left the center, it was six-thirty. She figured Wyatt and his crew would be long gone by then, but she was curious how much work they'd gotten done in a day, so she put on her jacket, closed and locked the doors and set the alarm, then headed around the corner to see what had been done.

It was dark, but the streetlight shed enough light on the project. They'd made a good start on the framing. She was impressed.

And Wyatt's truck was still parked on the street, a light on inside the trailer. She went over and knocked on the door. No answer at first, then Wyatt opened the door, his typical frown on his face.

"What do you want?"

She stepped up and came inside. "I thought I'd stop by to take a look. You did a great job today."

"Thanks."

He stood there, arms folded. She skirted around him to see what he was working on at the table. "Are these the blueprints for the room?"

He sighed. "Yes."

She leaned over the table. "Looks complicated." She lifted her gaze to his. "I could never figure this out."

His gaze met hers. "It's not that hard. Look. This is the frame of the room. This is electrical…"

He outlined everything in the blueprint for her, not that she was paying attention. She was close to him and he smelled like sawdust and sweat, a lethal combination. She leaned closer and breathed him in, her shoulder brushing against his.

"Calliope."

"Yeah."

"What are you doing?"

Fantasizing. "Trying to get a closer look. My prescription is old and I probably need to see an eye doctor to get new glasses, but I haven't had time." She bent closer to the blueprints—actually shifting closer to Wyatt.

"Any closer and you're going to be on top of my desk."

Wouldn't that be fun? She wondered what Wyatt would do if she climbed on there? Would it give him ideas? She wished she had something sexier on—like a dress—instead of jeans covered in spilled chocolate milk and a sweatshirt baby Ryan had spit up on. Not an alluring ensemble at all.

Still, she wasn't about to give up on him. She had her jacket zipped up to hide the spit-up and it was dark enough he might not notice the milk stain.

She turned around and leaned against the desk.

"Wyatt, do you ever date?"

His eyes widened. "What?"

"Do you ever date? You know…women?"

Wyatt damn near swallowed his tongue. Where the hell had that come from? He'd thought she'd left and he could spend an hour or so going over the blueprints to make sure they were on track with this project. But then Calliope knocked on the door of the trailer, forced herself inside and then threw herself all over his blueprints, practically draping her body over him. Her scent drove him crazy. He was sure if he'd walk her through the outline of the project she'd be satisfied and leave.

Instead, her curls brushed his cheek, and her hip nudged his, and then she flipped around and leaned against his table, making him think thoughts he had no business thinking, like bending her over his drafting table.

Her green eyes mesmerized him, and then she asked him if he ever dated?

She was driving him out of his mind and it was only the first day of the project.

"Calliope…"

"No, really. I know we haven't seen each other in a long time, but you don't seem very happy."

"Calliope, you need to leave."

She didn't look like she was going anywhere. She crossed her arms under her breasts. "Have you been out with anyone since you and Cassie divorced?"

"That's none of your business."

"That means no. Why not? It's been three years."

"Don't you have somewhere you need to be?"

"No. Why, do you?"

He wished he did.

"If you don't, we could go out."

He had no idea what to make of this woman. She was like a bulldozer. "What?"

"You know, go out. That thing you do when you're single."

"I know what it means. Are you asking me out?"

"Well, I wasn't, but sure. Would you like to go out with me?" She wasn't teasing or playing a game with him. She was honest to God asking him on a date. And she was beautiful and made his palms sweat and she was Cassandra's sister and no way in hell was he going anywhere near her.

"No."

He figured it would crush her. Instead, she cocked a brow, brushed an errant curl away from her cheek and continued to stand firm. "Why not?"

"You know why not."

She took a step forward. He took one back, but the trailer was small and there wasn't much room. He bumped the wall. She moved forward again and he was reminded of playing checkers with his brothers. He was backed into a corner with no place to go, and if he moved, he was going to be jumped by his opponent.

He suddenly couldn't remember why that was such a bad idea, especially when Calliope moved into him, tilted her head back and stared him down with her deep green eyes.

"I can't believe a big tough guy like you is afraid of a little thing like me, Wyatt." Then she stepped back, her gaze traveling halfway down and staring at the part of him she had no business staring at. When she lifted her gaze again, she grinned.

"I know you have balls in there. Why don't you try and find them? When you do, it's your turn to come ask me out."

She stepped out of the trailer and shut the door behind her.

Wyatt had never been so confused, confounded and downright irritated with a woman in his entire life.

No balls, huh? A man didn't take an insult like that from a woman.

He'd show her balls.

No, he wouldn't. He wasn't about to show Calliope anything, especially not his balls. If he was smart, he'd ignore her completely. She was his client, he'd been hired to do a job, and that was all he should do.

But no balls? He couldn't let that one go.

No way in hell.

FOUR

"You told him he had no balls?"

Tori tilted her head back and laughed, making heads turn all around them.

Ensconced in the booth at Lodge by the Lake, their favorite outskirts-of-town restaurant, Calliope and Tori ate their dinner and had their weekly gossip and catch-up session.

"I did tell him that."

Tori scooped up a forkful of pasta and slid it between her lips. A couple guys at the bar near their booth watched every bite Tori took. It always amused Calliope because Tori was gorgeous, with her flaming red hair and killer body. Men flocked to her, and Tori was immune. It was like she never even noticed men looking at her. Likely because she had the hots for Brody Kent, though Tori would never admit to it. She wasn't sure why Tori wasn't going all out for Brody. He was cover-of-a-magazine gorgeous, lean and sexy, and the two of them had combustible chemistry.

"So what did Wyatt say?" Tori asked.

"Nothing, because I never gave him the chance to respond. I just walked out of the trailer. That was four days ago and he and I haven't spoken a word to each other since."

Tori leaned back and took a long swallow of raspberry iced tea. "He's avoiding you."

Calliope nodded. "Like you wouldn't believe. He doesn't come inside the center at all, and whenever I pop outside to check on the progress of the addition, he ducks inside the trailer as if I caught him naked or something."

"That's great," Tori said. "You've got him on the run now. He must really like you. If he didn't care, he'd tell you to kiss his ass, or even worse, he'd ignore you, shrug his shoulders and go about his business. You've got him rattled, girl."

Calliope pushed her plate to the side and sipped her soda. "I'd like to think so. The man is simply too uptight for his own good."

"Don't I know it. I'm the one who has to work with him every day. He needs to get laid in the worst way."

Calliope sighed. "I'd love to be the one to take care of that for him."

"I have no idea why anyone would want to poke that bear. Get him all riled up and who knows what could happen."

Calliope knew exactly what. Her fantasies ran amok with the possibilities. "I can only imagine. If he hasn't had a woman since my sister, he's got all this pent-up passion inside just ready to explode."

"I hope you know what you're doing."

Calliope grinned. "No clue, but won't it be fun?"

AFTER DINNER AND girl talk, Calliope and Tori parted ways. It was still early and the weather continued to be unseasonably warm, so Calliope took a drive around the lake.

And, okay, maybe she was checking to see if Wyatt was home, since his house was near the restaurant. She drove by his house, the one he'd built for him and Cassandra.

Technically this could be classified as stalking, but what the hell. It wasn't like she was going to knock on his door. She loved his house.

It was a beautiful place nestled at the foot of the hills, surrounded by lush forest and the lake off to the left of the house. He'd built the house for him and Cassandra thinking they'd never have to move again. A two-story, it was big, rustic and gorgeous, with blue-and-gray trim and white gables.

Cassandra hated the house. She'd said it was too big, too remote. She hated the woods that backed up to the house, claimed it would draw wildlife.

Well, duh. That was the idea. Calliope could imagine watching deer while sitting on the back porch drinking coffee. How awesome would that be?

Their marriage had ended before the house had been finished. Wyatt had completed it anyway and moved in. She was surprised he hadn't sold the place. It was kind of big for one person.

She'd never known two people more wrong for each other. But both had been so stubborn and determined to make it work. That relationship had *failure* stamped on it from the get go. They'd wanted different things out of life, but Cassie had wanted Wyatt, and Wyatt had been head over heels in love with Cassie, so they'd both been blind.

His truck was parked in the driveway, and the garage door was open. Wyatt was in the garage, and since he'd looked up when she drove by, there was no sense in pretending he hadn't seen her. She pulled in behind his truck and got out.

He was under the hood of a pretty sweet muscle car—a Chevelle, maybe? It was some kind of Chevy. It was beaten up and had seen better days, but shades of its former glory could still be seen in the parts Wyatt was restoring. She didn't know a whole lot about cars, but she knew a great engine when she saw it. He'd already dropped that in and was working on sanding a fender, his body once again sweaty, greasy and smelling like motor oil.

What a turn-on.

"This is nice. Is it yours?"

"No, I stole it. I work part-time for a chop shop."

She leaned against the wall of the garage. "You've got a bit of the smartass in you, Wyatt."

He lifted the safety glasses from his eyes and glared at her. "You stalking me, Calliope?"

"Maybe a little. You've been avoiding me."

"Thank God you finally noticed." He grabbed his can of beer and emptied it in three swallows.

Undeterred, she followed him into the house.

For a big place, it was ridiculously devoid of furniture. Sofa and chair in the living room, big-screen television and that was it. Small kitchen table with two chairs. Everything looked garage-sale quality.

He went into the kitchen and grabbed another beer. Just one.

"I'd love one. Thanks for offering."

He frowned, then grabbed another and handed it to her.

"Thanks." She popped the top off her beer, waiting to see if he'd head back out in the garage. He didn't, instead took a couple long swallows and leaned against the counter, so she grabbed a stool at the bar and opened her beer, sipped and swiveled around to take a look at the house.

It was stunning despite the lack of furniture. High ceilings with natural wood beams. Tile and pale wood floors. Rustic, charming, and though it needed a few rugs and some decent furniture, it looked as though it had been made with a man's handcrafted expertise—someone who had taken their time and used a keen eye for detail, from the carefully constructed stone fireplace to the cornice at the bottom of the staircase.

She swiveled back around to find Wyatt staring at her.

"The house is amazing, Wyatt. Can I see all of it?"

"Why?"

"Because if it's anything like the family room, it takes my breath away."

Wyatt didn't want Calliope to like the house. He didn't want to show her the house. But dammit, something inside him made him push off the counter and start walking.

She followed silently, murmuring her appreciation as they went.

Somewhere along the way she'd shed her coat. She wore a sweater that clung to her body, outlining her spectacular breasts, and jeans that looked like they'd been painted on. He was going to try really hard not to notice that, though he supposed it was already too late.

Concentrate on the house. She only wanted to see the house. Quick tour and she'd be out of there.

Only it wasn't a quick tour, because she'd pause occasionally to run her fingers along the wainscoting, an exposed beam or a doorknob—small touches he'd put some thought or effort into that Cassandra had never noticed.

Never appreciated.

Calliope noticed. Appreciated.

Something inside him clenched as she paused at the stairs and inspected the way the wood wrapped around itself. It had taken him weeks to do that staircase. He'd wanted something elegant, yet sturdy, something beautiful that Cassandra would appreciate, yet stairs that would stand the test of time—and maybe a houseful of kids.

Cassandra had blown right by the stairs and never said a word.

"It's like music," Calliope whispered, her fingers a light caress over the wood. Her gaze met his, and her lips lifted. "It's amazing, Wyatt. You must have spent months on this."

He didn't know what to say, so he turned away and headed up, listening to the sound of her feet behind him.

The master bedroom was the only place he'd spent any money on, furniture-wise, since by the time he'd finished the house he and Cassandra were already divorced. He'd bought a big bed since he was a big guy, a double thick mattress and he'd made the headboard and footboard himself, grinding out his anger and frustration by creating the scrolled patterns in the wood.

Calliope leaned over and traced the pattern with her fingertips.

"This is beautiful. And the bed is so big." She turned to him and arched a brow. "For your harem of women?"

"Funny."

She wandered into the bathroom and gasped. "Oh my God. I'm moving in tonight and living in your bathroom."

He couldn't resist the smile as he entered the doorway and leaned against it.

"A tub made for four people. With whirlpool jets. And that decadent shower—Wyatt, that's just dirty and sexy. I want to get naked and get in there right now."

She was making his dick hard with that kind of talk and the corresponding visuals. He could already imagine her naked, the jets from all four showerheads spraying her, steam enveloping them both as he put his hands and his mouth all over her body...

Yeah. That train of thought had to stop. He turned around and left the room and started some complex algebra so his hard-on would go away.

He breathed in and out as he reached the top of the stairway.

"I always wanted to live in a big house," she said, grasping the railing in the sitting area at the top of the stairs. "I used to pretend I was a commoner—which I was, of course. That I was forced into servitude, but someday I'd meet a prince and he'd fall madly in love with me and carry me away to his huge castle where we'd marry and have children and live happily ever after."

When he didn't say anything, she turned to him and laughed, then pushed her glasses up the bridge of her nose. "I was a big fan of *Cinderella*."

"Obviously."

"And of course you've seen the house I grew up in. It wasn't exactly a castle."

Yeah, he had seen the house. It was a two-bedroom, about a thousand square feet. Small, built in the fifties. Calliope's parents still lived in the same house they bought when they were first married—the house her grandparents used to own.

"My mom and dad never had a lot of money, but we had love and a sense of family. It was always enough."

"For you, maybe." Not for Cassandra. She'd always bitched about wanting to get away from that cracker-box house, how much she'd hated it and how confined she'd felt living there. He'd often wondered if she spent so much time at his house—and with him—more as an escape than because she really cared about him.

He wondered about a lot of things. Like why he'd built this huge house with everything Cassandra could have wanted—and she'd hated it anyway.

Calliope must have sensed his thoughts, because she laid her hand on his arm. "You can't change the past, Wyatt. You have to let it go."

"Yeah, well, it won't let go of me."

She pushed off the railing and moved in front of him. "Maybe you don't distract yourself enough. Put something in your head besides my big sister."

"Like what? Her little sister? That's a little too close to home for me."

She tilted her head back, and instead of anger he saw the same bright-eyed smile she always wore.

"You need to separate me from Cassandra. I'm not her."

No, she wasn't. Cassandra always pouted. She was never happy, was always moody and the slightest thing would set her off.

Wyatt had been nothing but rude to Calliope. So far, she'd been nothing but sweet to him.

He brushed his fingers across her cheek. "You can't be real."

She inhaled, her breasts rising. "I am real. And it's about damn time you noticed me."

"Oh, I've noticed you plenty."

Her lips curved. "Have you? How?"

"I notice you're driving me crazy."

"Again. How?"

The invitation was obvious. One step and she'd be in his arms. He wanted to taste her so badly he licked his lips. Her gaze drifted to his mouth, then back to meet his eyes. The tightening in his jeans was almost unbearable.

It had been a really long damn time since he'd been with a woman. Hell, since he'd kissed a woman or touched one.

This woman in particular made him crazy.

And she was the wrong woman.

He took a step back instead of forward. "I need to get back to the car."

He caught the flicker of disappointment before she replaced it with a smile. He'd hurt her and he hadn't meant to. But he couldn't be what she wanted. He wasn't the man for her. She needed someone with an open heart, someone who'd appreciate her and be able to love her. Someone who wasn't damaged and bitter.

That wasn't him.

"Calliope."

"It's okay. I need to get home anyway."

They headed downstairs. She grabbed her jacket from the counter and slid into it. If he were a gentleman he would have helped her with it.

He didn't feel much like a gentleman right now, and if he got too close to her she wouldn't be leaving his house tonight. He'd have her naked and in that shower so fast her head would spin. And after he worked out some of the boiling tension tightening his insides, he'd never see her again.

Yeah, not the right guy for her.

He adjusted his jeans and followed her out into the garage. She turned around to face him, and he took that step back again.

She noticed, and her lips curved.

"I'll see you later."

It wasn't until she got into her car and pulled out of his driveway that he realized he'd been holding his breath. He wasn't sure if it was because he wanted her to be gone, or because he was waiting for her to turn around and come back.

He exhaled on a curse, then dragged his fingers through his hair and turned to face the car. He picked up the sandpaper, determined to take out his sexual frustration on the fender.

FIVE

The weather turned abruptly, their strange late November warmth obliterated by dark clouds and sharp wind that seemed to cut right through thick layers of clothing and heavy coats. The threat of snow hung in the air, and Calliope wondered how much work would be done on the addition before the bad weather moved in.

Wyatt and his guys had the framing finished, and had spent the past few days putting the roof on. Once that was done, the sheetrock would be next. Calliope hoped they'd get it all completed before it started to snow.

She'd already had to relocate the kids' playroom to another section so Wyatt could cut the hole in the existing wall to make the doorway, and for safety's sake the existing playroom was off limits until the project was completed. That meant they were crammed in like sardines in the other playroom. Not too bad when the weather was warmer and her staff could take the kids outside to run off some of that pent-up energy. Once it snowed, though, they'd all be stuck indoors together.

She wasn't looking forward to that.

Marcy was sick today, which meant Calliope was in charge of the three-year-olds. She had them out in the play yard right now, a perfect location to let her watch Wyatt and his guys as they put up drywall.

The wind was blustery. She pulled her hat down to cover her eyes. The kids bounced around and squealed with joy.

She was freezing. Wind was blowing out of the north and seemed to cut right through her jeans.

Where had that nice touch of sixty-degree weather gone? She wanted that back. Didn't seem to bother Wyatt, though, who worked on the roof in a short-sleeved shirt. Just the thought of it added goose bumps to her goose bumps.

She wished she had the time to lean over the fence and watch him, but not only did she have to keep her eyes on the kids, he and his guys almost had the roof finished and would be going inside soon, so she'd lose sight of him.

Too bad. She did enjoy looking at him.

"Miss Calliope, Jeffrey won't share the teeter-totter with me."

She glanced down at Lawrence's freckled face and smiled. "He won't, huh?"

Lawrence shook his head.

She slipped her hand in his. "Let's go see about that, shall we?"

Wyatt took a long swallow from his jug of water, trying not to watch Calliope with the kids.

It was hard not to be utterly taken in by the way she corralled a group of fifteen toddlers who couldn't be more than three or four years old. The kids were rambunctious, screaming and running wild on the playground. Yet when she bent down and called a couple of them over, she had their rapt attention. She didn't raise her voice, always smiled—like she did with him.

And she played with them. She didn't stand around and supervise. She ran around the yard with them, she climbed on the equipment, and she squealed as loud as they did. When they tackled her and she fell, she laughed, then got up and chased them until they were giggling.

He'd bet they'd all take great naps today.

Calliope obviously loved her work. Though it didn't appear to be work to her. It was clear she loved the kids, that it was more than a job to her.

Night and day difference from her sister. Cassandra had treated children like they all had communicable diseases. She'd wanted nothing to do with them, though he hadn't known that when they'd gotten married.

They'd wanted so many different things. How could he have not seen it?

Enough. He pushed Cassandra away, which was getting easier than it used to be.

He was going to have to go inside the center to start work from the existing playroom into the newly constructed doorway, which meant avoiding Calliope wasn't going to be an option.

He rang the bell at the front door. Beth the Bouncer, as he'd gotten used to calling her, opened the door and glared at him.

"I need to get to the playroom."

She opened the door. "Stay on the plastic runner so you don't spread that dust all over the floors."

He found himself smiling at her brusque tone. It reminded him of himself. "Yes, ma'am."

Kids were stuffed into the entryway, and stopped to gape at him.

"Who are you?" one little boy asked. He had dark curly hair and green eyes, with glasses. If Calliope had a son he'd probably look just like that.

He squatted down. "I'm Wyatt. I'm building a new room on to this place."

"You have hammers and stuff?"

"I do."

A little girl came up beside him. "You're dirty. Miss Beth will make you wash up before you come inside."

Wyatt lifted his gaze to Beth, who fought a smirk.

"And you'd better clean off your shoes, too," another little boy said.

"Miss Calliope doesn't care if you're dirty. She likes dirt."

"She gets dirty, too. She even plays in the mud with us."

A lot of giggles, then they ran off, his novelty wearing off. He straightened and walked down the hall. He caught sight of Calliope in another room with a handful of kids. She was on the floor playing with blocks. She looked up, pushed her glasses up, smiled and waved at him.

He couldn't help the smile that curved his lips or the involuntary wave back.

Or the warmth that filled him at seeing the way her eyes lit up when she saw him.

So she was Cassandra's sister. So what? She was obviously attracted to him, and God knew he wanted her in a way that defied all logic or reason.

Then again, was it illogical or unreasonable to want to be with a woman who was positive, bubbly, friendly and obviously loved kids? Wasn't Calliope the kind of woman he'd wanted all along, before he'd been seduced by the dazzling beauty of her sister?

Was that what he was afraid of—that the apple didn't fall far from the tree? She didn't seem at all like Cassandra—a one-eighty from her sister, in fact. Cassandra wouldn't be caught dead with muddy handprints on her jeans, or chalk on her face. She wouldn't spend five minutes of her day sitting on the floor coloring or reading a book to a bunch of three-year-olds. Getting dirty hadn't been on Cassandra's list of fun things to do at all.

He'd like to get dirty with Calliope. The thought of it had him hard and sweating, despite the dropping temperatures.

He'd let fear and failure rule him for so long he'd forgotten all the fundamentals. Like how to treat a woman. How to ask someone out on a date. How to let attraction take over and just go with it.

Why couldn't Calliope be a woman he'd met at random? That would make this a lot easier, because every time he looked at her, he made the connection to Cassandra, and then the big bad of his past kept rushing back to him.

Which was all in his head and not in reality. Calliope had nothing to do with the failure of his marriage. Maybe it was time to separate the sisters, think of Calliope as an individual and give himself a freakin' break.

But first he had to work. He focused his attention on the sheetrock and let Calliope slide to the background for a while.

Hours later, his crew had gone home and he was still in the center when he decided to call it quits for the night. The sheetrock had been finished. His crew had put up tarp on the outside to make sure any bad weather wouldn't ruin the work they'd done.

Wyatt walked into the adjoining room on his way out the door, stopping dead at the window.

It was dark outside—and snowing like crazy. From his guess, there was a foot on the ground already. He grabbed his phone. 8:00 p.m. No wonder his stomach had been growling.

Damn, where had his head been, and why hadn't Calliope come to tell him she needed to close up the center?

He saw a light on in her office so headed there.

Her back was turned as she studied her computer, furiously clacking the keys.

"You're still here."

She jumped, then swiveled in her chair. "Wyatt, you scared

me to death. It was so quiet in here, and I saw you were still working after everyone left, so I decided to leave you alone."

He leaned against the doorjamb. "You could have said something to me."

She shrugged and pushed her glasses up the bridge of her nose. "I had reports to do anyway. I didn't mind working late."

"There's a foot of snow on the ground."

Her eyes widened. "Really?" She got up and swiveled open the blinds in her office. "Wow. I knew it looked like it might snow earlier. Had no idea it was going to come down so hard so fast."

Now was his chance to not be an asshole for once. "Have you eaten?"

She lifted up a package of half-eaten peanut butter crackers. "A snack. How about you?"

"No."

"You're probably ready to get out of here then. I've locked the front door with the keys. I'll let you out." She grabbed the keys.

"You aren't leaving?"

She stopped in front of him at the doorway. "Yes, but I need to shut the computer down and grab my stuff."

"I'll wait."

"Are you sure?"

"I'll wait. Go shut down and grab your coat."

"Okay. Thanks." She went back to her desk, bent over her computer. He enjoyed the view of her butt as she did. She folded her crackers, slid them into the drawer and grabbed her coat, bag and keys.

"I need to turn off some lights around here, then I'll be ready."

He followed her around as she turned off the lights,

checked doors to be sure they were locked and went to the front door. He grabbed her coat and held it out for her this time. She gave him a look as she slid her arms into it.

"Better zip it up. Winds are howling."

She did, offering him up a smile. "Thanks."

"Don't you have a hat and gloves?"

"Yes. In my car."

He shook his head, threw on his coat, then slipped his knit cap over her head and handed her his gloves. "Put those on."

She looked down at the gloves, then at him. "But what about you?"

He cracked a smile. "I'm a pretty tough guy. I think I can handle it."

Wyatt was being nice to her? That was a change. Calliope didn't know what had come over him, but she wasn't going to question this rare gift of him in a good mood.

She slipped the gloves on, giggling as they flopped in her hands since they were three sizes too big for her. She squeezed her fingers in them to keep them on while Wyatt pulled the door open.

The wind slammed them hard, tossing snow inside and knocking Calliope against him. He put his hand against her back to steady her.

"Wow, that's some storm," she said.

Wyatt took her keys, pulled the door shut and locked it, then put his arm around her and helped her down the stairs. She really wished she'd brought her boots in from the car, but she hadn't expected an epic snowstorm. Now, snow slid into her socks and tennis shoes and she shivered.

It was hard to walk—at least for her. Wyatt had work boots on and had no problem. He grabbed her arm and led her to the street where her small car was buried.

She looked at the car. "Well, this will take some work. I have a shovel in the trunk."

"You aren't driving. We'll take my truck."

Snow had already covered his hair. It was coming down so fast she couldn't even see, and she wasn't about to argue with him. He led her over to the side street where his truck was parked. The effort to get there exhausted her. By the time he opened up the side door and helped her get in, her jeans and feet were soaked and freezing and she was shivering so hard her teeth chattered.

He turned on the truck's engine and hit the heaters full blast, then went back outside with a scraper to clean off the windows while she stayed inside. Her feet and ankles stung from the cold.

She should have handed him his hat and gloves back. The temperatures had dropped outside and he was doing the work bare-handed and without a hat. He must be freezing.

He climbed back in and looked at her. "Put your seatbelt on."

She did, noting his red hands. "You should have taken my gloves."

"I'm fine. I'm used to working outside in all kinds of weather."

He put the car in gear and pulled carefully away from the curb. The truck tried to fishtail, but Wyatt controlled it. The roads were hazardous, the snow thick and coming down so hard that even the windshield wipers on full blast couldn't clear the whiteout conditions enough to see clearly.

Calliope sat quietly and let Wyatt concentrate on the road. He made the right turn and headed down the narrow street. She was glad her house was only a couple blocks from the center, and even making it that far was treacherous driving.

There were no other cars on the road. This was a bad storm. He pulled into her driveway and she was glad it wasn't uphill.

"Got your keys ready?" he asked when he turned the engine off.

She'd already tugged the gloves off and handed them back to Wyatt. "In my hand."

Wyatt snagged the keys from her. "I'll open the door. You put the gloves back on. And don't get out of the car until I come over to your side to get you. You don't have boots on."

"You're coming in with me, aren't you? The roads are really bad out there."

He gave her one of those "You're kidding me, right?" looks that guys gave women sometimes when women thought men couldn't do something—like climb a mountain. "My truck is four-wheel drive. I can make it."

But she'd still worry like crazy about him being on the road. "I'll make soup."

"You're on."

She grinned and waited for him to come around and open the door for her, instantly shivering again as the cold blast of air, sleet and snow smacked her body. They made a mad dash for her front door—as much of a dash as two people could make in snow that deep. Wyatt unlocked the door and they rushed inside. He pushed the door shut and locked it.

She shuddered against the cold and stripped off the hat and her coat, then toed out of her soaked tennis shoes. "I need to change clothes."

Wyatt stood on her front hall rug and did his best impression of a snowman. "I'm just going to stand here and defrost."

She laughed. "You are not. Take your coat off and come into the kitchen. After I change clothes I'll make us some coffee and get started on that soup."

She ran into her bedroom and pulled off her wet clothes,

grabbed some sweats and dry socks, then made a quick stop in the bathroom to check herself in the mirror.

Oh, ugh. She cleaned the wet spots off her glasses, but otherwise there wasn't much hope for her wet hair, and she didn't think Wyatt would appreciate her taking the time to shower and put on some makeup. He likely wanted some coffee and homemade soup, not a glamour girl.

She fluffed her wet curls as best as she could, stuck her feet into slippers and went into the kitchen.

She inhaled when she walked in. "I smell coffee."

"I raided your cabinets and made myself at home."

Her stomach flipped in a decidedly warm way. "I'm glad. Sorry it took me so long."

"It didn't. I don't think you need to wait on me when I'm perfectly capable of making a pot of coffee."

He poured her a cup. She reached into the fridge. "Cream?"

"Yeah."

"How about sugar?"

"No, thanks."

She grabbed the sugar bowl on the kitchen table and scooped a spoonful into her cup, stirred and watched him.

There were never men in her kitchen. She dated on occasion, but never invited them home and sure as hell didn't have them in her kitchen making coffee for her.

Seeing Wyatt, his tall, lean body relaxing against her counters, was a little disconcerting. He was so big and her kitchen was small.

And speaking of the kitchen...

She took a swallow of coffee, then set it aside. "Let me get started on that soup I promised."

"You don't have to do that."

She bent down to grab her soup pot and grinned up at him. "Sure I do. I'm starving." She put the pot on her stove, then went to the freezer to dig out the chicken stock she was so glad she had on hand.

She put the container in the microwave to defrost, then opened the refrigerator, also happy she'd gone to the grocery store yesterday.

"What can I do to help?"

"How are you with a knife?"

He went to the sink and rolled up his sleeves to wash his hands. "Expert."

"Good." She laid celery and carrots on the cutting board. "Start slicing."

While he got busy with that, she tossed the chicken in the stock, added a little garlic and ginger and a few more spices. Soon the soup was bubbly and thick and she put a loaf of bread in the oven to heat up, then added the carrots and celery Wyatt had sliced.

She had a few minutes to rest while the soup simmered and the bread cooked, so she refilled her coffee. Wyatt was sitting at her table, one she'd found at a garage sale.

"You rent this house?" he asked.

She shook her head. "No, I'm a homeowner."

He arched a brow. "Really. This and the day care center."

"Well, this place is tiny. Only a one-bedroom. But it's a house and it's what I wanted when I moved here."

"Why not an apartment? I mean, you're young and single. I would think a condo or apartment would suit you better."

"That's just pissing money away every month."

He laughed. "A lot of young people do that."

She took a sip of coffee. "You make it sound like I'm sixteen and you're my dad. I'm twenty-six and I wanted the investment. I bought this little cracker box of a house because it was all I could afford. When my grandmother died and left half her money to me, I knew exactly what I wanted to do with it—invest it in the day care center.

"But I also wanted a house. I didn't want to throw money away every month on an apartment. I found this place. It was so small, but what else did I need? I'm single, have no kids, no husband, no boyfriend. So as an initial investment it was perfect."

He was staring at her with that unfathomable expression on his face that told her nothing of what he was thinking.

"What?"

"You surprise me."

She turned to stir the soup. "Yeah? In what way?"

"I always think of you as being a kid. But you're not. You're all grown-up."

"I've been a grown-up for a long time now, Wyatt. Maybe it's past time you realized that."

"Yeah, I guess it is."

She felt his gaze on her, but didn't turn around. He could just simmer on what she'd said.

The soup and bread were ready, so she served it up and they ate, drank, and what was most surprising of all—they actually talked.

Wyatt told her about the progress on the room addition at the center, as well as other ongoing projects their construction company had going. She could tell he really loved his family business, even though his brothers seemed to irritate him.

"I understand familial relationships," she said as they moved from the kitchen to her living room after they finished eating. She had poured them a snifter of her favorite winter naughty indulgence—brandy. Maybe she could get him drunk and take advantage of him. "Families can test you under the best circumstances, but underneath I know you love your brothers."

He nodded and swirled the brandy around the glass. "They try my patience—I'm sure on purpose at least half the time. Brody likes to tease and Ethan eggs him on. The two of them gang up on me."

"Most likely to irritate you on purpose because you're so naturally cranky."

He tilted the glass in her direction. "People who throw those kinds of words at me generally live to regret them."

She leaned back against the sofa and grinned at him. "Good thing I know your bark is way worse than your bite."

"Are you sure about that? I haven't bitten you—yet."

Whoa. Where had that come from? It had been a bonafide sexual come-on, and Calliope nearly self-combusted right there. Heat flared through every part of her. The whole room seemed to go up in flames, or maybe that was just her, and likely because of the way Wyatt's gaze burned into her. Her nipples tightened and everything that was female in her shouted for joy.

Usually never at a loss for words, she had no idea what to say.

Wyatt downed the brandy, then stood. "Well, I should go."

She shot off the sofa. "What? Are you insane? There's two feet of snow out there. You're not going anywhere tonight."

He arched a brow. "You thinking of holding me prisoner here?"

"I might if you come up with another dumbass idea, like trying to drive in that."

"It'll still be there tomorrow morning, Calliope."

"By tomorrow the road crews will have been out all night, spreading salt and plowing. The streets will be in more decent shape than they are right now. What if you get stuck getting back home? It's not like you'll have an easy time getting a tow tonight. I'm sure there are a lot of cars getting stuck."

He gave her a dubious look. "We don't live in a major city. I can call Roger. He owns one of the two wreckers in town to give me a pull."

She crossed her arms. "Or you can use some common sense and not be one of those idiots on the road tonight."

"I think you're trying to keep me here for your own nefarious purposes."

She laughed. "Yeah, all one hundred thirty pounds of me, plotting devious things against all—" she looked him over, "—two-ten of you?"

"Two-twenty-five."

"So you're nearly twice my weight. I'm sure I could pounce on you and take you down."

She saw his jaw clench.

"You could try."

"I could, couldn't I?"

It sure was warm in here, and the sexual innuendos were flying around the room like crazed bats. She supposed she could cut to the chase, but it sure would be nice if Wyatt came after her for a change. She was tired of being the one doing the chasing.

He finally settled back down on the sofa. "I'd rather you stop calling me an idiot."

"Since you're sitting and obviously staying, I'll refrain from further insults as to your state of mind." She grabbed his empty glass. "How about a refill?"

"Got any beer? That shit's too sweet."

"Sure." She refilled her glass while she was in there, handed him the beer and slid back onto the sofa, pulling her legs up behind her.

"Would you like to watch television?"

"Not much of a TV watcher."

"Neither am I."

He studied her. She pushed her glasses up.

"What do you do at night?" he asked.

"I read. I'm usually so exhausted by the time I get home, I eat dinner, take a hot bath and soak for a while, then curl up with a good book and generally pass out early."

"Kids are exhausting, huh?"

She laughed. "They can be."

"What made you decide to open a day care center?"

"That's easy. I love children. Always have, ever since I got my first babysitting job as a teenager. I knew then that I wanted to do something with kids."

Something flickered in his eyes. "Why not become a teacher?"

"I do have a degree in early childhood education, thought about becoming a teacher, but the little ones wrap me around their fingers and don't let go. I worked at a lot of day care centers while I was in college, and my career naturally progressed in this direction. I apprenticed under a director near my college, and worked as a director at one in Nebraska for a couple years. When the opportunity came up to buy out Miss Bettie, I leaped on it because I could own my own business, and it gave me a chance to come home."

"It's a lot of work."

She nodded. "It is, but it's so rewarding. The staff is amazing, and I feel like I'm doing something important. I can't imagine how worried these parents are, having to leave their little ones while they go off to work. I like to think I can ease their minds a little, knowing their babies are being well taken care of."

He took a long swallow of beer. She liked watching the way his throat worked, liked the beard stubble on his jaw, wondered what that would feel like on her face—and other parts of her body.

Again, that abrupt flash of heat scored her from the inside out.

She really should stop thinking of sex, especially sex with Wyatt. Especially when Wyatt sat less than a foot away from her. His fear that she might pounce on him? Not too far from the truth.

He laid his empty beer can on the table. She got up.

"I'll get you another."

He grabbed her hand. "I know where your fridge is. I can get myself another beer if I want one. You don't have to wait on me."

"I don't mind."

He released her hand and she hurried into the kitchen. What she really needed was a minute or two to catch her breath. She opened the refrigerator, letting the cool air bathe her face. She took a deep breath to calm down her riotous libido.

Geez, Calliope. You aren't sixteen anymore. Get a grip.

She stood, closed the door and turned around, then gasped when she found Wyatt standing right there.

"What are you doing here?" she asked.

"Wondering what the hell you're doing. Hell of a time to take inventory of the fridge, don't you think?"

"Oh. Uh. That wasn't what I was doing."

He placed his palm on the refrigerator door, right next to her shoulder. "Yeah? What were you doing?"

"Looking for this, of course." She handed him the beer.

He took it from her. "You're a little odd, Calliope."

"I prefer quirky." She skirted around him and headed back into the living room, conscious of him right on her heels.

Wasn't this what she wanted? Him going after her?

So why was she suddenly so skittish?

Likely because she was out of practice. It wasn't like she

had a parade of men chasing after her. Going after Wyatt was one thing, because she was pretty sure he wasn't going to take the bait.

Now that he seemed interested? Yeah, that was another story.

He was a lot of man. Could she handle him?

She blew out a breath and stared at the brandy.

"Calliope."

She lifted her gaze to his. "Yes?"

"Would you like me to take off?"

She shook her head. "No. I don't want you to leave."

"This is uncomfortable for you. For me, too."

Damn. She'd screwed it up. She'd hesitated. But she wasn't a quitter. She leaned forward. "I'm not used to having men over."

"Ever?"

"Uh...no." She'd never brought a guy to her house. It was too...intimate. Of course she'd had sex at college, and there had been Steve's apartment. Then there was that one time at the motel with Bobby. But no, she'd never brought a man here. She'd never had a long-term relationship because no guy had been...keepable.

"So you're a virgin."

Her head shot up. "I am not."

His lips quirked. "Yeah, I can tell you're full of experience." He got up and went into the kitchen.

Irritated now, she followed. "You can't tell anything about my...experience."

He tossed his empty beer can in the trash, then turned to face her. "Honey, you're like a lamb facing down a wolf."

She quirked a brow. "And you're the big bad wolf, I suppose?"

He grinned. "You got it."

"You think I can't handle you?"

"I know you can't handle me."

"Try me."

He laughed and moved past her. "I don't think so."

Now she was pissed. He was treating her like a child. "You prefer more experienced women."

"I don't want any woman."

"You lie. Ever since we met up again you've been dancing around your attraction to me. But because I'm Cassie's sister, you've held back because you've got some screwed-up notion that we're one and the same."

He looked her up and down, his gaze raking over her body. "Calliope, you are nothing like Cassandra. Not in appearance, not in actions, not in any way."

She knew how he felt about Cassie. It wasn't an insult.

"So you've given up trying to compare me to my sister."

He held up his hands. "Throwing the white flag on that one. You win."

Her lips curved. "I don't know about that, Wyatt. Seems to me we both win. So why not take what you want—what we both want—and quit fighting it?"

Her heart pounded as she stood in the middle of the room, her hands on her hips. Only a few feet of distance separated them, but she wasn't going to cross that distance. If he wanted her—and she knew damn well he did—he was going to have to bridge the gap.

He stared her down. He was mad, whether at her or himself she didn't know. Frankly, she didn't care. It was now or never because she wouldn't ask him again.

He came to her in two fast strides and jerked her into his arms.

And then he hesitated, his lips just inches from hers.

Don't walk away. Not again.

His gaze bored into hers and she nearly melted to the floorboards. She knew from the smoldering look in his eyes that he wasn't walking away this time. When his mouth came down on hers, the first contact of his lips stole her breath.

She went up in flames and her body exploded in a wild-fire of heat.

SIX

THERE WAS NOTHING gentle about this kiss. This was no sweet seduction. It was a full-on siege. Wyatt wrapped his arms around her, one hand gravitating to her butt to draw her against his erection. Calliope shuddered at the feel of him, so hard and ready as he plundered her lips. He slid his tongue inside and she moaned, arched against him, slid her hand in his hair and held on while his tongue played with hers.

She was lightheaded as sensations pounded at her. The softness of his lips warred with the scrape of his beard against her face and the steely hardness of his body as he moved against her. And when he cupped her breast, his thumb brushing her nipple, she whimpered at the sheer pleasure of it.

He pulled his mouth from hers, his eyes dark and full of hunger.

"Say no."

She blinked. "What?"

"Tell me to go."

"No."

He backed away. She grabbed his arms. "That's not what I meant. Don't go."

He raked his fingers through his hair. "If I don't leave now, I'm not leaving until morning."

She was panting, her breasts painfully full, her sex throbbing with need for him, and he wanted to have this discussion now?

"That's the general idea, Wyatt."

"If I stay tonight, I'm sleeping in your bed. With you."

She resisted the urge to suggest they likely wouldn't be sleeping much, instead stayed silent, her chest heaving with the force of her breaths. "Can we get back to the kissing part? I really like the way you kiss me."

"I just wanted you to be sure."

"I'm sure. And thanks. Now kiss me."

The smile he gave her was the kind any sane woman would call dangerous. He pulled her glasses off and set them down, put his hand on the nape of her neck and drew her close.

He hovered, his lips just an inch from hers. "You make me crazy, Calliope."

She palmed his chest. "Trust me. The feeling is mutual."

And then their lips touched again, and it was like a burst of fireworks. Wow, he really could kiss. Wyatt was formidable, no doubt about that. Her toes curled, her legs felt like jelly, and she was damn glad he had all that muscle in his frame to hold her up, because she sank against him, sighing against his lips as he overpowered her with his sheer masculinity. She breathed him in, the scent of outdoors, brandy and beer mingling together.

When he lifted her in his arms—and she was no lightweight—she felt small and feminine, and decided she liked that sensation.

He moved down the hall and bent to open her bedroom door, found the light switch and flipped it on, then settled her in the middle of her bed, coming down on top of her, his mouth taking hers again in a kiss that made her writhe with impatience. She wanted clothes off, needed to feel his bare skin against hers. She reached between them, pulling at his shirt.

He lifted, straddling her, and unbuttoned his shirt. She laid her hands on his thighs and watched as he pulled the flannel shirt off and the T-shirt underneath, leaving his torso bare.

She sucked in a breath. Wide shoulders, well-muscled chest
and arms, and flat, washboard abs, not from time spent at
the gym, she imagined, but from honest-to-God labor. She
snaked her hands along his stomach and farther down, where
a soft line of hair disappeared into his jeans. She reached for
his belt buckle but he snatched her hands away and placed
them on the bed.

"But you're not naked yet."

"I'll get there." He lifted her sweatshirt over her stomach,
leaned down and pressed a kiss to her belly.

His lips on her skin were just as flame-inducing as his
kisses. She wondered if spontaneous combustion was possible. She'd really hate to set him on fire, especially before
they had sex. But seeing his mouth on her stomach as he
gradually lifted her shirt and mapped his way north made her
heart pound so hard she was sure he could hear it. She knew
he had to feel it, because it ricocheted throughout her body.

"Lift," he said, and she arched enough so he could pull
the shirt over her head.

His lips curved, and he laid his hand over one of her
breasts, covered only by the flimsy, discount-store purchased
bra. Dammit, if she'd known she was going to have sex with
Wyatt tonight she'd have put her more expensive lingerie
on. She made a mental note to drag out the hot lingerie, so
she'd be prepared for future events. And there would be future events, because every touch of his fingers and hands to
her body was like she'd never been touched before. Her nipples peaked and hardened while she panted like the woman
in heat she was. He brushed a thumb over the bra and she
arched against him.

"Tell me what you want."

She lifted her gaze to his, saw the intensity, the hunger and need there. Yup. He was going to set her on fire before the night was over. "I want your hands and your mouth on me."

He reached under her and lifted her, undid the clasp in an instant and drew the straps down her shoulders, then laid her back down. He stared at her, not moving to touch her.

"You're beautiful, Calliope."

A heated flush spread over her body as he continued to look down on her like she was some goddess or something. She'd never thought herself particularly breathtaking, but she wasn't hideous, either. She was pretty in an average sort of way. She kept her body in shape—God knew running after kids burned a lot of calories. But her sister was the real beauty in the family, and Wyatt had been married to her.

Yet as his gaze burned into hers and she saw the lust in his eyes, the pure male appreciation, she knew then he wasn't comparing her to Cassandra. The desire he felt was for her.

She reached up and swept her hand across his jaw, tingling at the sensation of his beard tickling her palm.

"I think you're pretty hot, too, Wyatt."

He cupped her breast, then bent and took a nipple in his mouth. She sighed at the sheer pleasure of it, watched as he sucked her nipple, licked it, teased it with his tongue. Sensation shot south and she bit down on her lip to keep from whimpering. It had been an embarrassingly long time since she'd been with a guy.

Boys, really. That's what they'd been, while Wyatt was a man. A man who knew his way around a woman's body. A man with infinite patience. This wasn't about quickly stripping her clothes off so he could get right to the action. He worshipped her body, licking her nipples, teasing her into an absolute frenzy of passion until she was mindless, breathless and writhing without shame.

And when she thought she couldn't take any more, he

kissed her, so deeply and passionately she forgot all about getting right to the action. She lost herself in the taste of him, the different textures of his face. She reached up to touch the softness of his lips, the scratchiness along his jaw line, and the silkiness of his hair as she threaded her fingers through the strands to hold on for dear life while he fondled her breasts and kissed her until she lost all sense of time.

Only then did he caress his fingers along her ribs and stomach and make his way to her jeans, releasing the button effortlessly and drawing the zipper down in a way she found ridiculously sexy.

He didn't even bother taking her jeans off, just dove his hand inside and cupped the center of her, drawing out a low moan she couldn't contain. She was hot, wet and ready—had been for weeks now. She strained, lifted against his touch, meeting his gaze as release found her and he took her mouth, absorbing her cries.

He held her as she settled, then her jeans came off, her panties, and he moved down her body, put his mouth on her and amped her up all over again.

She'd never known a man like him before, so eager to please when she knew it had been a long time for him, too. But she lost herself in what he was doing to her, and after he gave her a second climax, she was limp.

When he climbed off the bed and shucked his jeans and boxer briefs, she rolled over on her side and sucked in her lower lip between her teeth, studying the utter beauty of his body. She rolled over and pulled a box of condoms out of the nightstand.

He arched a brow. "Have men coming and going regularly?"

She laughed. "Ha. Never. But I was hopeful about you so I figured I should be prepared."

He put his hand on his hips, and lord, he was magnificent. Powerful, hard and beautiful. She pulled a condom out of the box and he put it on, came to her and nudged her legs apart.

He stilled, watching her as he fit his cock inside her.

It was perfect, this moment everything she could have imagined as he filled her, swelling inside her. They fit together in so many ways, especially like this.

This time she didn't hold back, whimpering at the sheer pleasure of every sensation, every movement.

He brushed her hair away from her face, kissed her jaw, her nose, her mouth, then took her lips in a deep kiss as he moved within her. She wrapped her legs around him and lifted.

They strained together, murmured and kissed as passion ignited between them. Hands clasped, Calliope gave as much as Wyatt did, knowing this might be her only chance to show him what he meant to her—how much this moment meant as the tensions they both held united. He drove within her, relentless in his pursuit of her pleasure. She didn't think she was capable of it, but as he ground against her, refusing to give up until she did, she finally broke on a harsh cry, and he went with her, slipping his hand underneath her to tilt her close while he shuddered and buried his face in her neck.

She stroked his back and his hair, unable to believe this had really happened. When he rolled to the side he pulled her with him, adjusting her so her back was against him.

She wondered if he'd feel awkward. Wyatt was so quiet, but he kissed the back of her head, caressed her arm and cupped her breast in a lazy, playful way that made her smile.

He didn't speak—she knew he wouldn't—so she knew she'd have to be the one to break the silence.

"Well. That was pretty good."

His hand stilled. "Pretty good?"

"Yeah. For a first time and all."

He rolled her onto her back and she grinned at him.
"Not funny."

She laughed "I thought it was. Wyatt, you nearly killed me. I came three times. I don't think it gets much better than that."

She knew he fought it, but his lips curved in that supremely male satisfied way. "It's still early. Trust me. It gets better."

He leaned over and kissed her, and she sighed, shocked to realize she was ready to go again.

It was going to be a long night.

Wyatt left Calliope's house early the next morning before the sun came up.

She was on her stomach on the bed, buried under the blankets. Her face was flushed, her curls spread all over the pillow.

He'd never seen anything more beautiful.

She'd looked warm. He knew she would be. He could have shucked his clothes and climbed in the bed with her, woken her up by making love to her again.

Instead, he'd gotten dressed and left the house as quiet as he could so he wouldn't wake her.

More like so he wouldn't have to talk to her. Face her. Have that inevitable conversation about how this could never happen again.

Once had been bad enough. Though they hadn't really done it once, had they? More like three times.

He started the truck and let it warm up while he cleaned off all the snow. A couple feet on the ground at least. Damn good snowfall, but the salt trucks and plows had been busy last night so the roads looked passable. He should make it just fine, though he doubted any of the businesses would be open today, including Calliope's day care center.

He climbed in the truck and eased it away from the curb.

It pulled right off the frozen snow mound and into the street without a problem.

The main roads were even better than the side streets. He should stop at the office, see if anyone made it in, but he decided he needed to go home, take a shower, grab something to eat.

He should have left her a note.

Nah. He wasn't a note kind of guy. She'd figure it out. She was smart. Though it was rude to just leave.

Then again, she should be used to him being rude.

After all, she'd been nice enough to invite him in last night. She'd fed him. Hell, she'd slept with him.

And he'd just walked out on her this morning.

That made him an asshole. The kind of guy he'd been before. The kind of guy who'd been married to Cassandra.

Maybe he should stop being that kind of guy.

By the time he pulled into his garage at home, he'd decided too much introspection wasn't good for him. It didn't come out in his favor. He brewed some coffee and sat at the kitchen table, looking out at the piles of snow in his backyard, and wondering what the hell he was going to do with his day.

Right now he could be in bed with Calliope.

Instead, he was home.

Alone.

There was something inherently fucked about his decision-making.

SEVEN

CALLIOPE BLEW AN errant hair away from her face as she cleaned up one of the playrooms while the one-year-olds slumbered during nap time. The day care center had only been closed one day, and the kids obviously had snow fever, because they were all rambunctious and full of energy today. She was certain the parents were all happy to be back at work today and leave their wild little charges with her. The worst thing was the playground outside was still covered in snow, so they would have to deal with having the kids inside all day long.

Along with Wyatt and his men, who were working away inside the room addition.

He'd been gone yesterday by the time she woke. Normally a light sleeper, she must have been half-dead not to hear him dress and leave her house. Then again, they'd stayed up almost all night, and it wasn't like they'd been leisurely playing cards. She blushed as she remembered exactly what they'd been doing all night long.

He'd greeted her with a nod this morning, back to his usual gruff demeanor.

Yeah, that wasn't going to fly. She had a few things to say to him at the end of the day today. She was no mouse or doormat who would stand idly by and be treated this way.

She counted down the hours until the final child and the last of her employees left. Wyatt stayed behind after his two men headed out the door. She smiled at both of them, wished them a good-night, then locked the door behind them and headed into the new addition, determined to have a serious conversation about how you treat a woman after you've spent a night worshipping her body.

The existing playroom door was closed so none of the kids would wander in there. She opened the door at the same time Wyatt did.

He looked down at her. Frowned.

"Everyone gone?" he asked.

"Yes."

"About time." He moved her out of the room, away from the wind coming in from the addition, and closed the door. He backed her against the hallway wall and pressed his body to hers. "I've been waiting all damn day for this."

He slammed his mouth down on hers, obliterating all the righteous anger she'd worked up since he'd left her house yesterday. The kiss was dark and passionate and needy and made heat coil low in her belly. She melted against him, but then laid her palms on his chest and gave him a gentle push.

He drew back, his lips moist from their kiss. She wanted to grab his hair and pull him back, but she resisted.

"What was that all about?" she asked.

"The kiss?"

"Yes."

His gaze drifted to her mouth. "I've been thinking about it all day. Yesterday, too."

"You could have been with me yesterday, instead of sneaking out of my house while I was still asleep."

"Yeah, about that. I'm sorry. I shouldn't have left like that. It was stupid and inconsiderate. And I should have called, but once I left I felt like an ass, so I just...didn't."

This was new. An apology? "Okay."

He palmed the wall next to her head. "Look, Calliope. I'm not very good at this."

"This?"

"Relationships. Women. Dealing with them. I'll try to do better, but I'm probably not going to be good at it. You should know that going in, so you can change your mind if you want."

Her lips curved. As an apology, it kind of sucked, but it was honest. She couldn't ask for more. "It's okay, Wyatt. I understand."

He cocked a brow. "That's it? I'm forgiven?"

"That's it."

"You're too easy."

She laughed. "Not the best thing to say to a woman."

He laid his forehead against hers. "Shit. I told you I wasn't good at this."

She framed his face with her hands. "No, you aren't, but if you're honest with me, I can deal with everything else. Besides, you're a great kisser, and that forgives a lot of sins."

"Yeah?" He leaned in closer, grabbed the loops on her jeans and directed her toward her office.

When they got in there, he pushed her against the wall again, pulled off her glasses and tucked them in his pocket.

She might be old-fashioned, but she had to admit she dug his caveman moves.

"Oh, yeah."

He brushed his lips across hers, his breath a warm caress as he teased his tongue along her bottom lip, then went in for the kill, sliding his arm around her to draw her against him. He brought his mouth full force against hers, and kissed her until she forgot all about yesterday. All she thought of was right now, and the fact they were alone and the door was firmly locked.

And when he dropped to the floor, pulling her on top of

him, she went willingly, eager to pick up where they'd left off the night before.

"This is kind of wicked," she said as he swept her hair away from her face.

"Never done it at work before?"

She snorted. "I work at a day care center. I don't get many hot guys hitting on me here."

He popped the button on her jeans and drew the zipper down. "That's too bad. They should be lining up at the door."

Now he was making up for fumbling his words earlier. She felt warm all over, though maybe that was due to him rolling her over and touching her. He took off her tennis shoes and slid her jeans and panties down her legs.

By the time he'd removed her sweatshirt and bra, and gotten rid of his own clothes, she started to giggle. He frowned at her.

"This is no laughing matter," he said.

"I've never been naked at work before."

He grabbed a condom from the pocket of his jeans. "You should try it more often."

She rolled over on her side. "Oh? You make a habit of it?"

"Yeah. I wander around jobsites naked all the time. You haven't seen me on the news?"

She grabbed his shoulder. "Careful, Wyatt, or I might think you have a sense of humor."

"Don't worry. It doesn't come around all that often." He pulled her back on top of him and reached for her breasts, and all humor fled as she tilted her head back and lost herself in the magic of his hands.

Wyatt hadn't meant to start this. All he'd wanted to do was talk to Calliope tonight, to get her alone so he could apologize for acting like an ass and running out on her yesterday.

But seeing her as she opened the door, fury and irritation instead of hurt in her eyes, had primed the pump and made him forget everything he intended to say to her.

Anger had lit up her face, put a bright spot of color on her cheeks and made her eyes come to life. The only thing he'd thought about then was kissing her and getting his hands on her.

Okay, so maybe those were the only things he'd thought about since he left her house yesterday.

But now she sat on top of him naked. He didn't know if he'd ever seen anything more beautiful than her body, lush and flushed pink with arousal as she tilted her head back while he thumbed and teased her nipples.

She rolled against him, causing him no end of agony— the pleasurable kind. Buried inside her, he connected with her in the most primal way, reaching up to pull her against him, to take a nipple into his mouth, to touch her on a basic level so she'd feel what he felt.

He loved the way she responded, the way she looked at him so he knew she was as connected as he was. She gripped his shoulders as she rode him, as she raised and lowered on him, and when she climaxed, she kept that connection, digging her nails into him, her eyes widening as she tightened around him. He cupped his hand around the nape of her neck and flew with her, losing himself in her depths.

A part of him wasn't ready for this—this bond he felt with her. The last time he'd felt this attached to a woman had been Cassandra. And that hadn't ended well.

Calliope was like a hurricane—wild and turbulent. He wasn't sure he could handle her, but he wanted to see what she threw at him, and right now he just couldn't resist her. She was beautiful, a little scary, and he couldn't walk away.

"I'm hungry," she said, pushing up to look down at him. "You like pizza?"

He grinned up at her. "Sounds good."

"How about Rizzoni's?"

"How about we go to your place and order delivery? Fewer clothes involved that way."

She arched a brow. "Naked pizza eating could be dangerous."

"I live on the edge."

She climbed off him and started grabbing her clothes. "You're on, but hurry. Sex makes me hungry."

He grabbed his jeans. "I'll be sure to order an extra large pizza, then. You're going to need it."

EIGHT

"The party is scheduled for the sixteenth," Tori said, handing out the information sheet along with the menu.

Staff meetings at Kent Construction were his least favorite thing, but business had to be conducted. Discussing the annual holiday party was something he'd rather Tori handle. As the office manager, she dealt with the day-to-day running of the business, as well as all the financials. He'd much rather just get out there and work with his hands.

Unfortunately, when Tori called a meeting, you showed up. She might be only in her twenties, but she was formidable. When she bellowed, you came running or you'd never hear the end of it.

Wyatt took the information sheet and scanned it. "I assume there'll be meat at this party."

She rolled her eyes at him. "No. We're serving celery and carrots. Our clients like rabbit food."

"Har."

"We're having roast beef, chicken and pasta. There'll be hors d'oeuvres and an open bar, though I twitched at the open bar thing."

"We can handle it," Brody said.

"You say that now. Wait until you have to write the check. It's the holiday season. People like to drink."

"You like to drink, too, you lush," Brody teased. "Will I have to throw you over my shoulder and drive you home again this year?"

Tori glared at him. "That was one stinkin' year. And I

had just turned twenty-one. It's never happened since so I'd appreciate it if you'd never mention it again."

Wyatt's lips twitched.

"I saw that, Wyatt," Tori said, as if she had eyes in the back of her head. "Don't you dare smile."

"I don't smile. You know that. I'm the bad-tempered one."

Tori swiveled in her chair, narrowed her gaze at him. "You're almost in a good mood. What the hell is wrong with you?"

Ethan rolled his chair closer to Wyatt, inspecting him like he had ticks or something. "There is something different about you. What's up?"

"I know what it is." Brody leaned back and crossed his arms. "He's getting laid."

"What?" Tori's eyes widened. "How come I don't know about this?"

"You mean I know something you don't? What the hell, Tor? You having an off week?"

"Shut up, Brody." Tori narrowed her gaze on Wyatt. "What's going on?"

Shit. He knew he should have gone straight to the day care center this morning and bugged out of this meeting. "Nothing's going on, and if it was it would be none of your business."

"So he is getting laid." Ethan grinned. "Who is it?"

"Oh. I know who it is," Tori said. "And why she hasn't said anything to me is a subject I'll be taking up with her very soon."

"Who is it?" Brody asked.

Tori didn't say anything, just gave Wyatt a knowing smile.

"Oh," Ethan said. "It's Calliope Andrews."

Wyatt winced.

"Wow. Keeping it in the family, aren't you?" Brody asked.

"Shut up, Brody," Tori said. "This is none of our business. Let's move on with the meeting."

"Hey, you started it. Now we're going to take the ball and run like hell." Ethan nudged him with an elbow. "So... is one sister—"

Wyatt shot Ethan a look. "Don't go there. I mean it, Ethan."

Ethan kicked his chair back and raised his hands. "Hey, I was joking with you."

Brody leaned toward Tori. "A little sensitive, isn't he?"

"I'm not fucking deaf, you idiot."

"I mean it, Brody," Tori said. "You need to leave this alone. This is Wyatt and Calliope's business. Not ours."

Ethan shrugged. "Who am I going to tell? Besides Riley, of course. And she's out of town."

"It's not a big deal."

"Do you like her?" Brody asked.

Tori stared at him. He knew Tori and Calliope were friends. He'd have to be careful what he said. "Again, none of your business."

He knew this was going to be a problem, that once word got out he was seeing his ex-wife's sister people would start talking. He could trust his brothers and Tori...but other people? He didn't want to deal with the gossip. The talk after the divorce had been bad. And since he hadn't bothered to say anything, people had made up their own minds about what had happened between him and Cassandra. None of it had been true.

People could think whatever the hell they wanted to think, but he didn't want them talking shit about Calliope. It was best they didn't know about the two of them.

If he was smart he'd put an end to it now before things got out of hand, before people found out.

They finished the meeting and Wyatt grabbed his stuff. Brody stopped him.

"Hey."

He turned to his brother. "What?"

"You know we were teasing you in there. If you want to see Calliope, that's your business."

Wyatt nodded.

"If anyone's entitled to a life and some fun, Wyatt, it's you. And if that's with Calliope, then go for it."

"It's not that simple. She's Cassandra's sister."

"So? If she's the one you want…"

"Again, not that simple."

"Why? You worried about what people will think, what they'll say?"

He didn't say anything.

Brody frowned. "Screw that. We're behind you. Family sticks together and we'll kick anyone's ass who has something to say about it. Calliope's cool. And damn, man, you're the most relaxed I've seen you in years. It's about time you went out and had some fun. If she's the reason behind it, then don't let anyone stop you."

He nodded. "I'll think about it. Thanks."

He headed out the door and climbed in his truck, tossed his gear to the passenger seat.

Maybe Brody was right. Maybe he was worried too much.

Then again, he knew what small-town gossip was like. He knew his family would rally around him. It wasn't himself he was worried about. Anything people had to say, any whispers and innuendos were water off a duck's back to him. He'd heard it all after his divorce.

But Calliope was building a business. She dealt with families with small children. Rumors and gossip could hurt her and her business.

And that he wouldn't tolerate.

CALLIOPE STOOD AND laid her hands at the small of her back, stretching out her tight muscles.

What an interminably long day. She was glad it was Friday and the week was over. All she wanted was a hot bath, a good meal and her man. And a massage by said man. She wondered if she could convince Wyatt to give her a back rub. Maybe she could use her feminine wiles to wrangle a back rub out of him.

Or, she could just get naked. That should convince him.

Then again, they hadn't made official plans for tonight, or for the weekend. She'd assumed they'd see each other. He'd come over to her place or she'd gone to his after work almost every night for the past two weeks.

He and the other guys had left the addition about an hour ago, so she assumed she'd find him in the trailer doing some paperwork. She locked up the center and headed that way, frowning when she saw all the lights out in the trailer. She pulled on the door. It was locked.

Huh. She walked around to the front of the trailer and didn't see his truck.

He'd left. Without saying anything to her.

Okay, so maybe he'd had an emergency and didn't have time to tell her about it. She hoped everything was okay.

She drove home, tossed her coat and purse on the sofa and grabbed her phone, dialing his number as she kicked her shoes off.

He answered on the third ring.

"Hi," he said.

"Is everything all right?"

"Yeah. Why wouldn't it be?"

"I looked for you after I closed for the day. I thought you might be in the trailer but you had already left."

"Yeah. Cut out on time for a change. Had to head back to the office."

"Oh, okay." She took a seat at the kitchen table. "So what are your plans for tonight?"

"I thought I'd work on the car."

"Oh." She heard the definite brush-off signals in his tone of voice. "What about tomorrow? There's a new movie out I'm dying to see."

"I don't think so. I have a few things I need to catch up on."

Pain and irritation swirled around in her empty stomach, making her nauseous.

"Sure. I understand. I'll see you on Monday, then."

"Okay. See you."

She clicked off the phone and slid it across the table, angry with Wyatt, and with herself.

No. Not with herself. Definitely with him. They had a relationship. They'd been together every day for three weeks. That allowed her to make assumptions. He'd been happy, dammit. He couldn't just make an about turn and suddenly blow her off without an explanation.

An explanation she deserved.

She went into the bathroom and took a shower, washing off the day and some of her annoyance with it. By the time she'd dried her hair, she had the phone to her ear and Tori on the line.

"Are you busy tonight?" she asked.

"I was going to do a home pedicure. It doesn't get more exciting than that."

Calliope laughed, which was exactly what she needed. "How about a girl's night out?"

"Sounds fabulous," Tori said. "What do you have in mind?"

"Food and lots of margaritas."

"Bingo. I'm so game for that."

They made plans to meet at one of their favorite Mexican restaurants in town. She put on makeup, dressed in a pair of her tightest jeans, put on high-heeled boots, then slid into a sexy silk top instead of her day care center sweatshirts.

Tonight, she intended to party.

El Partido was a popular restaurant, especially on the weekends. In a small town, entertainment was limited. You went out to eat, you hit a bar, or you went to the movies. Though there was also bowling and ice-skating if you were in the mood for those activities.

Calliope was in the mood to drink, and she knew Tori was always game for a fun night on the town. They started out with a top-shelf margarita, settled in at the bar and waited for their name to be called for their table. Judging by the long line out front, it could be a while.

"I haven't seen you in like...forever," Tori said, her long earrings grazing her neck as she twisted her barstool around while juggling the oversized drink. "I've missed you."

"I've missed you, too. I'm sorry we haven't gotten together. I've been busy."

Tori lifted her brows. "Yeah? Busy doing what? Or should I ask...whom?"

"What do you know, or what do you think you know?"

Tori gave an innocent bat of her lashes. "I just know Wyatt has been a lot less grumpy lately. He even smiled. He might have cracked a joke. We thought the world was ending."

Calliope's lips curved. "Well, good for him."

"And you're saying his good mood over the past few weeks has nothing to do with you."

Calliope shrugged. "I'm not responsible for his moods."

"Uh oh. He's pissed you off. What did he do?"

"Nothing. He's not responsible for my mood, either."

"What a crock. Tell me everything."

She did, starting with the first night and every night since.

Tori leaned an arm against the bar and sipped her margarita, her expression changing as the story went on. By the time Calliope finished, Tori was frowning.

"What an ass."

"He has a right to his space."

"Bullshit. He sees you every night, and then suddenly blows you off with no explanation other than working on his car and some vague 'other stuff to do'? No. There's something else going on."

"He's not seeing anyone else. It practically took an act of Congress for him to have sex with me."

Tori snorted and signaled for a refill on their drinks. "Isn't that the truth? That man had a serious dry spell going. Hence his three-year bad mood. Thank God you came along and ended that."

"Yeah."

"So how's the sex?"

"Tori!"

Tori straightened in her seat. "What? I want to know how the sex is. Wyatt's gorgeous. Virile. Studly."

Calliope took the fresh margarita from the bartender and licked a spot of salt from the rim. "Yum."

"The drink or the man?"

She smiled. "Both."

"So he's good, right?"

"I wouldn't be sitting here pissed off at him if he wasn't."

"That's what I figured. I always knew he had some deep, smoldering sexuality simmering under the surface of that testy exterior."

"I'm surprised you even notice given the hots you have for Brody."

"I do not have the hots for Brody. At. All."

"You. Lie."

"First, I work for him. Second, I've known him since I was like…sixteen. Third…"

Calliope waited while Tori tried to come up with another objection.

Instead, Tori took a drink and Calliope laughed at her.

"What?"

"Why haven't you ever done anything about it?"

"About what?"

"Brody."

Tori rolled her eyes, then set her drink down and fiddled with the bracelets on her arm. "I am never doing Brody. We are not meant to be. The man gets on my last nerve. He's egotistical, loud, annoying, teases me too much and already has way too many women in this town who think the sun rises and sets on his perfect abs and great ass."

"And you're not one of them."

"Hell, no. I am not a member of the Brody Kent fan club. Besides, we're not here to talk about me. Nice try in deflecting, though. What are you going to do about Wyatt?"

"Nothing. I can't make him want to be with me."

"No, you can't. But why the sudden brakes on your relationship?"

"Maybe it's run its course."

"After a few weeks?" Tori shook her head. "I don't think so. There's something else, and you need to talk to him to figure out what it is."

"I don't want to talk to him. I want to drink my margarita, hang out with you, then have a giant enchilada."

"I think you'd rather have Wyatt's giant enchilada."

Calliope nearly choked on her drink. "Oh, my God, Tori. Don't do that to me when I'm drinking."

Tori grinned. "Just here to state the facts, my friend."

Calliope thought about what Tori had said all through drinks and dinner.

She wasn't a quitter, wasn't one to sit back and let things happen. Maybe all this togetherness had been too much too fast for Wyatt, but if so, she needed to hear that from him, not some flimsy excuse about stuff and cars. She'd told him from the very beginning the only thing she wanted from him in this relationship was honesty.

So she gave him the weekend to do whatever "stuff" he had to do. Monday morning he walked right past her office without dipping his head in, looking to see if she was in there or even trying to find her the entire day.

Yeah, something was definitely up.

If the relationship had run its course and he wanted to be done with it, then he owed it to her to have a face-to-face conversation with her and tell her.

So at the end of the workday, she stood at the entrance to her office while her staff shuffled the kids out the door to their parents. She waved to the other guys who were working on the room addition, and when Wyatt grabbed his tools on his way out the door, she stopped him.

"Wyatt. Can I see you in my office for a minute?"

"Kind of busy here, Calliope."

"Whatever you're busy with will have to wait. This is important."

He paused, looking toward the front door as if he considered a mad dash for freedom. "I'm dirty and full of dust. How about we do this in my trailer?"

"Fine. Let me lock up in here and I'll meet you there."

He nodded and walked out.

As soon as her staff left, she locked the door and headed over to his trailer. For a brief second as she rounded the corner she wondered if he would take off without talking to her, but he wasn't that much of a coward. The light was on the trailer. She opened the door and walked in. Wyatt was in there going over blueprints on the drafting table. He looked up, but didn't smile.

"What's going on?" he asked.

She leaned against the opposite wall. "Why don't you tell me what's going on?"

"Huh?"

"Things between us were great, and then suddenly you backed off. I want to know why."

"Calliope…"

"Don't." She pushed off the wall, came to the table and laid her hands on it. "All I want is the straight truth, Wyatt."

He looked down at the blueprints, then back up at her. She saw sadness and pain in his eyes and her heart squeezed.

"I don't want anyone to hurt you."

"What?"

"You started talking about going out, and you deserve that. But you know people are going to talk."

That wasn't at all what she expected to hear. He was protecting her? "Talk about what? That you were once married to Cassie and now you're dating me?"

"Yeah."

She rolled her eyes and slid her hand over his. "Wyatt. I don't care what anyone has to say about that."

"You know as well as I do it's the kind of thing that will get small-town gossip going. It doesn't bother me at all. I don't give a shit what people say. But you have a reputation to maintain. This could hurt you."

She snorted. "A reputation? Am I some kind of saint in this town?"

"You run a day care center. You can't be seen with me."

"Oh for the love of chocolate chip cookies. That's the dumbest thing I've ever heard." She moved in between him and table and palmed his face. "I want to be with you. In public. People can say whatever they want, gossip all they want about it. I'd be proud to be with you. If they care that you were married to my sister, that's their problem, not mine."

She saw the worry on his face.

"You know what they're going to say, all the things they're going to say."

"Let them," she said. "I won't be listening."

"What about the people who bring their kids to you?"

"If they're bothered by it, they're not the right kind of people. It's not going to hurt my business." She swept her hand along his jaw, tingling at the scratch of his beard. "But I love that you were worried for me. Thank you."

"I don't want to hurt you, Calliope. I'm trying not to be that guy anymore."

She tilted her head to the side. "That guy?"

"Never mind. It's not important. Look. I'm sorry. I warned you I wasn't any good at this."

She laughed. "You're only going to get so many free passes at using that as an excuse. If you want to be in a relationship, you have to work on your communication skills."

He wrapped his arms around her and tugged her close. "I'm not much of a talker. I'm more of a doer."

This is what she'd missed over the weekend. The rush of heat, the sudden flame of desire he could draw out of her with one touch.

"A doer, huh?"

"Yeah."

She looked over her shoulder. Her butt rested on the blue-prints. "You know, I've had this fantasy about your trailer and this drafting table ever since the first time I walked in here."

She felt the hard ridge of his erection as he pushed her against the table. "Do tell."

"It has something to do with you bending me over it."

He flipped her around so fast she was dizzy, his hands roaming over her breasts, her back, her butt. "I like the way you think, Calliope."

"Good. Then shut up. More doing, less talking."

NINE

WYATT WATCHED THE people around them as he escorted Calliope to their table at McCluskey's Restaurant. He intended to shoot visual daggers at anyone who gave Calliope even a sidelong glance.

So far they'd gone to a movie, eaten at her favorite Mexican restaurant, and gone out with Ethan, his wife Riley and their daughter, Zoey, since Riley was back in town after doing a recording session. As soon as Riley heard he was dating Calliope, she insisted on meeting her, so Ethan had suggested they all go out to dinner.

All this going out was wearing on him. Wyatt had spent so much of the past few years as a recluse he had lost the ability to be social. Fortunately Calliope was social enough for the both of them. She and Riley had talked for hours, and of course since Calliope loved kids she'd engaged Zoey in conversation, too. He and Ethan had kicked back and talked work while the three girls laughed together, talked fashion and music and the latest kid stuff.

Calliope was just damned...perfect.

He was in love with her, which scared the shit out of him.

The last time he'd fallen in love with a woman it hadn't ended so well for him. And this was Cassandra's sister. He couldn't imagine what her parents would think of all this. They weren't too fond of him because of what had gone down the first time. He didn't think they'd be overjoyed at the prospect of having him back in the family again.

"Wyatt."

He lifted his gaze to Calliope, who, along with the waitress he hadn't noticed standing at their table, gave him a look
of expectation.

"What?"

"What would you like to drink, sir?"

"Oh. Iced tea would be great."

"Thanks, Rachel," Calliope said, then turned back to
Wyatt after the waitress bounded off. "Where is your head
tonight?"

"Sorry. Was thinking about work stuff." Or proposing
to Calliope.

And where the hell had that come from?

He knew where it had come from. He was tired of being
alone. Calliope had filled a void in his life he hadn't realized
had been there. She was everything he'd ever wanted in a
woman. She was full of life and laughter, she loved kids, and
she didn't put up with his crap. She wanted the same things
he did, so what the hell was he waiting for, other than it was
all too familiar, family-wise?

It was too soon. He wasn't ready. He had no idea how she
felt. What the hell was he thinking?

"Wyatt."

He lifted his gaze. "What?"

She tilted her head toward Rachel, their waitress again.
"Sir, what would you like to order?"

Shit. He did a quick scan of the menu, ordered a steak and
handed her the menu.

"Are you even here tonight?" Calliope asked.

"Sorry. A lot on my mind."

She reached for his hand. "Would you like to talk about
it?"

"No." Hell, no.

"Well, there's something I want to talk to you about."

"Okay." This time he was determined to pay attention.

"The holidays are approaching, you know."

He lifted his lips and took a sip of tea. "Yeah, I have a calendar."

"Smartass. Anyway, I was wondering if you'd be willing to come over to my parents' house. They're having an open house this weekend."

He swallowed. Talk about tuning into his train of thought. "I don't know, Calliope. I'm not exactly their favorite person after Cassandra."

"I don't agree. They don't hold a grudge. Anyway, there're more."

"It gets worse?"

"I don't know if you'd call it worse. But I think if you and I are going to go anywhere with our relationship, there are some issues you need to put to rest."

He didn't like where this was going. "Go on."

"Cassie's coming home for the holidays."

And the train just jumped the tracks. "No."

"Hear me out on this."

"No. She and I have nothing to say to each other. Everything was said between our attorneys."

She squeezed his hand. "See? That's the problem. Neither of you had closure."

He pulled his hand away. "I had plenty of closure."

"Wyatt."

"Calliope. No. I don't want to talk about this anymore. I have nothing to say to Cassandra that hasn't already been said. I don't want to see her again, or talk to her again. Ever."

She opened her mouth to argue, but the waitress brought their drinks. Maybe she could tell by the look on his face, but she didn't bring up the topic again, at least until they left the restaurant and went back to his place.

They were curled up on the sofa together and she was unbuttoning his shirt, a slow seduction that was too damn slow in his opinion. He was more than ready to get to the good stuff, like her gorgeous naked body, with him inside her, hopefully rocking her world.

"What if you and I end up having…let's say a long-term relationship."

Fun halted. He took a deep breath. "Okay. Let's say we do."

"Eventually you're going to have to see my parents, come over to my house, hang out at holidays and birthdays and stuff."

He turned to face her. "My relationship is with you. Not with your family any more than your relationship is with my family. I care about you. Just you."

"But that isn't the way it works and you know it. You're trying to be simplistic and putting the two of us in a bubble. I don't want it to work that way, and I don't think you do, either. I like your family. I want our future to include *our* families—providing, of course, we have a future together. Do you want us to have a future together?"

He inhaled, let it out. "This is complicated."

"It doesn't have to be. You're making it that way by shoving this giant obstacle between us."

"Cassandra."

"Yes. And she doesn't have to be there. If you'd—"

He put his fingers to her lips. "I don't want my ex-wife in our lives, and I sure as hell don't want her between us right now. I don't want to talk about her or think about her. What I want right now is to kiss you." He put his mouth where his fingers had been. He much preferred kissing her to talking.

When she leaned against him, he felt her surrender. She

curled her hand around his neck and moaned against him. He'd won this battle.

But it was a temporary reprieve. This wasn't over, but he was content to let it go for now. All he wanted was this moment, and to have Calliope in his arms, to feel the softness of her body as she moved against him.

He reached behind her to the zipper of the incredibly sexy dress she'd worn to dinner. All he could think about was getting the dress off her. He dragged the zipper down, then drew the dress off her shoulders. She wore a black silk bra that made him hold his breath because her breasts nearly spilled over the top.

"Wow."

She grinned and pushed her glasses up.

Damn, she was one sexy woman. She slid off his lap, unhooked her bra then shimmied out of her panties. "You know what I really wish we could do?"

"If it has anything to do with sex, your wish is granted."

"Good. Because I want to take a shower."

He liked the direction of her thoughts. They made his dick pound hard against his jeans. He stood, scooped her up in his arms and carried her up the stairs, depositing her on the floor in the bathroom. He turned the shower on while he removed his clothes, loving the way Calliope watched him as he undressed. He was hard and aching by the time he pulled her inside the oversized shower.

"I told you the first time I came here that this shower gave me naughty thoughts," she said.

"And I want to hear all about them."

"Four showerheads? It's a woman's dream, in more ways than one." She stepped under one of the sprays, not at all self-conscious about her hair getting wet or her makeup running down her face. One of the things he loved about her.

Wyatt stood back and watched the water stream in rivers down her gorgeous body as she slicked her hair back.

He moved in and put his arms around her to tug her against him, let her feel what she did to him. She reached between them to stroke him, agonizing him with slow, careful movements that made him clench his jaw.

He pushed her against the wall and lifted her arms over her head, held them there with his hand while he used the other to roam over her body. Water poured over them both, steam shadowing them and making the temperature rise as his body heated to unbearable. He bent and took a nipple, licked it then sucked it between his lips. Her moans of pleasure and the way she rocked her hips toward him were an invitation for more.

He wanted more, so he straightened and cupped her sex, watching her eyes as he rocked his hand against her, found the tight nub and rolled it between his fingers and took her where she wanted to go. She gasped, her eyes widening when she came.

He grabbed the condom he'd laid on top of the shower and put it on, then pushed her legs apart and entered her. She held on to his shoulders as he thrust into her again and again, his passion as hot as the water and steam pouring over them.

She dug her nails into him. "More," she said, her voice a whisper, a sensual command.

He gave her more, and she tightened around him, then convulsed, and he shattered, wrapping his arm around her and lifting her. He took her mouth as the maelstrom of sensation wrecked him, left his legs shaking so hard he had to grab the top of the shower to hold them both steady.

He set her down easy, kissing her lips and her throat, stroking her hair while she threaded her fingers through his hair.

Neither one of them said anything. What they'd done, what they'd shared, had said enough.

They dried off and climbed into his big bed, but only used a quarter of the space because he tugged her close against him. She pulled his arm around her and he realized he liked having her here in his house. In his bed. In his life.

He'd do anything to keep her here.

Except the one thing he knew she wanted.

That, he couldn't—wouldn't do.

"I HAVE A PROBLEM, and I need some advice."

Tori tossed her oversized bag on Calliope's desk. "You've come to the right person."

Wyatt had a meeting with his brothers at a potential new job site, so he'd left early. Tori had agreed to pop over after work, so now that the day care center was closed, she and Tori had some quiet time to talk.

She'd let a week go by. Things with Wyatt were almost perfect. They were together all the time, and even though the room addition project was a couple days from being completed, she knew the two of them would continue to be together after it was finished. But still, things weren't quite whole between them, and she knew why. It nagged at her, refusing to go away.

Tori took a seat in the chair across from Calliope's desk.

"It's about Wyatt."

Tori smirked. "I figured. What's the problem? Is he being grouchy again?"

"No. Well, not really. He's…uncooperative about a particular subject."

"What subject is that?"

"His ex-wife."

Tori's eyes widened. "You do realize that subject is off-limits. None of us ever bring up the ex. I know she's your sister and all, but, honey, that marriage did not end well."

"I know." She pushed back from her desk and stood, looking out at the streetlights and cars passing by. She turned to face Tori. "The scars of that marriage are holding him back. It's holding us back. He can't let it go."

"Ugly things were said between the two of them. I wasn't privy to it all, but from what I heard, it was a bitter divorce."

"Yes, it was. Mistakes were made on both sides and they walked away without closure. Without forgiveness. Without talking to each other. They need that closure now. Without it, I don't think Wyatt will ever be able to move on with a clear conscience."

"And you want him to be able to move on. With you." She nodded.

"Honey, you know I love you. But some things—some people—can't be fixed."

"I don't want to fix him. I want him to be happy."

"Doesn't he seem happy? With you?"

"Yes and no. I feel like there will always be a wall between us."

"Meaning Cassie."

"Yes. He needs to get past her, really let her go, before he can ever be truly happy."

"You do realize this could be a deal breaker for him."

Calliope nodded. "I know. But I love him, and I know that on the surface he's happy with me, but Cassandra will always be between us. Which means I have to try. And if that means he walks away from me, then I guess we were never meant to be."

Tori stood, came over and hugged her. "So what do you want to do?"

"I have an idea."

"That Wyatt won't like."

"He'll hate it. He'll be angry with me."

"And you need my help to make it happen."

"Yes."

Tori nodded. "You know I love you both. So what can I do?"

TEN

WYATT HATED PARTIES. It required more socializing, and God knew he'd done enough socializing the past couple months to last him a lifetime.

But it was part of what they did for business, and the annual Kent Construction holiday party included inviting their clients. Treating clients to a night of fun, dinner and dancing was good for their business. So he'd suck it up, put on a smile and a suit, and down enough whiskey so he could numb the pain.

At least this year he'd have Calliope by his side, so he wouldn't have to huddle in a corner with some drunken businessman he'd have to end up driving home at the end of the night.

Trying not to strangle on his tie, he pulled into Calliope's driveway and got out, went to her front door and rang the bell.

"It's open," he heard her holler. He opened the door.

"How do you know I'm not some serial killer?" he said as he walked in. "Lock your damn door, woman."

"There are no serial killers in this town," she said from the bedroom.

"I'm sure the last person to be killed by a serial killer in a small town thought that, too."

"Fine. I'll have a key made for you and I'll start locking the front door."

She came out, and he forgot all about the lecture he was going to give her about locking the door.

Dressed in a black dress that swept across the tops of her knees, her shoulders were bare, the dress sparkled, clung to her amazing breasts and every curve of her body. Long silver earrings hung from her ears, her hair was swept up and into some kind of sparkly clip, curls dangling down her back. She even wore different glasses, black ones with tiny crystals on the side. Sexy as hell. Her shoes made her legs look miles long and all he could think about was getting her out of that dress later on tonight.

"I can't breathe, Calliope."

She frowned and walked toward him. "What's wrong?"

"You're so goddamned stunning you take my breath away."

She paused, and her lips curved. "Really?"

"Yeah." He came to her, lifted her hand in his and pressed a kiss to it. "I'm going to make every man at the party jealous."

"Stop."

"No. You're truly beautiful. I'm a very lucky man."

She grinned. "Thank you." She adjusted his tie. "You look so handsome in a suit. Black suits you. We make a fine couple."

"Thanks. I'm uncomfortable."

"Suck it up, hot stuff. It's only for one night."

"You ready?"

She inhaled, let it out, and he couldn't help watching the rise of her breasts.

"You keep looking at me like that and we won't make it to your party tonight."

"And that would be a bad thing…how?"

She laughed. "I'll get my coat."

CALLIOPE'S STOMACH WAS twisted up in knots. The venue was beautiful. She found Tori and told her she'd done a fantastic job.

"Thank you." Tori squeezed her hand. "We have so many people here tonight. I'm so nervous."

"Don't be. This is amazing."

Tori took a sip of champagne and looked around. "We have such a great turnout. I'm glad we booked on a Friday night. I think people were ready to party, let loose before the holidays."

"And you look gorgeous." Tori's flaming red hair was in an updo, with tendrils framing her creamy face. She wore diamond studs in her ears, and a knockout, tight-fitting red dress that showcased all her assets. "Has Brody seen you yet?"

"Brody who?"

Calliope laughed. "Deny all you want, but that is an impress-a-man dress."

"How do you know it isn't for Jimmy Redding of Redding Tools?"

Calliope snorted. "If you had the hots for Jimmy Redding I'd already know about it."

Tori shrugged. "I'm on duty tonight, making sure our guests have a great time."

Calliope saw Brody frown in Tori's direction, and head their way.

"We'll see what Brody has to say, since he's coming at you like a runaway freight train."

Tori turned. "Huh. Oh, look, there's Jimmy Redding now. Gotta go."

Tori skirted away in a hurry. Calliope had no idea what kind of game Tori was playing with Brody, but from the steaming mad look on Brody's face, she'd guess that game was going to reach a conclusion soon.

Calliope dug her phone out of her purse, then palmed her stomach to calm the nervous jitters.

This had to work. If it didn't, her relationship with Wyatt would be in serious jeopardy.

She spotted Ethan and Riley along with Ethan's parents, so headed over there to say hello. Riley looked gorgeous in a pale cream dress, her hair cascading down her shoulders.

"I love a good party," Riley said. "And these aren't the industry type of parties I'm always stuck going to. Small-town parties are always the best."

"You didn't always think so," Ethan said, sliding his arm around her waist.

She leaned her head against Ethan's shoulder. "I'm reformed now. I might have to be on the road a lot, but there's nothing better than coming home."

Calliope grinned. Ethan and Riley had gone through a lot to be together. Seeing them so happy together now gave her hope.

"Calliope," Stacy Kent said, taking her hands. "It's so wonderful to see you here."

"Thank you, Stacy. It's nice to be here."

Stacy looped her arm in Calliope's after Ethan and Riley moved off. "Can I say thank you?"

"Why?"

"For giving life back to my son. He hasn't had much of one since the divorce. Until you."

Calliope smiled. "Can I tell you a secret?"

"Of course."

"I'm head over heels in love with your son."

Stacy hugged her. "He's very lucky to have someone like you."

Obviously Wyatt's mom had no problem with her being

Cassie's sister. That was one Kent in her corner, at least. Her fingers were crossed this was going to work out.

She'd made a calculated decision. A tough one. One that might blow up in her face and cost her the man she'd fallen madly, hopelessly, irrevocably in love with.

But she didn't see any way around it, because this needed to be done. Not only for Wyatt and her, but for her sister, whom she loved.

It was time to bury the past, forgive the sins and move on.

She just had to get Wyatt on board.

The evening passed with little fanfare. There was food, drinks were plentiful and Wyatt seemed to be having a great time. He wasn't drinking a lot—mostly water, so that was good. She didn't need him drunk and difficult to deal with. This night was going to be tough enough as it was.

She pulled her phone out, judging the time. She wandered around the party, saw Tori and Brody in a dark corner engaged in a heated discussion. Tori's hands were flailing like they always did when she was pissed off. Brody towered over her, his voice raised. Calliope wondered if she should go over and intercede, see if Tori needed any help, but then Brody jerked Tori into his arms and planted one seriously hot kiss on her.

Uh. Wow. That was some kiss. Tori didn't seem to be fighting it either. In fact, she grabbed the lapels of Brody's jacket and tugged him closer. Calliope pivoted and walked the other way, her lips lifting in a wide smile.

Go, Tori.

Intending to find her own hot kisser, she searched the crowd, found Wyatt engaged in conversation with a few of his clients. She slid her arm through his. He looked down and grinned at her, then excused himself from the conversation.

He pulled her into his arms and kissed her, making her

entire body swirl with warmth and emotion. A little over a month ago he wouldn't have even wanted to be seen with her. Now he was kissing her in public. Not only in public, but surrounded by his family and friends.

That was some serious progress.

"People are watching us, you know."

He brushed his lips across hers again. "Don't care. Let them watch. You're mine and I want everyone to know it."

Her stomach tightened. She didn't want to lose Wyatt over this. "I like being yours."

"Let's dance."

He dragged her out on the dance floor and pulled her into his arms. The music was slow and his body was all muscle. They fit together perfectly.

Other couples were out there, but Calliope didn't notice. All she saw was Wyatt, the way he looked at her, as if she was the only woman in the world for him.

She wanted to be the only woman in the world for him. That's why she was doing this tonight.

It was now or never. "I hope you don't mind, but I have a surprise for you later."

His brows lifted. "I hope it has something to do with you and me finding a private room somewhere so I can see what you're wearing under that dress."

She let out a soft laugh. "Yes, there's that, too. But there's another surprise. After the party's over."

He cocked a brow. "I can't wait."

They finished the dance and Wyatt pressed his lips to hers. He hovered, as if he wanted to say something, but one of his clients came up and the moment was broken.

"Go ahead," she said. "We'll catch up later."

He wandered off and she tried to find Tori, who seemed to have disappeared. So had Brody.

Interesting.

Maybe the two of them went off to have their own private holiday party.

If they had, it was about time.

She ran into Ethan and Riley.

"Have you seen Tori?"

Riley looked around. "No, I haven't as a matter of fact."

"I was looking for Brody earlier," Ethan said. "I can't find him."

"You don't think—" Riley's eyes widened. "Did the two of them run off to some dark corner together?"

Calliope refused to answer that one, but Ethan and Riley put two and two together and grinned at each other.

"I guess I can stop trying to hunt down my brother," Ethan said with a knowing smile.

Calliope had no idea what was going on with Tori and Brody, but she hoped whatever it was, it was a good thing and nothing bad.

The party wound down and guests had begun to leave. By midnight, the place was empty. Still no sign of Tori and Brody. Wyatt's parents had already gone home, and Ethan and Riley had to go pick up Zoey from the babysitter.

Which meant she and Wyatt were the last ones standing. She made the call. It was now or never.

"You ready to head out?" Wyatt asked.

"Not yet. I need you to follow me."

His lips curled. "Are you planning to drag me to some dark corner for sex?"

She laughed. "Uh. Not exactly."

She took his hand and led him out of the main ballroom. Her heart pounded and her pulse began to race. Her legs felt weak and she pondered calling a halt to this whole thing, but as soon as they reached the lobby, she was standing right there, right on time.

Cassandra had always been punctual.

She had left a party of her own at the hotel next door, promising Calliope she'd show up.

Wyatt's hand tightened in hers. He stopped, looked at Cassie, then down at her.

"Why? After I told you no, why? You have no business interfering in my life."

She saw the hurt and anger on his face, but lifted her chin.

"I have every right to interfere in your life. I'm in love with you. I want you to be happy, and as long as this animosity lingers between you and Cassie, you'll never be free."

He turned, started to walk away, but she grabbed his hand. "Wyatt, don't. Don't walk away. Not this time."

"I asked you not to do this. I trusted you. The last time I trusted a woman she screwed me over. I guess it runs in the family, doesn't it?"

His words were like a stab in the heart, but she knew it was just his fear talking. She refused to let him push her away. Instead, she was determined to stand and fight.

"Grow up and act like a man, Wyatt. Once you do you'll realize I'm the best damn thing that's ever happened in your life—a life you'll never be able to wholly live until you let go of the past." She pointed down the hall at her sister. "That's your past. I'm your future. Pull your head out of your ass and figure out what you want. A life of regret and anger, or a life with me."

She turned and walked away.

WYATT HAD NEVER been more furious about anything in his entire life. Not even when things had been at their worst with Cassandra had he felt as betrayed as he did right now.

He'd asked Calliope to stay out of it, not to put him and Cassandra together.

He'd trusted Calliope to honor his wishes, yet there Cassandra was, the nightmare of his past.

Fuck a Christmas turkey. What the hell was he supposed to do now?

Cassandra didn't look any happier about this than he did. In fact, she looked downright miserable. Not angry. Miserable.

Shit.

He'd never wanted to see her again, talk to her again, think about her again, but all he'd been doing for the past three years was think about every goddamn thing that had gone wrong in their marriage. And he'd done a lot of blaming—mostly blaming Cassandra for his failures.

Maybe Calliope was right, and it was time to talk it out. If he and Cassandra could have a civil conversation that lasted five minutes.

He strolled toward her, and she came toward him, looking as wary as he felt.

She was still as beautiful as he remembered—even more so, her long blond hair straight and pulled back into a ponytail. She wore heels, some fancy black coat and a party dress.

"You come from a party?" he asked as they stopped a couple feet from each other.

"Real-estate event, yes. A holiday party, like yours."

"How's business?"

"Good. I hear yours is going very well."

"It is."

"Wyatt. Is there someplace less...busy...where we could talk?"

He raked his fingers through his hair. "Yeah." He led her through the lobby and into one of the private ballrooms that wasn't having an event tonight, flipped on the lights and pulled up a chair at a dressed-up table that was set up for some luncheon tomorrow.

She slipped off her coat and he grabbed a chair, straddling it to face her.

"It's been a long time," she finally said.

"Yeah."

Neither of them said anything for a while. Wyatt didn't know where to start, what to say. For years he'd thought of nothing but the words he'd say to her if he ever saw her again. Angry words. Hurtful words. Now, seeing her, she looked small, vulnerable, not the pit viper he'd conjured up in his head all these years.

"Calliope forced me to come here," Cassandra finally said. "She browbeat me, said the two of us left things…open. That there was so much animosity between us, neither of us could move on with our lives until we had closure."

"She's good at pushing people into doing what they don't want to do."

Cassandra laughed. "She's pushy. Always has been."

"I love that about her," he said, then lifted his gaze.

"It's okay. I know you two have been seeing each other for a while. It's all right, Wyatt. I think it's well past time we both move on, don't you?"

"Yeah."

"You two are a good fit. You and I never were."

"You're right about that," he said, and found himself falling into conversation with her easier than he thought he would. "I fell in love with the prettiest girl in town. I put you on a pedestal, and projected everything I wanted out of life on to you, expecting you to toe the line. I was blind to the fact the things I wanted weren't the same things you wanted."

For the first time, she smiled. "I did the same thing. You

were the boy all the girls in town wanted, so I set my sights on you. Then I thought I could turn you into the man I wanted you to be, but you were never that man. I was wrong to try and change you."

"So we both screwed up."

She laughed then. "We should have never gotten married. We were never right for each other."

"I'm sorry I hurt you."

Her eyes glistened with tears. "I'm sorry, too."

This wasn't what he expected. She wasn't what he expected. All these years, he'd had an image of her in his head, and she wasn't that person at all.

"Are you happy now?" he asked.

"I am. I'm getting there. I love my job, and where I live. I'm seeing someone who treats me well, and we do want the same things. I've learned to be honest about what I want—and what I don't want. I have learned from my mistakes."

He inhaled, let out a long breath. "Yeah, I'm still learning, obviously."

She laid her hand over his. "Do you really love my sister?"

"Yes."

"No hesitation. I like that." She stood. "I love her too. She's perfect for you."

He needed to ask, needed to know. "Does that hurt you, that I'm in love with Calliope?"

She paused, tilted her head. "Not at all. I think maybe we're both moving on, don't you think?"

"I think so." They both stood and he helped her with her coat. "I'm sorry for the pain."

She hugged him, and he realized he felt nothing. No anger, no bitterness, nothing at all.

She turned around and smiled at him. "I wish you happiness, Wyatt. And I'm so glad Calliope forced us into this. I

hope we can work on being friends someday. Maybe even…
in-laws?"

He smiled back at her and walked her out.

Now he needed to go find Calliope, because he had a
few more apologies to make, this time to the woman who
really had his heart.

ELEVEN

CALLIOPE PACED ON the back steps of the hotel, switching from angry to hurt back to angry again, then tossing in worry and angst for good measure.

Her stomach was a ball of knots. She could use her best friend and a tall margarita right now, but Tori was otherwise occupied somewhere with Brody. She made a mental note to call her tomorrow for a full recap of what that kiss had been all about.

She was going to give Wyatt another half hour—mainly because she was freezing her ass off out here—but also because he needed to cool off and so did she before they talked again.

"You didn't leave."

Her head shot up at the sound of his voice. He was standing at the top of the stairs.

"You're not wearing a jacket," she said.

"What?"

"It's freezing out here. Where's your coat?"

"Inside."

"Then let's go inside before you freeze to death."

"Calliope. Aren't you mad at me?"

"Furious. But I don't want you to get sick and it's cold out here. I'll yell at you inside."

He shook his head and helped her up the stairs and inside.

"Where would you like me to yell at you?"

He punched the elevator button and they rode up in silence to the penthouse floor. She noted the floor, but otherwise stayed silent, figuring she'd have plenty to say when they got to wherever they were going.

When he pulled out a key card and slid it into the penthouse suite's door, she turned to him. "Really?"

"Yeah. Figured we'd live it up tonight."

"Huh." He pushed the door open and held it while she walked in. When he flipped the switch, she resisted the urge to gasp.

The room was opulent. She'd always wondered about the penthouse suite at this hotel. Now she didn't have to wonder anymore. It was lavish, decorated in creams and blacks, with marble flooring, floor-to-ceiling windows and more square footage than her entire house.

"Would you like a drink?"

"No, thank you," she said, pulling off her coat and laying it over a chair. As she rubbed her chilled hands together, she walked to the window, surveying her entire town in one sweep. Beautiful.

But she wasn't here to enjoy the view, so she turned to face him.

"I know I meddled, that you asked me not to contact Cassie and have the two of you meet. But here's the problem, Wyatt. I love you. And you're never going to be whole until the past is firmly in the past where it belongs. And maybe I don't do things the right way all the time, but I'll always have your back. I'll always want what's best for you. So you know what? What's best for you is me."

"You're right."

She pause her train of thought. "What?"

"You're right. About all of it. I did need to talk to Cassandra. We both needed to exorcise the past. We both did things that were wrong, but I was the worst. I had it in my head that she was the enemy, and all this time I carried this giant grudge. She wasn't the enemy. She was just the wrong woman for me."

"You talked to her."

"Yes. It's over for good now. We mended fences."

Some of the tension dissolved and she dropped her shoulders. "Oh. Well, I'm glad. Better now?"

He came toward her. "A lot better. I feel light now, Calliope. Like a weight was lifted off me."

She nodded. "Good."

He picked up her hands, slid his thumbs over them. "The past is gone now. All I want to think about is the future. The only person in my future is you."

Her heart squeezed.

"I love you, Calliope."

"I love you too, Wyatt."

"I'm sorry for what I said earlier. I'm probably going to say I'm sorry a lot over the next fifty or sixty years, so get used to it."

Her heart did a little song and dance, fluttering in her chest. "Okay."

He dropped to his knee. "I want to marry you. I want to have kids with you. A lot of kids. I want you to move into my big house that you fell in love with, and raise those kids with me there. I like dogs. Do you like dogs?"

She swiped at the tears that rolled down her cheeks. "I love dogs."

"Good. Will you marry me?"

"Yes. Of course. Yes."

He stood and pulled her into his arms, kissed her in that way that never failed to make her feel a little bit faint.

"I love you, Wyatt. I want to marry you. I want to make babies with you—FYI, as soon as humanly possible. I want as many dogs as you can tolerate underfoot—kids too, for that matter. I'm yours."

He smoothed his hand over her hair, her face, her lips. "You are the rarest gift. I'm a very lucky man to have found you, and it isn't even Christmas yet."

She gave him a wicked smile. "No, but you might be getting your gift early. Wait 'til you see what I'm wearing under this dress."

He reached for the zipper in back of the dress and pulled it down. "Now that's a challenge I accept."

Her skin broke out in goose bumps, her body flaming to his touch. Her dress unzipped, he drew it off her shoulders and let it pool at her feet. She stepped out of it, and Wyatt's eyes widened.

"Merry Christmas to me," he said, his eyes roaming appreciatively over her body.

She'd splurged on a fire-engine-red, lace-and-satin thong with a matching demi-bra that barely contained her breasts. With her shoes still on, she knew she looked like a wicked temptress. She felt like one. And when she dropped to her knees to undo Wyatt's belt buckle, he let out a litany of curses that only served to drive her arousal to danger levels.

He kicked off his shoes while she unzipped and removed his pants and boxer briefs, then took his shaft in her hand and stroked it before taking him in her mouth to show him how much she loved every part of him.

He tangled his fingers in her hair, removing the clip she'd put her hair up with earlier. He wound his hand around her hair and held her while she engulfed him, taking him in deep, until he let out a low groan and pulled her to a standing position and swept her into his arms.

"When I come, it's going to be inside you."

"Without a condom," she said as he laid her on the bed.

"You would risk me knocking you up before we're married?" he asked, his expression one of mock horror.

She laughed. "Well, I am still on the pill, but you did catch the ASAP part of my speech about kids, didn't you?"

He drew her panties off, his eyes gleaming with heated desire. "Yeah, ASAP works for me, too. In more ways than one."

He crawled between her legs, spread them and put his mouth on her. She bit down on her lip to keep from screaming as he used his tongue to take her right to the peak, and then over. When he moved up her body and entered her, he cupped her butt, lifted her against him and took her right to the edge again with slow and easy strokes.

"I love you," he whispered as he brushed his lips across hers, using his mouth and his body to take her so close she thought she'd die from the sweet pleasure of it.

She rubbed her palm against the quickly growing stubble of his beard. "I love you too." She wrapped her legs around him and brought him home, and when they both came together, she couldn't think of a more perfect way to cement their love.

After, he held her against him and she listened to the sound of his heart beating against her ear.

"You really want kids right away?" he asked.

She lifted her head and turned over onto her belly to look at him. "I do. Do you want to wait?"

"No. I've waited my whole life for you. For this. I want to get married right away. How soon can you do that thing that women do?"

She arched a brow. "That thing that women do?"

"You know. The whole putting together a wedding thing."

She laughed. "Oh. I don't know. Six months?"

"So I have to wait six months to get you pregnant?"

"Hey, pregnant brides are the new black, you know."

"Huh?"

"In other words, knock me up, stud. I'm ready."

He rolled her over onto her back. "Have I ever mentioned I take direction really well?"

"Now who's the rare gift?" she asked with a laugh.

But that laughter turned into something else as he kissed her, and they got down to the business of making their future.

★ ★ ★ ★ ★

Dedication

To Angie—Thanks so much for the opportunity to write this series. It's been so much fun.

THE BEST THING

ONE

"You need to fix Tori. She's broken."

Brody Kent frowned at his brother Wyatt. "What the hell are you talking about?"

They had an early-morning meeting at Kent Construction Company, which meant their office manager, Tori Lewis, wasn't there. Which was why they were talking about her. Because normally Tori had acute hearing, and you couldn't whisper anything she couldn't hear.

"I'm talking about what you did at the company Christmas party a year ago," Wyatt said, looking to their brother Ethan for confirmation.

Ethan crossed his arms. "I didn't see it, but I heard about it. You know—that kiss. The one that screwed up Tori and made her hate you. And apparently us by proxy. For the past year we've been walking on friggin' eggshells around here."

"More like walking on fire," Wyatt said. "And we're all getting burned because she's turned into a fire-breathing she-dragon. It's unpleasant, Brody. Fix it. Fix her. Make her not hate you anymore so things can be normal again."

"She doesn't hate me," Brody defended, though it had seemed that way over the past year. Ever since that night at the Christmas party last year. They'd been having one of their usual arguments over—hell, he couldn't even remember what they'd been arguing about. The only thing he could remember about that night was how beautiful Tori had looked with her fiery red hair pulled up, pieces of it spilling down her neck. He really liked her neck—there was a sprinkling of freckles there that had always caught his attention.

Oh, now he remembered. She'd accused him of staring at her neck, and they'd argued about that. He was so damn tired of her always picking fights with him about the stupidest shit. And maybe he'd had a few beers and he'd wanted to shut her up, so he'd grabbed her, hauled her against him and had done what he'd wanted to do every time she opened her smart, sassy mouth—he'd kissed her.

It had been an accident. Or maybe it hadn't been. But that accident had been a two-way street, because she'd kissed him back. For a full minute. With tongue.

Until she'd taken a step back, and she'd run like her dress had suddenly fallen off, which it hadn't, because he would have definitely noticed if it had.

She'd avoided him the rest of the night. Hell, the rest of the year. She hadn't even come to his family's house for Christmas that year, something she'd done ever since she'd joined Kent Construction four years ago.

So maybe the guys were right, because ever since that night, things had been different. A lot different.

Like she'd avoided eye contact. She'd gotten quiet, and Tori was never quiet. She was loud and brassy and kind of obnoxious in a lot of ways—all the things he liked about her. But it was a fun loud.

That Tori was gone. The Tori of the past year did her job efficiently, as always, but it wasn't the same Tori they'd all grown to—

Well, the one they'd gotten used to.

And when she wasn't quiet, she was mean. Not fun and sarcastic, just downright bite-your-head-off mean.

"If she doesn't hate you, she sure doesn't like you," Wyatt said. "Things are tense now. I don't like it tense. Nobody

does. And you must have your head up your ass not to notice what's going on."

Brody preferred denial to actually figuring out how to
deal with Tori.

"The only place my head is right now is on these bids.
Can we get back to work?"

Ethan pulled up a chair. "Are you going to fix Tori?"

He didn't want to talk about Tori, or think about Tori.
He wanted to think about work, which was uncomplicated
and not difficult and definitely not emotional or a woman.
Or pissed at him. "There's nothing wrong with her."

"There is. Even Mom and Dad have noticed and keep asking me what's bothering her. She doesn't come over to visit
and hasn't been to any of the family functions. They keep
asking what they did to make her angry." Wyatt gave him
a pained expression. "And Calliope tells me about all the
conversations she has with Tori, since they're best friends.
Though Tori isn't really talking about you. All Calliope tells
me is that Tori is unhappy. I have to hear all the time about
how unhappy she is, and isn't there something I can do to
make this better. Come on, man, give me a break here."

Brody wasn't going to fall into this trap. It wasn't his fault
Tori treated him like a pariah. It had been just a kiss, for
God's sake. Nothing life-altering, even if the kiss had been
everything he'd expected it to be. And more.

"What are we, a bunch of women here? How about those
bids?" Brody gave both his brothers a stern look, and they
finally dropped it and got back to work.

At least until Tori swept in two hours later wearing her
normal skintight jeans, sweater and boots, her shocking red
hair a riotous mess on top of her head.

She always looked good. More than good. Sexy without
trying to be sexy. And she smelled good, like something ex-

otic he wanted to taste, but he didn't know what it was. Not that he noticed or fantasized about her or anything.

What he did notice was the mood went from joking and friendly to instantly arctic. And dead quiet.

"Morning, Tori," Ethan said.

"Morning, Ethan." She set her bag down, went to the coffee pot and grabbed a cup before settling in at the conference room table, giving their spread-out mess a glacial once-over. "You started without me."

"We had bids to go over," Wyatt said.

Tori fixed them all with a cold stare. At least she gave Ethan and Wyatt a stare while glossing over the top of Brody's head. "And what? I'm suddenly too stupid to sit through a bid meeting?"

"Nobody said you were stupid," Wyatt said. "We're all due out on jobsites this morning so we wanted to discuss the bids before we headed out."

"Which didn't really answer my question, did it?" Tori said. "Who do you think is going to be submitting these bids?"

"Maybe we thought you might want to sleep in instead of attending a meeting at five-thirty in the morning."

She gave Brody the most cursory of glances before opening her laptop. "Maybe you should do less thinking and let me do my damn job."

Wyatt and Ethan gave him the Kent eat-shit-and-die look.

Okay, so maybe she was broken. She'd always had a smart mouth, but she'd been fun, had joked around with them, teased them.

This Tori wasn't fun anymore.

So maybe it *was* time he did something about that.

He didn't know exactly what that "something" was going to be, but he'd figure it out.

MIDWAY INTO THE DAY, Tori acknowledged she had turned into a raging bitch over the past several months. She'd nearly bitten Ethan's head off this morning, had snarled at Wyatt and, as usual, pretended Brody didn't exist.

She sighed and packaged up the bid Ethan would deliver on a potential new building on the west side of their small town, then started to work on the numbers for Wyatt's project. Business was flush at Kent Brothers' Construction, all the guys were busy, and her job as office manager was secure. She should be happy.

Instead, she'd been decidedly unhappy for almost a year now, ever since Brody had kissed her at the last company Christmas party. Everything had changed then, because that silent dance they'd done around each other for years, and all the look-but-don't-touch fantasies she'd had about him had become a definite reality.

She thought all her feelings had been one-sided, that she could simply adore him from afar and be content with that. And then they'd been in the middle of an argument and he'd kept staring at her mouth and suddenly his lips had been on hers and it had been all whoa—so incredibly amazing her world had turned upside down in the space of a heartbeat.

His body had gone flush against hers, his hand had dove into her hair and his mouth—oh his mouth—had been everything she thought it would be—and more.

Which was the worst thing that could ever happen, because she loved her job, adored his family, and getting involved with Brody Kent, who never met a girl he couldn't date, sleep with and summarily dump, would be nothing short of the end of her security. There was no way she'd ever become a Brody Kent statistic, no way she'd jeopardize this job she held so dear or her relationship with the Kent family—the only family she knew.

The problem was, that kiss still burned on her lips all these months later, the feel of his rock-hard body pressing against hers still lingered in her thoughts and her nightly fantasies, and she absolutely hated Brody for crossing that line and making her want him even more now than she did before.

When the door to the office opened, she prayed it was either Wyatt or Ethan.

It wasn't. Brody came in. From the first day she'd hired on at Kent Construction—hell, even before that since she'd known the Kents in high school—she'd had a massive, soul-searing crush on Brody. He didn't know it, of course. No one did. It had been a secret she'd been keeping for over ten years, and one she'd intended to take to her grave.

Brody looked around, as horrified to find them alone as she was. "The others aren't back yet?"

She shook her head and firmly planted her gaze somewhere in the middle of the spreadsheets on her laptop.

"Oh. Uh, I need to grab my blueprints for the Handy Market job."

She didn't look up. "Not stopping you."

He made a wide berth around her desk as he headed to the other end of the office.

She hated this tension between them. Before, they'd had easy banter. He teased her mercilessly and she shot him down with cruel barbs. It had been fun—usually the high point of her day.

Now it was just miserable. She felt him behind her and she closed her eyes, wishing things between them could go back to the way they used to be.

Before the kiss that had changed everything. Before she'd erected this wall of protection.

"Tori."

She tensed. "Yeah."

"Turn around."

She swiveled in her chair to face him. "What?"

"Let's talk."

Uh-oh. "About what?"

He leaned against his desk. "The Christmas party last year."

"We're not talking about that. Ever." She turned her chair around.

He came over to the front of her desk. "It's been ten months. Don't you think you should tell me why you're so pissed off at me about one little kiss?"

He so didn't get it. Typical guy. "I'm not pissed off at you about that kiss. It didn't mean anything."

"Bullshit. You've practically stopped talking to me. Everything changed after that night."

Her stomach hurt. She needed to get out of here. She stood and grabbed her purse. "I'm hungry. I'm going to grab lunch. I'll be back in an hour."

Instead of letting her by, he grasped her by the arms. But his voice was soft and low when he said, "Look at me."

It had started like this the night of the party. They'd argued. She'd yelled at him and he'd grabbed her. And then their lips had met. She stared at those lips now, hers still tingling at the memory of his mouth coming down hard on hers, the way his tongue had invaded, the hot rush of pleasure that had made her legs tremble.

Maybe she should have just gone with it, indulged in the desire that had burned so all-consuming for him all these years. But she couldn't. Not with so much on the line. She'd shoved him and run like hell.

Just like now. She shoved him. "We're at work, Brody."

He let her go. "I know where we are. But I've tried to

talk to you. I've called you. I've texted you. You refuse to talk to me."

She edged around him and headed for the door. "That's because there's nothing to talk about."

"We kissed. And it changed everything between us."

She had her hand on the doorknob, ready to walk out. "It changed nothing. Do you hear me? Nothing is changed. Everything stays the same."

He cocked his head to the side and stared at her. "Tori, nothing ever stays the same. Sometimes things have to change. We all have to change."

Not her life. She liked it the way it had been. Safe. Predictable. "I can't accept that. I have to have a certain order in my life, and you disrupted that."

"Well, you're disrupting things at work."

Her stomach tightened. There it was. The change she didn't want to happen. She finally met his gaze. "Are you saying my job's in jeopardy?"

He moved toward her and she inched close to the door, afraid if he touched her again she'd cave and spill her feelings to him.

"No. Of course not. Whatever gave you that idea?"

"Come on, Brody. You and your brothers own this company. I'm just an employee. If something goes down—something bad—you know I'll be the first to go."

Brody gaped at Tori. That's what she thought? That they'd fire her because of this? "Tori. That's not going to happen. That's never going to happen. You're an invaluable resource to Kent Construction. You're like—"

He was about to say family, but hell, she wasn't family. He felt no brotherly bond to her. From the first time she'd stepped foot into the offices of Kent Construction, there'd been an attraction between them. She'd been very young then, so he'd ignored it. Okay, maybe he'd tried to ignore it. There were always plenty of women around his social circle, but that didn't mean he didn't notice Tori's beauty, her flaming red hair, mesmerizing green eyes and her cocky confidence and attitude that he found so sexy.

They'd been playing this game for four years now and on impulse, he'd taken advantage at the last Christmas party. He just didn't understand why it was such a big deal to her. Until now.

"You think if you and I—that you'll lose your job?"

She shot him a look. "Come on. You think I won't? Screwing one of the bosses doesn't scream job security to me. Besides, you're not exactly known for hanging on to a woman after she slides between your sheets. Once you're done with me, do you really think you're going to want to see me in the office day in and day out year after year? How freakin' uncomfortable would that be? Furthermore, would I want to see you? Not that I'd have sex with you anyway."

His mind was in a tailspin as he tried to process what Tori had said. "Just what kind of reputation do you think I have?"

"It's not the reputation I *think* you have, Brody. It's the one you *do* have. Everyone in town knows you sleep with any woman who's available. And you don't keep them. You get bored after a week or so—if they even get to hang around that long. Then it's dumpsville, and on to the next one."

He frowned. "I do not."

"Uh yeah, you do. So, no thanks, not interested in being just another notch on the great big bedpost of the infamous Brody Kent. I like my job, I love your family, and I don't want to lose either, no matter how allegedly awesome your reputation in the sack is, though I'm sure that rumor is highly exaggerated. I'm going to lunch."

She shut the door behind her. Brody stared at the closed door, dumbfounded.

So that's what everyone thought of him? That he was a womanizing douchebag who didn't give a shit about women or their feelings?

And what the hell did she mean by "allegedly awesome"? There were rumors about his performance?

He dragged his fingers through his hair. Christ. He had no idea.

Wyatt opened the door and came in, saw Brody and grinned. "Oh, good. You're here. Ethan's pulling in, too. I'm starving. Want to have lunch?"

Brody lifted his head. "What do you know about my sex life?"

Wyatt's gaze went blank. "Uh. Nothing. Thankfully. And don't start sharing now."

As Ethan walked in, Wyatt tossed his briefcase on his desk. "Hey, Ethan, what do you know about Brody's sex life?"

Ethan stopped dead, looked at Wyatt, then Brody. "What? Have you been drinking?"

"No. But I think Brody has."

"I haven't," Brody said. "But I just had the oddest conversation with Tori."

Ethan rummaged through his desk, but stopped to shift his gaze to Brody. "You talked to Tori?"

"Tried to."

Wyatt took a seat in his chair. "And you somehow got on the topic of your sex life?"

"Yeah. Though I don't know how."

"You probably brought it up," Ethan said with a smirk.

"I didn't. I was talking to her about the Christmas party, and our lack of communication. I think I may have that part figured out. Or at least some of it. I don't know, I'm still working on that. But did you know that I apparently have a reputation as some kind of manwhore who has sex with women and then dumps them?"

"Oh, yeah, I've heard that about you," Ethan said.

"You are kind of a dick to women," Wyatt said.

Brody just stared at his brothers. "Seriously. You both think this."

"When was your last serious relationship, Brody?" Ethan asked.

"You mean like a long-term girlfriend?"

Ethan shot Wyatt a look. "Clearly the term is foreign to him."

Wyatt shook his head.

"Okay, so I've never had one."

"And you're what? Thirty now?"

"So? I've been busy."

Wyatt snorted. "Yeah. Busy screwing a bunch of different women. No wonder they all think you're an asshole. When was the last time you brought a woman home to meet Mom and Dad?"

Brody thought about it. "Uh...high school, maybe?"

Wyatt looked at Ethan. "Case closed. He's a douche."

Ethan nodded. "Agreed. Let's go have lunch. I'm hungry."

"Hey," Brody said. "I'm not that bad."

Ethan and Wyatt headed for the door. "Keep telling yourself that, bro. You coming with us?"

"No. I'll eat something from the fridge here."

Wyatt wrinkled his nose. "The fridge of moldy mystery? Good luck with that, man. We'll be back in an hour."

After they left, Brody leaned back in his chair and pondered what Tori had told him.

So he had a lousy reputation with women. He could accept that. He'd been no Boy Scout, but he couldn't recall any of the women he'd dated complaining about it, no late-night teary phone calls from women claiming they were broken-hearted over losing him. He never made promises to any of them, never wanted a relationship, not while he'd been busy with his brothers building the company.

He'd had fun. He wouldn't apologize for that. But maybe he'd led these women on somehow, led them to believe there'd be something more when he'd never had any intention of doing anything more than just let off some steam and have a great time.

Then again, maybe none of the women were all that upset about being left by him. Maybe it was him that was lacking.

Ah, hell. This was why he never did the whole romance and relationship thing. He had no idea how to do it or how to do it well. Short-term flings were more fun and more his style.

But the way Tori looked at him, and the things she said…

She'd looked horrified at the thought of losing everything that mattered to her just because they'd kissed. Getting involved with him was that big a risk? It had more to do with the possibility of losing her job—he knew it did. But in order to find out what was really bothering her, she'd actually have to talk to him.

"Screw it. Why do I even care?" He dragged his fingers through his hair and went to scrounge through the fridge. Tori was just going to have to be someone else's problem. He had enough issues to deal with.

Except as he walked by her desk, that exotic perfume of hers lingered in the air, and he realized that she was one big damn problem that had been stuck in his head for a long time.

She wasn't going away, and she really was his problem to deal with.

TWO

"I'M NOT KIDDING, CALLIOPE. He cornered me in the office and wanted to talk about the Christmas party last year."

Tori's best friend sipped on her margarita and feigned a look of horror. "Must have been awful for you. The bastard."

Tori narrowed her gaze at Calliope. "You are not being sincere. I can tell."

Calliope pushed her glasses up the bridge of her nose, then leaned her head on her hand, the effects of two margaritas on an empty stomach obviously already taking their toll. "First, I'm glad it's Friday night because I'm getting a little buzzed. Second, I think I'm getting a little buzzed. Did I say that?"

Tori fought back a grin. "Yes."

"Okay. Third, eventually you and Brody are going to have to have 'The Talk.'"

"I don't want to talk to him. I have nothing to say to him."

"Ignoring him isn't going to make the problem—or your feelings for him—go away, you know." She pulled the stirrer out of her glass and pointed it at Tori.

"I don't have any feelings for him."

"You lie. You've had feelings for him since you were fifteen years old and he was the hot quarterback senior at the high school."

Tori narrowed her gaze at Calliope. "See, this is what happens when I confide all my deep dark secrets to my best friend. You throw them back in my face."

Calliope shrugged. "No, I'm throwing your honest feelings back at you, my friend, just like you did for me when I was falling in love with Wyatt."

"It's not at all the same thing."

"Isn't it? You've been madly in love with Brody for years. Isn't it time you acknowledged it and did something about it, like I did with Wyatt?"

Tori shook her head. "Your situation with Wyatt is nothing like my situation with Brody. Wyatt was hurt over his divorce from your sister and you helped him heal from that and in the process he fell in love with you. I'm not going anywhere near Brody because he's a manwhore with a notorious reputation for dumping every woman he gets naked with."

Calliope snorted and took another drink. "He does have a bad reputation. A bad reputation for being great in the sack. Wouldn't you like to own that? Maybe you can redeem him and turn him into a one-woman man."

Now it was Tori's turn to let out a decidedly unladylike snort. "Fat chance of that happening."

"Is that right? Has he been with anyone since that night of the Christmas party?"

"How should I know? I don't schedule his liaisons with women."

"Oh, please. This is a small town. Everyone knows who everyone is sleeping with. Gossip runs rampant. And with hot stuff like Brody, the rumor mill is on alert every time he's seen around town with a new woman on his arm. Have you heard anything—anything at all about him hitting on a woman since the night of the Christmas party last year?"

Tori chewed on her bottom lip and thought about it. "Well, actually...no."

Calliope pointed the stir stick at her again. "Aha! And that's because he wants you."

"He does not. He never even asked me out."

"Because you've been such a mean bitch no one wants to get within twenty feet of you. Can you blame him?"

Okay, maybe Calliope had a point about that. She couldn't help her natural self-preservation instincts. But she still thought Calliope was crazy. Brody was a sought-after commodity. All the women flocked to him. Surely there'd been someone in all these months...

Then again, maybe there hadn't. There was a network of gossip—especially when it came to who Brody was sleeping with—that would rival network entertainment sites. Some of the women in this town had such finely honed stalking skills they could easily get jobs as paparazzi. If Brody had been sleeping around, or sleeping with anyone since last December, it would have made the rounds of the gossip mill and Tori would have heard about it.

"You know what, Calliope, you might be right about that."

Calliope lifted one half-drunken brow in question. "I am? Right about what?"

"Brody. Not having been with anyone since December."

"'Course I'm right, Tori. Told ya. You should jump him."

Tori laughed. "And I'm cutting you off margaritas. Let's have some dinner."

Calliope frowned. "Buzz killer. I had a hard week. Children are evil, you know."

"You love those kids at the day care center. And you adore your job."

"I do." Calliope grinned. "And I love Wyatt. And you. And my sister. And Wyatt's whole family. And..."

Tori rolled her eyes and signaled for the waitress. Definitely time to put some food into her inebriated best friend.

After some food and several glasses of water, Calliope had sobered up—at least a little, though she did order a post-dinner margarita. And why not—it was Friday night, after all, Calliope had had a miserable week, and her friend deserved to let loose a little.

Tori had thought a lot about what Calliope had said about Brody. Her job would be a lot easier if she and Brody could at least go back to the way things used to be. What had happened between them had been a fluke—a onetime kiss and nothing more. He'd obviously put no expectations on her, she hadn't lost her job, so nothing had really changed. There was no reason to act as if the world was coming to an end just because they'd kissed, and he never needed to know how she felt about him.

Men were easily clueless, since most of the time they didn't want to know the truth that was right in front of them anyway.

She decided she'd go back to being her normal self on Monday.

By the end of dinner it was obvious Calliope was not going to be able to drive herself home. When she got back from the restroom, Tori said, "Since you picked me up, I'll drive you home. Then I'll bring your car back to your place tomorrow."

Calliope shook her head. "I already called for a ride home. I'm very smart and I know better than to drive myself home when I've been drinking."

"I'd have driven you home, Calliope."

"It's okay. There's my ride now."

Tori looked up and her stomach dropped.

Brody. She'd called Brody to drive her home.

THREE

Brody hadn't expected to run into Tori tonight, but when Calliope had called saying she'd had some cocktails and needed a ride, he had no problem giving it to her, especially since Wyatt was on an out-of-town job this weekend.

What he hadn't expected was for Tori to be with her, though that shouldn't surprise him since Calliope and Tori were best friends.

He pulled up a chair at their table. "Celebrating tonight, Calliope?"

She nodded, her curls bouncing. "Yup. I'm celebrating an end to a hellish week. Parents are mean."

He laughed and tugged on one of her curls. "They can be sometimes. This is a good place to unwind though. Great margaritas."

Calliope grinned. "I had four."

"Awesome." He looked over at Tori, who surprisingly wasn't ignoring him, just studying him. "How about you?"

"I figured I'd have to drive the lush home, so it was iced tea for me tonight."

"Hey. Not a lush. I was sober enough to give you love advice, wasn't I?"

Tori glared at Calliope. Brody gave her a quizzical look. "Love advice?"

"Drunk talk. You ready to go? Calliope picked me up, so I can drive her car home and I'll bring it back to her house tomorrow."

"It's okay. Just follow me to her place and we'll drop her

car. Then I'll drive you home. Save you a trip back over there tomorrow."

"It's not a problem."

"I need my car early, Tori," Calliope said. "I have a meeting."

She hesitated then nodded at Brody. "Okay, fine. I'll meet you at Wyatt and Calliope's house."

Brody scooped Calliope out of her chair and led her to the parking lot.

"Calliope, do you want to ride with me in your car?" Tori asked.

"Oh. No, I'll ride with Brody. See you at the house." Calliope gave Tori a wave.

Tori gave them a worried look, then said, "Uh, okay. See you there." She headed over to Calliope's car and Brody put Calliope in his truck. She started to sing and he rolled his eyes. Wyatt owed him for this one. It was a good thing he adored his sister-in-law, because he'd left a warm house and a football game on TV for this.

"You need to talk to Tori," Calliope said as they made the turn down the highway toward Wyatt's house.

"Huh?"

"Just...well, I can't say more than that, other than you need to talk to her."

"Is this about the Christmas party again?"

"Sort of, but it's about a lot of things, Brody. Open your eyes."

"My eyes are wide open, Calliope."

While they sat at a stoplight, she looked over at him, her glasses askew on her face. She slid them up her nose and gave him a stern look. "Men's eyes are very rarely wide open. You only see what you want to see, not what's really there."

"What the hell are you talking about? See, this is the problem with women. You talk in metaphors instead of straight talk, then we're supposed to figure out what the fuck that all means."

She laughed. "I know. But Tori's my friend and I can't say any more than that. But trust me, you want to talk to her."

"I've already talked to her. She won't give me the god-damn time of day."

Calliope looked out the window. "Try again. She might know the time now."

"There you go again. Fucking metaphors."

They pulled into the driveway and he helped Calliope slide out of his truck. Brody walked her to the door and helped her find her keys in her purse. She giggled—a lot.

"You really did have a good time tonight, didn't you?"

She tilted her head back. "Have I mentioned I had a shitty day today?"

"Yup."

"Then yes. I had a good time tonight."

"Sounds like you needed it."

Her head bobbed up and down. "You have no idea."

He opened the door and turned on the lights, then made sure she got safely inside. By then Tori had pulled Calliope's car into the garage, so she met them in the kitchen.

"Thanks for picking me up," Calliope said, giving Brody a hug and a kiss on the cheek. "You're the best brother-in-law ever."

"Anytime. You know that."

Calliope threw her arms around Tori and hugged her, then whispered in her ear. Tori shifted her gaze to Brody, her eyes widening.

"Okay. I'm done for. I'm going to bed. Love you both and lock the door on your way out."

Brody shook his head as he watched Calliope's weaving form disappear down the hall. "Night, Calliope."

Tori gave him a look. "Give me just a second. I'm going to run upstairs and make sure she's okay. If you don't mind?"

"I don't mind. Go ahead."

He made himself at home by heading into the living room and turning on the television. The game wasn't over yet, so when Tori came downstairs he asked her to wait as the last few minutes ticked down. When the game was over, he clicked off the remote and turned to her. She was perched on the edge of the leather sofa.

"She okay?"

"She's out. Not much of a drinker anyway, so when she decides to put one on, it generally throws her for a loop. I just wanted to make sure she wasn't going to end up sick. She got into her pajamas and she's already snoring."

He laughed. "Good. Everyone needs to cut loose every now and then."

"True. She had some snooty parents at the day care center to deal with this week who decided to inform her how they thought she should run things. Real know-it-all types and just relentless perfectionists who think their kids don't ever poop or have boogers."

Brody snorted. "Yeah, I know the type. In every business there are customers like that. You just have to grin and bear it, when all you want to do is smash a fist in their smug faces."

"Exactly. And you know Calliope—she's as sweet as they come, but even she folds under the pressure every now and then. And with Wyatt being out of town, I could tell by her tone of voice at the end of the day today she was ready to explode, so I suggested we go out tonight."

They closed the front door and Brody made sure everything was locked up before making their way to his truck.

"I'm glad you could be there for her so she could let off some steam and vent it out."

"That's what friends are for. We're there for each other."

They got into the truck and he backed down the driveway to make his way back to town. "I guess she's always there for you, too."

Tori stared out the window. "Always."

"Yeah. Like she gave you love advice tonight?"

Her gaze shot to his. "No she didn't."

"She said she did."

"She was drunk."

He was silent for a while as he drove toward town. So was Tori, who stared out the window.

"I didn't know you were seeing someone," he finally said.

"I'm not seeing anyone."

"So she gave you advice on how to ask someone out?"

She sighed. "Let it go, Brody."

He heard the subtle pleading in her voice and decided he should probably let it go. But something twisted in his gut at the thought of Tori dating some random guy. Or any guy, for that matter. She hardly ever went out, and when she did, it didn't last. She was pretty selective with guys she dated. He wondered why.

"You haven't had a boyfriend in…hell, Tori, I don't remember you ever dating anyone seriously."

She shot him a look. "Why? Do you have a friend you're thinking of setting me up with?"

He frowned at her. "Hell, no."

Her lips curved in a hint of a smile.

"Is that funny?"

"No. Not at all."

"I have great friends."

"I know you do."

He thought about all the guys he called friends, the times they'd all gotten together, and which ones had given Tori a second look. Probably all of them, considering she was gorgeous. "Is there one of my friends you want to go out with?"

"Nope."

That relieved him a little. But only for a second, because he knew damn well that what Calliope had said about the love advice hadn't been made up, and usually people who'd had too much to drink spilled a little too much of the truth.

When he pulled into Tori's apartment complex, he got out of the truck and opened her door.

"Thanks for the ride."

"It's late. I'll walk you up."

"That's not necessary."

"I'll walk you to your door, Tori."

She blew out a breath. "Fine."

As they walked up the back stairs, he frowned. "Lots of foliage around here. And you're on the second floor."

She fished into her purse for her keys. "And?"

He waited while she unlocked her door, surveying the remoteness of the area. "How long have you lived here?"

"About a year."

"I don't like it."

"Gee, Brody, thanks."

"I mean it doesn't look safe. You should move."

She rolled her eyes and stepped inside. "Thanks for the ride home. I appreciate it. Good night."

He put his hand on the door. "Seriously, Tori. This isn't the best neighborhood in town. And this apartment is at the end of a remote corridor. Not the best location."

"It's the best I can do, you know?"

He looked down at her. Always so tough, with that "I

can take care of myself" attitude. He knew she had no one to take care of her.

Hell, she probably didn't need anyone to take care of her, but right now maybe he needed it.

He braced his hands on either side of the doorway. "Ask me to come in."

Her eyes widened. "What?"

"Let me come in, Tori."

"Why?"

"I want to see your place."

"Why?"

"Quit asking why and ask me to come in, Tori."

She shook her head. "That is so not a good idea, Brody."

"I know. In fact, it's a really bad idea. Ask me to come in, anyway."

FOUR

Tori's heart beat so fast she could feel the pounding in her chest.

Brody wanted in her apartment. What could that mean? A huge mistake, was what it could mean. She should say no. Then again, maybe he was just being chivalrous and wanted to see if the boogeyman was in there. One quick check and then he'd leave.

But the way he looked at her, his sexy gaze giving her a look that said they had a lot to talk about—or maybe that there'd be no talking at all once she invited him past her threshold—definitely gave her pause.

She'd kissed him once and all these months later she couldn't forget the taste of him. She couldn't afford to mess with Brody, couldn't handle letting him take her to bed and then deal with the repercussions of that.

Ridiculous. She was overthinking this, which happened every time she got anywhere near Brody. Then again, this was part of his modus operandi. He messed with your head, and before you knew what was happening, you were naked.

And then he dumped you.

"No."

He cocked a brow. "What?"

"You can't come in."

"Why not?"

"Because…I'm tired."

He inched a little closer and she breathed in the scent of him. Cool and crisp and ever so male, she wanted to reach out, grab his jacket and haul his mouth against hers, then kiss him until neither one of them could breathe. Oh, why couldn't she have what she wanted, damn the consequences?

"Tori…you don't look tired. You look…really good tonight." He reached out and tugged on one of the curls that always seemed to be falling out of the top knot where she twisted her hair up. "Have I ever told you how much I like your hair?"

"Um…no, you haven't." See, there went her brain cells. Everything that screamed intelligent, logical woman had traveled somewhere south, which was now throbbing and screaming his name and begging him to take her and undress her and do wicked things to her.

He took a step closer. "I really like your hair. It's soft and sexy and God, that red makes me crazy."

She swallowed, or tried to, but there was currently a boulder in her throat making it impossible. "Brody, what are you doing?"

"Invite me in. You always have such careful control over your life. Tonight, let go. I just want to see if that kiss last Christmas was really as explosive as I thought it was. Did you think it was?"

"Yes."

"So that was a yes." He crossed her doorway and pushed the door shut behind him, gathered her in his arms and put his mouth on hers.

Oh, God. He was right. It was an explosion as his fingers dove in her hair and his lips claimed hers and she suddenly couldn't breathe as everything in her body ignited. She could do nothing but grab on to him, because Brody was a force to be reckoned with. He turned her around and pushed her up against the door, then fit his body against hers while he explored her mouth with his lips and tongue until she was dizzy with the delight and wonder and realization that this—this was what it was like to be thoroughly kissed and man-handled in the absolute best way.

And his body, pressed full up against hers, was a thing of beauty. She snaked her hands along the firm ridges of muscle that lined his biceps, and let out a soft moan that caused him to deepen the kiss until she was certain she'd have dropped to a heap on the floor if his body hadn't been wedging her against the door.

It wasn't fair, this mastery Brody had over women, the way he tangled his fingers in her hair and released the clip holding her hair up. His hand dove into her scalp and fur-ther enflamed her senses as he rocked his pelvis against hers.

It was too much—all too much, just like that first kiss last winter. He overloaded her senses and made her want him, made her body weep with joy and need and all the things that were dangerous and bad.

She pressed her palms against his chest and he groaned and God, she didn't want to stop, wanted to see where this would go. She already knew where it would go—straight to her bedroom, where the two of them would end up naked and entwined. She'd entertained that fantasy so many times it was embarrassing.

But it wasn't going to become a reality.

She tore her lips from his. "Brody. Stop."

To his credit, he did. He pulled his head back and looked at her with heavy-lidded eyes that melted her and made her wonder why she hesitated.

She knew why. In some part of her sex-addled brain, she knew why.

He dragged his thumb over her bottom lip. "Yeah, this kiss was just as good as the first one, Tori. Don't you think so?"

God, yes. Even better, in fact. So much so she knew it

could never happen again. She couldn't lose everything that meant so much to her. Her job, Brody's family, her friends. Him.

"You should go," she finally managed to say.

"You should talk to me about why you're hesitating."

"No, it's the last thing we should talk about."

He took a deep breath and a step back, the evidence of his passion for her deliciously visible against the zipper of his jeans. Her fingers flexed. She wanted to snake her hands down his body and touch him, spend all night mapping his body with her hands, her mouth, her tongue.

Dammit, she wished she didn't care so much about all those things that she really did care about. Because right now all she craved was one night with Brody, just one night to explore those epic fantasies that had fueled her for so many years.

Instead, she opened the front door, the blast of cool air doing nothing to ice down her raging libido.

Brody looked at the open door, then back at her.

"At some point, Tori, we're going to talk about what's holding you back."

She laid her head against the door and didn't say anything.

So Brody leaned in and brushed his lips across hers. "I think you'll be surprised what a good listener I am. Night, Tori."

She watched him walk down the stairs. When he disappeared from sight, she shut the door and locked it.

As she headed to the bedroom, every part of her body throbbed with unfulfilled sexual desire.

No, there'd be no conversation with Brody. He could never know her fears.

Or how crazy in love she was with him.

FIVE

"HEARD YOU DROVE my wife home the other night," Wyatt said as they sat in a morning staff meeting.

"Yup. She was well and truly wasted, man."

Wyatt grinned at Brody. "She said she had a great time with Tori—thanks for that, by the way," he said to Tori. "She needed it after a shitty day."

Tori smiled. "It was my pleasure. She had the mother of all hangovers the next day."

"She told me that, too. She said it was well worth it."

"Sometimes you just need to tie one on," Tori said. "Especially after a crappy week at work."

"Surely you're not saying you've ever had a bad week here." Ethan handed her a file. "We treat you like the queen you are."

Tori snorted. "You're all a giant pain in my butt. I have to drink heavily on the weekends just to survive this job."

Wyatt rolled his eyes. "Yeah, you're so mistreated around here. I don't know how you bear it."

"It's true," she said. "The things I must suffer for a pittance of a paycheck."

"Speaking of that pittance," Wyatt said. "It's time for your annual review. I guess one of us will have to do that."

"I was going to mention it." She looked at her laptop. "Ethan did it last year."

"We usually rotate. I did it the year before," Wyatt said. "So that means Brody's up."

Brody had been busy going through safety guidelines for

his current job and had only been paying half attention. "I'm up for what?"

"Tori's annual review," Wyatt told him.

"Oh." He looked over at Tori, whose smile suddenly died.

"If you don't have time, I'm sure one of the other guys can handle it," she said, looking hopeful.

"I have time." He scanned his schedule on his laptop. "Let's do it Friday. That'll give me a few days to go over things with Wyatt and Ethan, and if your performance sucks, it's a good day to fire you."

Ethan snickered. "Great idea. Friday's always perfect for a pink slip. We could even take you out for drinks."

"Oh. Margaritas. I'll alert Calliope," Wyatt added. "You know, just in case things don't go well for you."

Tori glared at him. "You are so not funny. None of you are. In fact, you all suck."

Brody laughed. "Now you're going to be nervous all week long, aren't you?"

"Not at all. The ones who should be nervous are the three of you. I'm half tempted to go find another job. And then what would you all do? Why should I put up with this abuse every day?"

"Because we're your family?" Ethan asked. "Because we're like your annoying brothers who you can't help but love?"

Her gaze shot to Brody. "You are definitely not my brothers."

"Definitely not," Brody said. He knew their parents had taken her under their wing and unofficially adopted her as family when she'd hired on at Kent Construction four years ago, barely twenty-two years old at the time and with no family to speak of. She'd been quiet but efficient, and as soon as she'd grown comfortable with the family she'd become brassy and opinionated and they'd all fallen crazy in love with her.

Well, not in love, love. Just…

Hell, he didn't even know what he was thinking anymore where Tori was concerned. And that kiss the other night still hung on his lips, unforgettable as hell.

He wanted more. He wanted her.

At least she was semi-sort-of talking to him again, though it was only about work-related stuff. But still, that was a breakthrough. Now if he could just get her to talk to him about important issues, like why she'd stopped the kiss when he'd thought it was going so well. There was serious heat between them, they got along well, he teased her, she shot back with some barb. It was a great relationship. He had no idea why she wouldn't want to take it to the next level.

He understood that he was her boss, but she had to understand he'd never jeopardize her job. She'd always have that. Hell, they'd be lost without her.

Maybe that was the holding point for her. He'd have to talk to her about that. Maybe after they did her review on Friday, he'd take her out for drinks, in a non-work environment and they could discuss her reservations about the two of them.

Tori pushed aside the thought of sitting with Brody for her review the entire week. In fact, by Friday, she'd totally forgotten about it. Being busy always helped with forgetting things she liked to forget, like that kiss they'd shared.

Okay, maybe she hadn't forgotten that. Maybe she thought about it every night as she lay in bed, when it was quiet and dark and all she had were her thoughts. Then she couldn't shove him aside like she could during the day when the phone was ringing and paperwork piled up on her desk and she had a million things to do to fill her brain, so it was easy to forget about Brody.

At bedtime, though, he wouldn't go away. Not virtually, anyway. Resulting in a lot of restless nights spent watching reruns of her favorite television shows while eating ice cream, which kept her up all night. Which meant one cranky Tori the next day. Frankly, she didn't know how the guys put up with her.

It should make for an interesting annual review, which brought her back on topic of Brody.

Oh, why did it have to be his turn to give the review? She could sit through it if Ethan or Wyatt was giving it to her. But not Brody. Their day-to-day interactions were brief, and she could deal with that. A review was intense, going over her work performance for the entire year. It would last at least an hour and would be one on one, just the two of them. Eye to eye, shoulder to shoulder.

Gah. She should just tell him she was sick and going home early.

Except she wasn't a coward and putting it off wouldn't do any good. They'd have to do this eventually. Besides, she was kind of hoping for a raise, which she needed so she could get out of that hellhole apartment. She'd blown off Brody's suggestion that she move immediately because the area wasn't safe, but he wasn't too far off in his assessment of her current neighborhood. Her neighbors to the right fought all the time, and not just loud arguing, but knock-down, drag-out, throw-the-furniturevkind of fighting. The two dudes who lived on her left had people coming and going all the time. Despite Deer Lake being a small town, drugs still crept in, and she could swear those two guys were dealers. Either that or they were *very* popular.

She'd settle for a nice, quiet place. Maybe she could finagle her way into a senior citizen's center. Or maybe Brody's parents would let her bunk at their house. She loved Roger and Stacy Kent. When she'd first gone to work for Kent Construction, she'd been closed up, emotionally as well as physically. But Ethan, Wyatt and Brody—and especially Stacy Kent, the guys' mother—had changed all that, had given her the bond of a family she'd so desperately craved her whole life and never had. Her own family had certainly been lacking. Cold and remote, her father had never been a presence in her life, and had taken off permanently after her parents had divorced. Not only had he not wanted her mother, he'd clearly had no use for his daughter, either. Her mother, on the other hand, had leaned heavily on Tori after the divorce, her emotional upheavals a burden that had been difficult for a young Tori to bear.

Tori hadn't regretted leaving that suffocating atmosphere as soon as she'd been old enough. Her mother had latched on to a new guy and she and Tori rarely spoke anymore, which suited Tori just fine.

Stacy'd been more the parent than her mother had been. So getting close to the Kents, especially Stacy, had been like grabbing on to a desperately needed lifeline.

She loved the Kents. They were the *normal* family she craved. She really did think of Wyatt and Ethan as her brothers.

Changing the status quo in any way could put her out in the cold again, leaving her all alone.

She'd had plenty of alone and it sucked. She'd rather not do that again, especially not for someone like Brody, who changed women as often as he changed his underwear. It was too bad she was crazy about him and thought about him constantly. Why couldn't she be immune?

Then again, was any woman in Deer Lake immune? Judging from his past interactions with the women in this town, it didn't appear so. And she had no interest in becoming another statistic. Likely the only reason Brody appeared interested in her was because she kept shutting him down. Once she let him in, he'd no doubt drop her in a hurry.

The door opened and Brody walked in. She'd spent the day by herself since all the guys were out on jobs.

"Sorry I'm a little late," he said, taking off his coat and slinging it on the chair. "I had to drop Ethan and Zoey off at the airport."

"No problem. They get off okay?"

He cracked a smile. "Yeah. Zoey's all kinds of excited to go see her mom in concert in Nashville this weekend."

Tori leaned back in the chair and grinned. "I'm sure she is. I talked to Riley on the phone earlier this week. She really misses Zoey and Ethan when she's on the road. She's thrilled this is the last road trip she'll be on for a while."

He nodded. "Ethan said he's pretty happy she's closing out her tour in Nashville. Now that she's pregnant, she'll be able to settle back for a while and concentrate on the baby. Ethan's been nervous as hell with Riley insisting on finishing her tour while she's pregnant."

Tori laughed. "Well, she is in her eighth month, but she's been super healthy and the doctor's been monitoring her regularly. But you're right. She's finishing up now and she can rest and start nesting."

"I'm glad it's all worked out for them, considering their rocky start. Zoey loves Riley like she's the only mother she ever had."

"The only one she remembers now. And you can't tell Riley that Zoey isn't hers. It's a good fit for all of them. With the new baby almost here, I can't think of a happier couple, or a happier family."

This was a new side to Brody, seeing him all mellowed out and grinning about his brother's contented family life. "You'd think all that wedded bliss and family life would make you twitchy. Your younger brother is married with a baby on the way, and your older brother just got married this year to his ex-wife's sister. So much...settling down going on around you. Doesn't it freak you out?"

He cocked a brow. "I have nothing against marriage and family, you know."

"Of course you don't." She couldn't resist the smirk. "All your relationships with women lasting so long and all."

"Hey. I just haven't found the right one."

"Uh huh." She took a long sip of her giant soda she'd bought earlier. "You are the king of denial, aren't you?"

"I can do a relationship."

"Careful, you might break out in hives. Or maybe your nose will start to grow. I should get out my tape measure and check it out."

"You wanna check out something with a tape measure..."

She shook her head. "So inappropriate for the office. And you being my boss and all. I should report you to your brothers."

"Whatever. Let's go."

"What? Where?" Somewhere she could measure him? The thought both appalled her and flamed her senses.

"Out of here."

"What about my review?"

"You're doing a kickass job, like you have been since we first hired you. We're jacking up your pay twenty percent. I've got a write-up about your glowing skills in my file as well as a goals sheet for the next year. I'll email it to you and copy my brothers. Any questions?"

Her eyes widened. A twenty percent pay raise? Hell no she wasn't going to question that. "Uh, no. No questions."

"Good. Let's go."

She grabbed her purse and her coat, curious about where he was taking her. He locked the door behind her, but when she headed toward her car, he grasped her arm.

"We'll take my truck."

Shrugging, she climbed into his truck and he drove off. He was quiet as he drove down Central and turned onto the highway.

"You're brooding," she said as she studied his profile.

"No, I'm not."

"It's because I insulted you, isn't it?"

"Doubtful, since you're always insulting me. You really can't hurt my feelings, Tori."

"Oh, I'm sure I could if I tried harder."

That at least got a curve of a smile. God, he was devastating when he gave that sexy half smile. She'd love to see that smile close up, like when he was hovering over her, both of them naked...

Stop that. Hadn't she spent the time before he came into the office reminding herself of all the reasons why they *couldn't* be together? Fantasizing about making love with him was the wrong direction for her thoughts to go.

It was a while before she realized he'd hit the highway, that they were leaving Deer Lake.

"Brody, where are we going?"

"Out of town."

"So you're kidnapping me?"

"Not exactly."

It took about fifteen minutes to get to Botswell, the next town over. He pulled into a one-story—shack, was the only way she could think of to describe it. She supposed it was a

bar, with the headache-inducing half-blinking neon sign pro-
claiming it as Ed's Bar and Grill. Though the grill part was
suspect, since the place resembled an oversized shed. She'd
come into Botswell on occasion, mainly to do some shop-
ping, never to hit the bars.

This one seemed—interesting, in a she'd-never-stop-here-
without-a-guy kind of way. Or even *with* a guy, for that matter. She half expected a brawl to tumble out the front door
any second.

When she climbed out of his truck and met him around
the front, she cocked her head and looked at him. "Seriously?"

"Best beer and burgers I've ever had."

"I hope this isn't a date, Brody, because if this is where you
bring your women, your taste is sorely lacking."

He cracked a smile and grabbed her hand. "You have such
little faith in me, Tori. Just trust me."

She snorted. Trust him? Borrowing a line from one of her
favorite movies ever—as if.

The inside didn't look much better than the outside. Old,
worn tables were scratched with wear and tear. There were
a few pool tables scattered around, and those were taken up
by people who must be regulars. A couple older-model televisions sat above the bar that several people who'd bellied
up were watching.

A couple food tables were full, but Brody had spied one
in the corner, so he grabbed her hand and, despite her dragging her heels the whole way, tugged her along. She feared
for her life as she took a seat in a rickety chair.

"Come on," he said. "It's not that bad."

She wasn't exactly a prima donna as far as the places she
hung out, but Ed's was as low on the dive bar food chain as
she'd ever gotten.

A waitress hustled over. She was older, in her fifties maybe, with faded-out blond hair that she'd over-teased, over-bleached and gathered up in a haphazard ponytail. And she didn't look happy to see them, because she didn't smile as she grabbed a pencil from her hair and pulled the pad out of her apron. "What can I get you to drink?"

Brody ordered the specialty beer. Tori looked at him.

"Try it. It's great."

Tori nodded. "Okay, I'll have one of those. And can we see a menu?"

The waitress, whose nametag said "Pat", snickered. "Honey, we have cheeseburgers, or cheeseburgers without cheese on them. If you're feeling adventurous you can have a hot dog. That comes with or without chili and the works. I'll be back with your drinks and you can let me know what you want."

Tori shifted her gaze to Brody. "Limited menu."

"People come here for the beer and the burgers. The hot dogs kind of suck."

"Thanks for the warning. I guess I'll have a burger, then."

"Good call."

When Pat came back with the beer, Brody said, "We'll both have the cheeseburgers."

"Smart idea. Everything on them?"

Brody looked at her. Tori said, "Sure. Why not?"

Pat finally shocked her by patting her hand and grinning. "You're gonna love these burgers, honey. And once you eat them, you're gonna come back again and again. Enjoy your beer."

After Pat hustled away, Tori looked at Brody. "Oh, my God. She seemed almost human there."

He laughed. "Pat has tons of attitude. She and Ed have

owned this place since they were in their twenties. He brews the beer himself, along with his sons now. Taste it."

She took a drink of the beer. It was mellow, with a honey flavor. "Oh, it's good."

"Told you. They're a small operation, but this place is never empty. I stop by for lunch a lot when I'm driving through town on a job."

"For the beer?" she asked with a smirk.

"For the burgers, smartass. Though after a shitty day, I can pound down a few beers."

She preferred margaritas with Calliope after a bad day. She wondered who Brody unloaded on when he had problems. His brothers? Or was the familial bond too close, the fact that they all worked together too much to share troubles. Who did he tell his problems to?

"So when you have a bad day at work and you want to let off some steam and have a few drinks, do you grab your brothers and go out for beers to talk it out?"

He looked horrified. "Hell, no. It's bad enough I grew up with them, and now I work with them. Half the time it's them I'm pissed off at. The last thing I'd want to do is unload my problems on them."

She swirled her finger over the top of the glass. "So...who do you talk to?"

He shrugged. "Nobody."

"Surely you have friends to talk to."

"I have friends, yeah. But we aren't like girls, Tori. We don't have to have...chat sessions or whatever you women call them where we discuss every problem we have."

"You hold it all inside."

"I didn't say that."

"You didn't have to. You don't talk to your brothers or

your friends, and you being a man and all are obviously not going to talk to your parents when you have a problem."

He let out a laugh at that one.

"Okay, so that means you keep all your problems bottled up inside and don't talk to anyone about them, right?"

He finished off his beer and set the mug to the side of the table so Pat could refill it for him. "I don't have a lot of problems. I'm generally a pretty content guy."

"Please. Everyone has problems. Even if it's just a bad day at work, a job doesn't go right. Someone pisses you off—like your brothers. You have to let off steam. How do you do that?"

"I have ways of letting off steam."

He gave her a look that melted her to the chair. "Well, yes, there is that. But I mean talking."

"Oh, I like talking. Verbalizing is good."

This was not helping to cool her off.

Fortunately, their food arrived and Brody dragged his very direct gaze away from her to offer his trademark grin to Pat. After that, she dug into her cheeseburger and tried to shift her thoughts away from one very sexy man to the incredibly delicious burger. She ate every bite, had another beer to wash it down and wasn't even embarrassed about picking the last crumb off her plate with her fingers.

"You were right. This is the best cheeseburger I've ever had."

Brody crumpled his paper napkin and laid it on his empty plate. "Told you it was awesome. I wouldn't let you down, Tori."

The way he said it made her cock her head to the side, as if he'd meant something else entirely, and wasn't talking about burgers anymore.

Probably her imagination. "You're right. It was a great meal. Good beer and good burgers. Thank you."

"I actually brought you here to talk to you."

She laughed. "We have been talking."

"I meant I brought you here to talk about something else."

"About what?"

"Us."

Uh-oh. "What about us?"

The words had spilled out before she could correct herself, correct him and tell him there was no "us."

"Why did you stop that kiss the other night? What are you so afraid of?"

She looked around, but televisions were blaring, people were playing pool and engaged in their own conversations. There were no people around them listening in. Still, she leaned forward. "I don't want to talk about this."

He leaned in, too, and grasped her hands. "I do. And it's time you stop running from it. From what the two of us could have."

Her eyes widened and she tried to tug her hands away, but he held firm. "Brody, I don't want to do this."

"I think you do, Tori, but something's scaring you off. Talk to me. Tell me what's bothering you. Is it something I've done in the past? Some way I'm not measuring up? I think you and I could have something, if you'll just give me a chance."

Oh, God. Smartass Brody she could handle. Funny, jokester Brody she could deal with. Teasing Brody she knew well. But earnest, honest Brody wanting to have a heartfelt conversation with her about having a relationship? She'd never known this side of him and she couldn't handle it.

He was handing her everything she wanted, everything

she'd always dreamed of. All she had to do was meet him half way.

But she didn't trust it, didn't trust herself.

She didn't trust him.

Because she had so much to lose.

Everything to lose.

She finally freed her hands and pushed back. "I need some air. I'm sorry."

She grabbed her purse and made a beeline for the front door.

SIX

THAT WENT WELL.

Nothing like opening yourself up to a woman and seeing a look of horror on her face, followed by a world-record dash for the door.

Brody had never thought of himself as repulsive. Women were always attracted to him. He had a pretty healthy ego, but seeing Tori run for her life when he offered to have a relationship with her had given his self-esteem a severe hit tonight.

Something was up, and he wasn't about to give up on her. He needed to figure out what the hell was going on.

He signaled Pat, paid the bill and left a generous tip, then made his way out the door. Tori was leaning against his truck, arms folded in front of her like a protective shield. When she saw him approach, she lifted her head and cast him a miserable gaze.

Okay, so maybe out in the parking lot of Ed's wasn't the place to have a talk about this. He unlocked the truck, helped her inside and got in. They made the drive back to Deer Lake in silence. Tori huddled on her side, looking out the side window, as far away from him as she could get.

Great. How was he supposed to handle this one? He was no expert on women, except in the bedroom. He was really damn good at pleasing them there. At seduction he was a pro, and he could read sexual signals like a master. But emotion and conversation about feelings and all that shit? Not his area.

But there was no way in hell he was dropping her off at her car and leaving things the way they were. This past year had been hell, and he wasn't about to make things worse by letting her run on him again.

So instead of taking her back to work to fetch her car, he went with instinct and drove her to his place, where she wouldn't be able to run.

When he pulled into the driveway of his house, she finally straightened.

"What are we doing here?"

Instead of answering her, he came around to her side of the truck and opened the door. "Come on, Tori. We're going to talk."

She cast him a wary look.

"It's time. And there are things that have to be said. You can't run from it forever."

He held out his hand. If she refused to come in, he wouldn't force her. He wasn't that kind of guy.

The call was hers to make.

With a shaky sigh, she slid her hands in his and he helped her down from the truck. He slid his key in the lock and opened the door, hoping like hell he hadn't left his place a mess.

He switched on the light, relieved as he remembered his cleaning lady had been in today. Thank God.

"I don't think I've ever been in your house before," she said, her voice low, almost a whisper as she took in his living room.

He turned to her. "I don't entertain much here."

She shot him a look. "Yeah. I'll bet you don't."

"Okay. I meant parties and that kind of thing. It's just where I crash."

She walked around, then turned to him. "It's a nice place, Brody. Lots of room. You should throw a party or two here."

He dragged his fingers through his hair. "I got a great deal on it, and hated living in an apartment. I like open space."

He took in the expansive living room, with its two couches that faced each other and the chair flanking them, all the furniture kind of cozy with the stone fireplace and all. He'd loved the place when the Realtor had shown it to him. It had seemed so…big, especially after living in that cramped apartment. Plus, with four bedrooms, he knew he could make it home for a long time.

"You want to see the rest?"

For the first time, she smiled. "I'd love to."

He showed her the kitchen, and she gasped. "This is amazing. Do you cook in here?"

"I can do breakfast and I cook on the outside grill."

She laughed. "That's it? This kitchen is going to waste." She ran her fingers over the granite countertop and started making some noises about state-of-the-art appliances. He knew a woman would like this kitchen, though he hadn't thought about it when he'd bought the place. He'd just wanted big and spacious in everything, because where he'd lived before had been so damn claustrophobic.

Same thing with the bedrooms. All of them were big. One of them was set up as his office, the other two were vacant, and the master was enormous, something else he liked because he'd bought a king-sized bed.

He flipped the light on in there and Tori's eyes widened. "Wow. How many people sleep in that thing?"

He slid his hand along the nape of her neck and whispered in her ear, "Just me. I like a lot of room. I had a double bed in my old apartment and it sucked. My feet hung off the end and I couldn't sleep. So when I bought this place I found the biggest damn bed I could and bought it."

He heard the rumble of her laugh, which made his dick twitch.

"I understand that," she said. "My apartment is tiny."

She walked into his bathroom and she made a murmur of approval. "I love the tub, especially the window over it." She turned to him. "It needs some flowers or something. You can tell a guy lives here."

His stomach tightened as he thought about Tori being here, and all the feminine touches she'd bring. Like flowers in the bathroom window. "Yeah. Or something."

They finished downstairs. She turned to face him, her features much less tense than they'd been when she'd walked in. "It's a spectacular home, Brody."

"Thanks. Would you like something to drink?"

Tori swallowed. The tour of Brody's house had delayed the talk he insisted on having with her, the one she'd avoided by embarrassing herself and running like hell out of the restaurant.

"Sure. A drink sounds great."

They made their way back into the kitchen, where he opened that incredible refrigerator. She hated to admit to being jealous of his appliances, but she was.

"I have beer...uh, beer, and water. Oh, and soda."

Needing the bolster of courage, she said, "I'll have a beer, thanks."

He popped the tops off the bottles and handed her one. She took a couple long swallows, then followed him into the living room, taking a seat on one of the ultra-comfortable sofas. She liked the big double windows in the living room, could already picture a giant Christmas tree there, covered with lights and ornaments.

"Do you cut a real tree to put in that window?"

He followed her gaze. "Huh?"

"For Christmas. You have such high ceilings, and that window is perfect for your Christmas tree."

"Oh. No, I don't put a tree up."

She frowned. "Why not?"

"Who's going to see it, Tori? It's just me here."

"So?"

"Do you put a tree up in your apartment?"

"Yes. It's only a foot tall since I don't have any room, but of course. It's Christmas. You have to have a tree."

"No, I don't."

"Scrooge."

He laughed.

"Seriously, Brody, you need a tree. This place is begging for a tree. It would look beautiful there."

"And again, no one would see it."

An idea formed in her head. "Your house is so big. We should have the company Christmas party here."

He gave her a blank look, then shook his head. "No."

"Why not? There's plenty of room here. I haven't booked the venue yet. That was on my schedule for next week." She shifted, looking around the room. "The kitchen is enormous, you have that game room off the garage with the pool table and arcade games. People would love it. I've often thought we should make our parties a little less stuffy and a lot more fun."

"Not a good idea. At all. I don't want all those people here."

"Why not?"

"Because…"

She waited for his good reason why not. It didn't come.

"See? It's a great opportunity for you and your brothers to start inviting your clients into your homes. It makes your relationships with them more personal. Wyatt has a perfect home for it, too. There's plenty of room there, too. And with Ethan and Riley building that big new house, he can take a turn, too, though I think you and Wyatt should go first, since they're going to be busy the next couple years with the new baby."

He leaned back on the sofa. "Just planning our lives away, aren't you?"

She lifted her chin. "No. I'm planning the company Christmas party. You and your brothers make the final decision on that. If you absolutely hate the idea, just shoot it down."

"I didn't say I hated the idea. I need to think about it. We'll discuss it at the meeting on Monday. And I don't want to talk about work." He swept his knuckles across her cheek. "I want to talk about that Olympic dash you did out of the restaurant."

She looked down, studying her jeans. She was hoping he wouldn't bring that up, but how could he not? "Yeah. About that. Sorry."

"It's okay. I didn't pick the right place to have that conversation. It was my fault."

She tipped her gaze to his. It was nice of him to take the blame, when she knew it fell squarely on her. "No. It wasn't. You were trying to figure out what the hell was wrong with me. It was all me. Trust me, I know this."

He let out a soft laugh. His touch was gentle as he swept a stray hair behind her ear. "Tori, there's nothing wrong with you."

If only he knew. It was best he didn't. She liked things the way they were, but as they sat here, she knew—one way or the other—things were going to change, starting tonight.

But which way? She could either talk to him, tell him everything, or she could choose another way. She could stop fighting what she'd wanted all along.

She shifted, leaned into him and laid her hand on what was a spectacularly solid thigh. His face registered surprise for a fraction of a second, but then he pulled her closer, his hand coming around to cup her neck.

"You sure?"

"Yes. I'm tired of fighting it."

He traced her bottom lip with the pad of his thumb, making her shudder, her senses alive with need for him.

"It shouldn't be a fight, Tori."

She took a deep breath. "Just shut up and kiss me."

Fortunately, Brody was a man of action. He kissed her, and everything inside her went instantly hot. And damp. It was just like the Christmas party last year, just like that night in her apartment. Brain cells began to burst, she lost all sense of time and place, and she focused only on the way his lips took command of hers, the way his tongue wound around hers. He wrapped an arm around her and dragged her onto his lap, the feel of all that solid muscle underneath her shocking her.

And when he began to move his hand over her ribcage, her heart stuttered, then raced. He paused, no doubt waiting for her to push him away and make a run for the front door. But she covered his hand with hers and brought it over her breast. He molded his hand there, teased her by brushing his thumb over her, making her nipple harden and tingle, promising what she could have if she surrendered.

She'd surrendered the minute she walked through his front door. She didn't have the energy to fight this anymore. Not when it was what she'd wanted for so many years.

With a low growl, he brought her closer to him, cradling her against his chest as he deepened the kiss. He was everything she wanted, knew she shouldn't have, and tonight, she just didn't care anymore.

And when he made a swift move and slid her underneath him, his big body covering hers, she wrapped her legs around his thighs, aching at the intimate contact. He rocked against her and she wanted to weep. It felt so good, and she needed release desperately. She'd denied herself for so long—stupidly, foolishly holding on to the notion that if she kept herself from having what she wanted, time would stand still and nothing would change.

But the world did change. She'd changed, and tomorrow, so would her life, which she wasn't going to worry about tonight, because the only thing she was going to concentrate on tonight was having Brody.

He lifted, giving her the opportunity to finally be close enough to look her fill of him, to touch him in all the ways she'd denied herself for so long. She laid her hands on his thighs, swept them inward, biting her lip as she zeroed in on one very sizeable erection.

Her gaze swept to his and he cocked one of his famous grins at her, then laid his hands on either side of her head and bent to give her a smoldering kiss that rocketed her senses. He lifted her shirt, his hands big and warm on her belly as he snaked them upward.

"Too many clothes," he said, raising her shirt over her head. For some ridiculous reason, she blushed, likely because she'd allowed very few guys to see the goods. She was damn picky about who she slept with, and of course there was the ridiculous torch she'd carried for Brody all these years.

But him looking at her? Yeah, she'd fantasized about this moment. She had a rockin' body and she knew it. She worked out so she could eat whatever she wanted. She was curvy in all the right places and she loved her curves. Obviously, Brody liked what he saw, because his eyes darkened and he traced a finger around the swell of her breast, dipping his fingertip inside the cup of her bra.

She suddenly found it hard to breathe as his touch sent wild sensation rocketing throughout her nerve endings.

"God, you're beautiful, Tori."

He bent, kissed the swell of her breast, and she was afraid her heart would burst. She breathed heavily and she knew he could hear her but there was honestly nothing she could do to stop the dizzying heights the touch of his lips to her breasts took her to.

He dropped down beside her and she was ever so grateful for this oversized couch, because Brody wasn't a small guy. She heard his boots drop to the floor—he must have toed them off, so she kicked off her shoes, and suddenly their feet were entwined. That made her smile, because there was something both playful and yet so intimate about it.

He didn't seem to be in any hurry to get to the good stuff, another thing that surprised her. He lazily drew circles over the swell of her breasts with his fingertips, while he played with her feet. He still had all his clothes on and she still wore her bra and jeans. Somehow, she had expected this explosion, with clothes flying everywhere, the two of them falling to bed and having a quickie. Yet here they were, lying on his sofa side by side while he mapped her breasts.

Brody constantly surprised her.

"You're quiet," he said.

"I'm…shocked."

He lifted up on his arm. "Yeah? Why?"

"I don't know. I thought this would go…faster."

He laughed. "You have an appointment later that you need to get to, or a curfew?"

She smacked his shoulder. "No."

"Then we have all night, don't we?"

"I guess we do."

He kissed her shoulder. "I've thought about you—about

this—for a long time, Tori. I want to get to know your body. I'm not in any hurry."

She let out a sigh. He was just too damn perfect, which ratcheted up her anxiety level to the nth degree. Why couldn't he be a jerkwad who dragged her to the bedroom, screwed her brains out and dumped her back at her car with a pat on the butt and a transparent promise to call her tomorrow? It would make this so much easier.

Instead, he was putting slow seduction moves on her that were shattering her from the inside out.

He reached behind her and undid the clasp of her bra. Her breath caught as he drew it down, his gaze on hers as he grabbed the other strap and pulled her bra off, baring her breasts.

He cupped one, lazily brushing his thumb over an aching nipple, then bent to take it between his lips. She arched into him, a part of her unable to believe that she was here, that he was touching her, had his mouth on her. She tangled her fingers in his hair and held him there, hoping this moment would never end. The pleasure was unbearable, and when he lifted and smiled that devilish smile at her, every female part of her tightened.

He smoothed his hand down her stomach, popping the button on her jeans with ease. He eased the zipper down and she reached for his wrist to stop him.

"I'm not going to be the only one with no clothes on," she said.

He grinned, and rose up on his arms to climb over her. "I can fix that."

He held out his hand and drew her off the sofa. "Let's go play on that big bed."

With a shaky sigh, she let him lead her into the bedroom. He flipped the light on and pulled her into his arms, kissing her so thoroughly she was lightheaded, before depositing her on the edge of the bed.

He drew his shirt over his head, and she sucked in a breath at his wide shoulders, expansive chest and those abs—oh, dear God his stomach. She always ogled the male fashion models and their six-pack abs, figuring they were an anomaly. Apparently not, because Brody had a stacked eight-pack going on. She reached out to smooth her hand over his rippled muscles.

"Damn," she said.

He grinned. "Thanks. You have a pretty hot body yourself, though I can't wait to get you naked so I can put my hands and mouth all over you."

She shuddered at the thought. "Let's get you naked so we can get me naked and move on to the fun stuff, then."

She loved that he was in no hurry to get to her body. And when he unzipped his jeans and dropped them to the floor, leaving him in just his boxer briefs, she wondered what the hell he was doing in construction, when his gorgeous face and body could be blazing the billboards just like those athletes and models. With no sense of modesty he shucked the briefs, and she sent up a short prayer of thanks that she was going to have sex with this amazing man tonight.

She unashamedly looked her fill, then her gaze drifted up to his face where he quirked a smile.

"Now it's your turn," he said.

She reached for her jeans, but he pushed her back on the bed.

"It's more fun if I get to do that."

He peeled her jeans down her hips and over her legs, then draped her clothes over the chair next to the bed.

"These are nice," he said, smoothing his hand over her peach-colored silk-and-lace panties. He drew her legs over the edge of the bed and cupped her sex, then dropped down to his knees between her legs.

He pressed a kiss to her hip bone, slowly dragging one side of her panties down. Then he moved to the other side, kissed her hip bone again, drew her panties over her hips and pulled them down her legs. He flung them over his shoulder and spread her legs. Tori breathed deeply as he looked up at her.

"Has anyone told you how beautiful you are?" he asked.

"Not lately."

"I've always thought you were beautiful," he said, smoothing his hand over her thigh and down her leg. He pressed a kiss to her knee. "But, Tori, you're beautiful everywhere."

She couldn't breathe as he pressed kisses to her inner thighs. And when he put his mouth on her sex, she nearly died from the pleasure. She arched her hips upward, lost in the sensations as he played a masterful game with his tongue that took her right to the very edge of oblivion.

He gripped her hips and she reached for him, holding on to his hands as his expert mouth brought her so close to orgasm she bit her lip to keep from coming. Because this was pleasure she'd waited seemingly a lifetime for, had fantasized about, and now that it was real, she wanted to hold on, to savor the moment. But oh, he was so good, and she couldn't stop the rollercoaster of her climax as it plummeted her right over the cliff.

She cried out as she came, and Brody stayed right there with her, clasping her hands and using his mouth to heighten her pleasure until the pulses died down and she lowered her hips to the bed.

Brody raised up and scooted her further onto the bed as he climbed up her body, his mouth coming down on hers in a blistering kiss that stole what few senses she had left.

He let go of her only long enough to grab a condom and

put it on, and then he rolled her underneath him and slid inside her. She gasped as he filled her.

He stilled, and she held on to his arms, watching him, feeling him expanding inside her.

"Fucking perfect," he whispered as he brushed his lips against hers.

Emotion swelled and she pushed it aside. This wasn't emotional. It was sex and nothing more. And as he moved against her, nearly shattering her again, she shielded her heart and closed her eyes, focusing only on the incredible sensations every stroke he made evoked.

"Tori."

Her heart clenched at the soft timbre of Brody's voice, like a caress, licking at the core of her soul.

"Tori, look at me."

She opened her eyes and he moved inside her.

"Stay with me."

He surged within her and grabbed one of her hands, lifting it above her head. He ground against her, slow and easy, the movement so intimate as he locked gazes with her. She felt each stroke all the way to her toes. What this man did to her tore her apart. Somehow she knew it was going to be like this—consuming every part of her and beyond just the physical. And as he brushed his lips across hers, the searing tenderness of it was her undoing. A cry tore from her and she shattered, tightening around him as she came.

With a low growl, he thrust into her in rapid succession, clenching her hip as he buried himself deep and shuddered with his own climax. She wrapped her legs around him and held him, lost in the sensations—lost in Brody.

She'd long ago lost her heart to him. Making love with him had only cemented the love she had felt for him all these years. And as he rolled her over to her side and wrapped her

tightly against him, she wondered how she was going to survive this with her heart intact.

Brody had expected great sex. Tori was fiery and passionate in everything she did, and he knew that would extend
to the bedroom. What he hadn't expected was the lightning
bolt of emotion that had hit him when she'd turned those
emerald-green eyes on him, the connection he'd feel to her
when he was inside her.

He liked sex—a lot. It released endorphins and hey, it was
fun. What wasn't to like about it for both parties? But he'd
never connected emotionally to it, because he'd never been
attached to anyone before.

Until now.

And as he held Tori and stroked the softness of her skin,
he wondered what the hell he was going to do about everything he was feeling right now, because this was new territory. Normally he'd cut and run, because he liked to keep
things light and easy and non-complicated.

But this was Tori, whose middle name was complicated.

Which left things between them—where, exactly?

He tipped her chin and brushed his lips across hers. She
smiled up at him, her eyes half lidded and sleepy. She snuggled up against his chest and pressed her body against his,
where she fit perfectly.

Typically when a woman insinuated herself into his bed
for the night, he'd start to think about how fast he could get
her out of his house in the morning.

With Tori, he didn't feel that way. He felt...comfortable
with her here. In his bed, and in his house.

And maybe in his life.

He should go to sleep before he started to think too much
about what the hell that meant. There was already too much
going on in his head as it was.

SEVEN

WHEN TORI WOKE the next morning, she had a few seconds of disorientation. First, she was in a very comfortable, over-sized monstrosity of a bed, so it definitely wasn't hers.

Second, underused muscles were sore, and then she remembered last night.

And Brody, which reminded her where she was.

In Brody's bed, with no Brody in sight. But she smelled bacon. And coffee. And her stomach growled in response.

She started to throw the covers off to get dressed, but Brody came through the door right then with a tray.

"Don't get dressed," he said. "I have coffee and breakfast."

"In bed? I can come into the kitchen."

"No." He set the tray down and poured a cup of coffee that he filled with two dollops of cream, then added a spoon-ful of sugar, just the way she made hers. He handed her the cup. "I want us to eat in bed."

She inhaled the brew, then took a sip. "Mmmm. Deca-dent."

While he poured his coffee, she admired his lean physique in his low-slung sweat pants and no shirt. He was barefoot, too.

"Aren't your feet cold?"

He looked down at his feet. "Uh, no. I don't get cold. I'm used to working outside in the winter and it's plenty warm in here. Are you cold? I could turn the heat up."

She raised her knees. "I'm plenty warm." And heating up fast as she ogled him.

"Good. I made pancakes and eggs—scrambled—plus bacon and sausage and hash browns."

She arched a brow at the smorgasbord he presented her. "You lied last night. You *can* cook."

"I'm no master chef, but I do have to eat to survive, so there are a few things I know how to fix. What would you like?"

"Pancakes sound great. And bacon. I love bacon."

He grabbed a piece of bacon and held it in front of her lips. "Bite."

She took a taste. It was crispy. "Perfect," she said after she'd swallowed.

He took the next bite, then her. Sharing the meal together was intimate, and she had to admit, fun to eat in bed. Naked. Though she was the only one naked, a fact she was reminded of every time Brody glanced at her breasts. It made breakfast an interesting experience.

"Lots of syrup or only a little?" he asked after they polished off the bacon and eggs, which he'd also shared with her by feeding her.

"Lots."

He poured syrup on the pancakes, then scooped some onto the fork and slid it into her mouth.

"Oh, that's delicious."

"Thanks. It's my own recipe."

"Not a box mix?"

He looked horrified. "Bite your tongue. Pancakes are sacred."

She laughed, and when he hovered near her lips for the next bite, syrup dripped over her breasts.

She looked down. "Oops. Did you bring napkins?"

"Yeah, but I'll get that." He laid the fork on the plate and bent down to lick the drops of syrup from her breast, then ended by capturing her nipple between his lips and sucking.

She gasped, then held his head there while he tasted her. When he lifted his head, he said, "You taste much better than the pancakes."

He grabbed the bottle of syrup and poured another few drops over both breasts, letting some dip between the valley and over her nipples. Breakfast forgotten, Tori leaned back against the pillows and Brody dropped his sweats, his erection a much better appetizer than the bacon.

He climbed onto the bed and licked along the valley between her breasts, moved to one nipple, then the other, cleaning the trail of syrup he'd mapped. By the time she was clean, she was hot, and more than wet in another strategic area.

"Brody," she said, capturing his head between her hands. He moved up her body to kiss her, his lips and tongue sweet like the syrup.

He cupped her butt and shifted her sideways on the bed, laying her flat under him, grabbing a condom from the nightstand. She was throbbing and ready for him when he entered her. He rolled to his side and she lifted a leg over his hip, giving him deeper access as he thrust into her with quick, fierce movements that made her rake her nails down his back.

She was so close so fast, his syrup foreplay driving her to the brink in a maddening instant. And when she came, he went with her, his loud groan eclipsed by her shattering cries.

He rolled again, this time pulling her on top of him so he could stroke her back and butt. She loved his hands on her, loved the feel of his body underneath her.

She was afraid she was never going to get enough of Brody, that there would never be enough time to get him out of her system.

"I think we're stuck together," he finally said.

She lifted, and he was right. The syrup had made both their chests sticky. She laughed. "I guess a shower is in order."

She climbed off and he led her into the shower, where he showed her another trick or two about his lovemaking prowess. And to prove how utterly decadent she could be on a weekend with Brody, after that they climbed back into bed and made love again, then took a nap.

She decided as he played with her breast and she drifted off into a lazy slumber that she might live in this fantasy forever and never come back to reality.

Because in this fantasy, Brody belonged to her.

And she belonged to him.

EIGHT

MONDAY WAS AN ugly reality, especially since Brody had to bring her to work.

Time had escaped her and she'd lost all track of it in Brody's arms and in his bed. He'd driven her to her apartment on Saturday so she could grab some fresh clothes. They'd hung out at his house all weekend watching movies, cooking, eating, playing video games, and mostly having the most amazing sex of her life. It was like the dam had burst and she'd let go of everything she'd held back all these years.

She'd never had more fun.

Until his alarm had gone off at five-thirty Monday morning.

What had she been thinking? Her car was still parked at Kent Construction's office. What if Wyatt or Ethan got there first? She should have had Brody take her back to her car Sunday night. Then she could have gone home and no one would ever know except the two of them.

Even worse, they'd spent the entire weekend so lost in each other, they hadn't once had a serious conversation about what this had meant, or what it would mean come Monday, when reality set in and they went back to working together.

Obviously, it meant nothing. It was a fantasy weekend, and now everything would go back to the way it had been before. But she'd been in such a sex-induced haze of pleasure and giddiness she'd forgotten to set ground rules, the first and most important being, Don't Tell Anyone In Deer Lake That We Slept Together.

Now she was in his truck and she was exhausted—though

happily exhausted—and Brody wasn't saying anything and neither was she. Though he didn't seem tense or nervous as he casually drank his to-go cup of coffee. Apparently she was the only one about to implode.

"You sure you don't want me to drop you by your apartment for more clothes?" he asked as they drove down Central toward the office.

"No. I'm fine. I grabbed extra when you brought me by my place over the weekend."

He laid his coffee in the cup holder and took her hand. "I had a good time this weekend."

She tried not to look out the window, half expecting to see someone peering in at them. "I did, too."

"You want to stop somewhere for breakfast?"

Was he out of his mind? Someone might see them together and…assume things. "Oh, no. I'm good."

"How about I drive through Marjorie's for donuts, then? We can buy a bunch for the staff meeting."

He was acting so…normal. "Sure. That sounds great."

Maybe she could hop out and hide in the bed of the truck so no one noticed her.

He pulled into Marjorie's, her favorite coffee and donut store. They waited in line, since Monday mornings were Marjorie's busiest time.

It was early and the sun wasn't out yet, but she dragged on her sunglasses.

"Are you okay?" he asked.

She pulled her gaze away from other cars and looked at him. "I'm fine. Why?"

"You seem tense." Then he grinned at her. "I thought we worked all that tension out of you this weekend."

She smiled back at him. "I'm not tense. I'm just trying to get back into work mode."

"Okay."

It was their turn at the window. Marjorie was the worst gossip ever. This was going to be an epic disaster.

"Morning, Brody," Marjorie said, her raven-and-gray hair pulled back into a bun as usual. "Hey, Tori."

So much for the sunglasses as a disguise.

"Mornin', Marjorie," Brody said. "We'll take a dozen mixed." He turned to Tori. "You want a coffee?"

She'd need it to get through this day. "Yes. An extra large, please, Marjorie."

She waited for the winks, knowing looks, or the questions. Instead, Marjorie said, "Coming right up."

Nothing. She'd gotten nothing at all. No sly looks, no questions, just the box of donuts and her coffee and then they were on their way.

Huh.

Which didn't mean Marjorie wouldn't be calling or texting everyone she knew about the fact she and Brody had been seen together in Brody's truck at six-thirty in the morning.

They pulled up to the office and she breathed a sigh of relief. Neither Ethan nor Wyatt had arrived yet. She nearly bolted out of the truck, her keys in one hand, coffee in the other, to open the front door.

"I'd have come around to open your side," Brody said as he met her at the door.

"Sorry. I, uh, need to pee."

"Oh. Okay. Go right ahead."

She didn't have to go, but she fled to the privacy of the ladies' room for a few minutes to catch her breath. Okay, so far so good. She checked her face in the mirror. It was flushed.

Calm down, Tori. You might just make it through this day.

She booted up her laptop and set the donuts on the con-

ference room table, then started a pot of coffee while Brody
gathered up paperwork. They worked efficiently side by side
as Brody asked her to pull some files and blueprints they'd
talk about at the morning staff meeting.

Everything was back to normal, which made her ache with
loss. She wanted to slide her arms around him and hold him
close, feel his heart beating against her as it had the past few
nights. She wanted to kiss him, to feel his lips touch hers.
She wanted his hands on her again.

But that was over. He'd had his fill of her and they were
done now, just as she'd suspected.

And when Wyatt came in, followed shortly thereafter by
Ethan, it was like the final nail had been driven in the coffin.

"Morning," she said, lifting her chin and pasting on her
brightest smile. She wouldn't give in to her emotions. She'd
known what she was doing the other night, knew what it was
going to cost her. If she was heartbroken, she had no one to
blame but herself. She knew what kind of guy Brody was.
He was a serial woman chaser, and once he caught a woman
and had her, he was done and on to the next one.

She couldn't blame him for what he was.

Once the guys had all had some coffee and shared some
mundane chit chat, they all gathered in the conference room
for the staff meeting. Tori made notes and discussed financials for an upcoming project that Brody would be heading,
which was gutting and rebuilding one of the town's major
supermarkets.

"It should be set to gear up after the holidays," Brody said.

"I'm damn glad we won that bid," Ethan said. "If the Johnson brothers had taken that one out from under us, I might
have had to resort to violence."

"I'd have been right behind you on that one," Wyatt said.

"But it's ours and it's a big project. We're going to need to add to our labor force."

Brody nodded. "Already on it." He motioned to Tori, who passed out a sheet she'd prepared.

"We estimate we're going to need to add about fifteen to this project. I'm already in contact with some of our labor force people about the people we'll need, and have contacted the local union for the steel portion of the project. They've got a meeting set up with Brody next week."

"Good," Wyatt said then turned to Brody. "How about the Hansen Sporting Goods job over in Mission City?"

"It'll be finished before this one starts up."

"Great. Any other business?"

"The Christmas party," Tori said. "It's time to start planning for that again."

Wyatt groaned. "I assume you'll be handling it. Do we even need to participate in discussions?"

"Actually, I was thinking since you and Brody have such big houses, and Ethan is building a big place, all three of you have plenty of room to start hosting these events at your homes. I thought this year we'd start at Brody's, then next year at Wyatt's, giving Ethan and Riley time to first finish their place and second, with their baby on the way, they won't need to have a turn for a couple years."

Ethan cocked a brow. "Why at our houses?"

"First, it's more economical. Second, it's more intimate and it'll bring you closer to your customers. Third, having it at your homes gives us more flexibility on dates to have the party since we're not at the mercy of a hotel or restaurant and their busy holiday schedules."

Ethan looked over at Wyatt and Brody and shrugged. "I don't have a problem with it. I doubt Riley will, either. What do you guys think?"

"I guess it's all right with me," Brody said. "Wyatt?"

"I'll have to discuss it with Calliope, but that woman loves a good party, so I can't imagine she'll say no. And she'll help you with the planning, especially when it's at our house. Hell, she'll help you this year at Brody's."

Wyatt looked over at Brody. "You're the single guy. You sure you're fine with this?"

Brody's gaze leveled on Tori and he quirked a smile. "Yeah, I'm fine with it."

She tried to tamp down the emotions battering at her. She dragged her gaze away from Brody and instead focused on his brothers. "Great. I'll start planning. I'll email all of you with potential dates for the party. Get back to me as soon as you can."

They went on to a few more last-minute topics, then wrapped up the meeting so the guys could get out to their jobsites for the day. Ethan and Wyatt were on the phones while simultaneously packing up their gear.

Brody stopped at her desk. "You sure about this Christmas party thing at the house? That there'll be enough space?"

She tilted her head to look up at him. "Definitely. I wouldn't have suggested it otherwise. But I think, depending on the weather, we rent a fire pit and heaters for the back deck. If it's warm enough, people might want to spill outside."

"You order whatever you think we'll need. I trust your judgment on this."

"And you'll need a Christmas tree for that front window."

He cocked a brow. "This was all a ploy to get me to put a tree up."

She laughed. "Hardly. But it's a perfect spot for one. And you can't have Christmas at your house without a tree, Brody."

"Fine. But you'll have to come over and help me decorate it. I don't even have ornaments."

He was inviting her over again? She didn't know what to make of that. Was it in a professional capacity, or something more personal? "Okay. Sure. I'll be happy to help you set up the place. Trust me, I'm not going to leave it for you to handle."

He bent over and whispered in her ear, "I'm not talking about just the Christmas party, Tori."

She leaned back, her gaze shooting across the room to a gaping Wyatt and Ethan. "Brody. Your brothers are watching."

"Let them watch." He brushed his lips across hers, a long slow kiss that melted her to the chair. She clutched his shirt and soon forgot where they were. She might have even forgotten her own name.

"Get a room," Wyatt said.

"Jesus, is it hot in here or what? I need to go outside, where it's cold," Ethan said.

Brody pulled his lips from hers, his smile and sparkling eyes as devilish as always. "Screw you guys," he said without looking at them. "I'll call you later," he said to her.

"Okay." She released the death grip she had on his shirt and watched him as he grabbed his coat and his bag and walked out the door, his brothers following behind. They both gave her a knowing grin as they left her.

She finally exhaled.

Well. That was unexpected. And she supposed she should stop worrying about all the things she'd worried about this morning. Like whether anyone in town would find out. From their trip to the donut shop to Brody kissing her in front of her brothers, that cat was most definitely out of the bag.

As far as the weekend spent with Brody being a one-time-only thing? From the kiss he just gave her, she'd guess probably not.

Brody had changed everything.

She just didn't know what to make of it all.

"WHAT THE HELL was that about?" Ethan asked as they walked out to their trucks.

Brody clicked the remote on his key ring. "What was what about?"

"You might look dumb, but we know you're not," Wyatt said. "That kiss with Tori in there."

"Now who's dumb?" Brody threw his briefcase in the passenger seat and turned to look at his brothers.

"So what's going on?" Ethan asked.

"None of your business."

"If it's Tori, it's definitely our business." Wyatt laid his briefcase down and folded his arms. "So, spill."

"Whatever's going on with Tori and me doesn't concern the two of you, so butt out." He climbed into his truck, but before he could shut the door, Wyatt grabbed it.

"She's family, Brody. Don't screw this up."

"And don't hurt her," Ethan said.

Brody rolled his eyes. "Don't you two have jobsites to get to?"

"I'm serious," Ethan said. "She means something to us."

"She means something to me, too, so leave it alone, okay?"

He finally pulled the door shut and his brothers walked away. As he drove off, he shook his head.

First they wanted him to make peace between him and Tori. Now that he had, it was like they wanted him to back the hell off.

Christ. He raked his fingers through his hair as he made the turn onto the highway.

First he pissed her off and he was the bad guy. Now he brought her in close and he was still the bad guy.

It was a no-win scenario, and no matter what he did he was going to be skewered.

He and Tori had had a great weekend, even better than

he could have imagined. He wanted more time with her, because a few days of her sweet smile, her genuine laughter, her smartass wit and her gorgeous body just wasn't enough.

He had no idea where it was going to lead, and he didn't waste time imagining the future. He preferred to live in the present and let things roll out how they were going to roll out. There was no sense in trying to predict how a relationship was going to go.

Hell, he never even had relationships, so this was uncharted territory for him. Hopefully he and Tori could just take it a day at a time, without anyone butting their nose in and offering unwanted opinions.

He eased into the fast lane and hit the gas, switching his mind over to business, where it belonged.

Though a certain redhead kept popping into his head, making him smile as he worked throughout the day.

That was a first, because once he settled on business, that's usually where his mind stayed. But stray thoughts of Tori kept filtering through. Her laugh, the way she looked naked, her competitive nature when they'd played video games, or the soft way she snored when she'd fallen asleep while watching movies.

He'd never realized how alone he had been until he had her with him all weekend, or how much he'd enjoyed spending time with her.

Usually he was all about getting women out of his house.

Now all he could think about was when he could get Tori back there.

NINE

MONDAYS WERE ALWAYS BUSY, so by the time Tori got home, she was exhausted, not only from work, but from her nonstop ringing and texting cell phone.

Word was out that she had been with Brody, and there had been more calls and texts from Calliope than anyone.

She knew Calliope had her hands full at the day care center, so for her to take the time to send her approximately seven million texts meant that it was urgent. And for Tori to send only one back, which said "We'll talk after work tonight," meant that Tori was being a big fat coward.

She couldn't face anyone, didn't want to talk about this thing with her and Brody.

Whatever this thing might be, which was probably no thing at all, which was why she didn't want to talk about it.

She hadn't been home more than a half hour when her phone buzzed.

She looked at it, saw that it was Calliope again and pressed the button.

"Hey."

"You might be the queen of avoidance, but I'm the queen of I-will-stalk-you-until-you-talk-to-me-because-we're-best-friends-dammit."

Tori smiled at that. It was true. "I'm sorry, Calliope. It was a hellish day at work."

"I'm sure it was. Now answer your door."

She frowned. "There's no one at my door."

"There is now. Me."

Tori went to the door and looked through the peephole, laughing when Calliope stuck her tongue out. She opened the door. "Oh, my God, you really are a stalker."

"Told you. I was afraid you were going to ignore my calls again." Calliope came in and Tori shut the door.

"I did not ignore your calls."

"Of course you did." She threw her purse on the chair and flopped down on the sofa, her curls bouncing as she did. "Trying to process your hot, sex-filled weekend with Brody and couldn't come to terms with it enough to talk about it yet?"

Tori laid her phone down and fell into the nearby chair. There was no sense lying anymore to Calliope. Her best friend knew her facial expressions and body language better than anyone. "Yes."

She propped her feet on Tori's coffee table. "Spill. And I mean everything. Well, you can spare the intimate sex details because that's between you and hot stuff. But how did it happen?"

"I don't know. He took me out to dinner. We were supposed to go over my annual review. We talked. I bolted from the restaurant when it got personal and he wanted to talk about the two of us."

"Coward."

"I know. But then he took me back to his place and gave me the option of coming in or not."

"And you took option I-want-to-sleep-with-you."

"I don't know that I consciously took that option, but I knew the two of us had to talk and clear the air."

"Bet you didn't do much talking, did you?"

She laid her head in her hands. "Not particularly."

Calliope clapped her hands together. "Well, it's about time. You should have jumped Brody's bones years ago."

She lifted her head. "No, I shouldn't have done it at all. This only made things worse."

"Yeah? How so?"

"We work together. You know how entrenched I am with his family. When things end between us—and they will, because you know how he is—I'll lose my job and my connection to his family."

"Oh, aren't you Miss Negative today? What if things don't end badly, or God forbid you think positively, what if they don't end at all? What if you two end up together, like forever and ever?"

Tori snorted out a laugh. "Brody doesn't do forever and ever. He doesn't even do two weeks."

"Brody's grown up now. He's not the same guy he was before."

"Before what?"

Calliope gave her a smug smile. "Before you, honey."

She didn't want to think positively. She didn't want to hope that things would work out between her and Brody, because the crushing fall would be unbearable.

"We just had a weekend, Calliope. Nothing more."

"And then he kissed you in the office this morning. In front of his brothers, no less."

"You know about that?"

"I'm married to one of said brothers, you know. You think he wouldn't tell me?"

"Okay, right. Forgot about that."

Calliope laughed. "Wyatt called me from the truck with one of those 'You're not gonna believe this shit' kind of phone calls. I figured it would be a jobsite thing, and nearly fell off my chair when he told me Brody planted a hot one on you right in front of Wyatt and Ethan. What was your reaction when he did that?"

"Honestly? I was so focused on Brody kissing me, it was like no one else was in the room. I didn't even think about it until after."

Calliope gave her a nod and a smug smile. "Oh, you're in deep."

"I know." It was already too late to guard her heart against the break. "And I don't think I can handle it."

Calliope came over to her and shoved herself into the chair next to Tori. "You can handle this. Love is scary business, Tori, but it's worth fighting for. I think you and Brody could have something special."

Tori looked at her. "I'm scared."

"I know you are. And I know you think you have a lot to lose, but at some point you have to either close yourself off to him, or throw yourself headlong into this and trust Brody not to hurt you."

She shuddered at the thought. Could she do that? Could she trust him, given his past track record with women?

It was a huge leap of faith.

She didn't know what to do.

Calliope's pocket buzzed. She shifted. "Hang on a sec." She looked at her phone and then at Tori. "Oh, it's Brody's mom."

"Hey, Mom…" She looked at Tori. "Really? That sounds fun. I'm actually at Tori's right now and I know she'd love to help."

Tori's eyes widened and she shook her head.

Calliope grinned. "Yes, tomorrow night is perfect. We'll be there. Love you."

She hung up and Tori asked, "What did you just volunteer me for?"

"Mom wants to have a baby shower for Riley since she's epically pregnant. She wants us to help her with the planning and execution."

"Oh." It warmed Tori's heart to be asked to help. "Sure, I'll be happy to do that."

"Great. We're going over tomorrow night to help Mom with the planning." Calliope climbed out of the chair. "I need to go home and fix dinner."

She led Calliope to the door. "Thanks for coming over and beating me up about Brody."

Calliope hugged her. "It's for your own good." She grabbed her arms. "Trust in yourself, Tori. And in Brody. I don't think he'll let you down."

She nodded and closed the door after Calliope left. She fixed dinner, took a hot, relaxing bath, then climbed into her pajamas and into bed. She hadn't had much sleep over the weekend and she was beat. Not that she was complaining.

As she stared up at the ceiling, she realized she ached for Brody. He was out of town the next three days on a job. She wondered if he would have asked her out tonight if he'd been home.

Probably not. They'd spent three nights together, which likely exceeded his spend-time-with-a-woman rules anyway.

But then there'd been that kiss this morning, which had blown her away.

She sat up and punched her pillow into submission, suddenly not as tired as she'd thought. She rolled over and stared out the window, hoping the passing clouds would lull her into sleep.

When the phone rang, she startled. It was only nine o'clock, though. She grabbed the phone, her stomach doing a mad leap when she saw Brody's name come up on the display.

"Hey," she said as she punched the button.

"Hey, yourself. What are you doing?"

"Lying in bed, actually."

"Oh. Were you asleep?"

"No. I was tired earlier so I went to bed, but now I can't sleep."

He laughed. "I guess we didn't get much sleep the past few nights, did we?"

Her toes curled just thinking about it. "No, we didn't." She shifted onto her back. "What are you doing?"

"Going over some paperwork for tomorrow's build. Boring stuff. My mind was wandering and I thought about you, so I wanted to give you a call to tell you I wish I was home. In bed. With you."

If he kept talking to her like that she was going to have to throw open a window to let some icy cold air in. "I wish you were here, too. How did your day go today?"

He told her about the project, complained a bit about some delays, and made her laugh about a meeting he'd had with some of the other contractors. She realized he was sharing his day with her, which made her smile, especially when he asked her how her day had been.

"Has your phone been blowing up with people asking about the two of us?" he asked.

"Sort of. Calliope stalked my door as soon as I came home from work."

"Figured Wyatt would blab to her."

"Also, I'm going to your mom's tomorrow night. She asked me to help plan Riley's baby shower."

"That'll be fun for you. I guess."

She laughed. "I'm looking forward to it. Girl stuff, you know."

"Yeah, I know. Well, I'll let you get some sleep. I'm about to hit it, too. I've got an early morning."

"Okay."

They both went silent.

"Brody?"

"Yeah?"

"Thanks for calling."

"You're welcome."

Another silence.

"Tori?"

"Yes?"

"I missed you today."

She sucked in a deep breath, her heart tightening. "I missed you too."

"Night."

"Good night."

She clicked the phone off and laid it on her nightstand, then curled under her covers, wishing she was in Brody's bed right now so she could inhale his scent.

God, she had it bad.

She was deeply in love with Brody and this was going to wreck her completely.

TEN

THE PAST FEW weeks had been spent in a whirlwind of work, prepping for the Christmas party, and nights spent with Brody. The best part of those few weeks had been the time Tori had spent with Brody.

Now she looked forward to days at the office, because he'd make time for the two of them to have lunch together. And when he was in town, they'd go out to a movie or to dinner.

It was like they were dating. A real couple. She was having a hard time getting used to him actually being fully in a relationship, expecting the other shoe to drop any moment and for him to say that he was tired of her. But that hadn't happened yet.

And it was probably a good thing she stayed busy with other things, like Riley's baby shower. The house was decorated in the most adorable shade of baby blues to welcome the new Kent baby into the family.

It had only taken a couple weeks to plan the shower, and Tori was convinced that nearly everyone in town had RSVP'd saying they were coming.

Okay, maybe not everyone in town, but Tori was glad when Calliope suggested they have the shower at her and Wyatt's house instead of at Stacy's, because Calliope's house was much bigger, affording them the opportunity to broaden the guest list.

And it was much less stress on Stacy, though she was throwing herself into the new grandchild bit with as much enthusiasm as any grandmother-to-be. And with Ethan's

eight-year-old daughter Zoey assisting Stacy, Tori and Calliope, it was a joy to behold the finished product.

Zoey proudly sported her *I'm The Big Sister* T-shirt today,
which of course was a baby blue shirt.

"Hey, Zoey, can you come here a second? I need your
help."

"Sure! What can I do?"

"Hold the end of this paper so I can hang it above the
fireplace."

Zoey carefully climbed on the stepladder, with her daddy's
ever-present help, and held the sign they'd had made that
said Welcome Baby Boy Kent.

"Put the tape on that end."

Ethan helped her, but Zoey grinned when she saw it up
there. "That's for our baby," she said to Ethan.

He kissed the top of Zoey's head. "It sure is."

Riley waddled into the room. "Ugh. How can my ankles
be swollen in December?"

"You should sit down, Mommy," Zoey said. "You look
like you're about to bust a giant alien out of your belly."

Riley snorted out a laugh. "You're right, Zoey." She carefully eased herself into a comfortable chair in the living room.
"Come sit with me and we'll read a book before the guests
start to arrive."

While Zoey ran to her backpack to get a book, Tori sat
next to her. "How can you be thirty-seven weeks pregnant
and still look so gorgeous?"

Riley took her hand. "Ethan paid you to say that, didn't he?"

She laughed. "He did not. It's true. Your hair is luscious
and beautiful and you still have a great body."

"Minus the huge stomach."

"Tori's right," Ethan said, grabbing a seat on the other side
of her. He laid a hand on her stomach. "You're beautiful."

"He tells me this every day. God, I love this man."

Zoey returned with a book, so Tori excused herself and let the family have a few minutes of quiet time together before the madness. As she shifted away, she turned and admired the love they had for each other.

"I'm so happy for them," Stacy said from behind her. She put her arms around Tori. "They've worked so hard for their happiness."

She wrapped her arms around Stacy's. "I know. It warms my heart to see them become a family, to know they're adding a baby." She turned around. "You can just feel the love pour from them. Sappy, I know."

Stacy's eyes filled with tears. She grabbed Tori's hand and pulled her into the kitchen. "It's not sappy at all. I love seeing my children happy and fulfilled, and Riley has always been like one of my own. Just like you."

Tori took a deep breath. "Thank you, Stacy."

"Now sit. Let's have a glass of wine together before the craziness ensues."

Stacy poured a glass for each of them. Tori lifted hers. "To Ethan, Riley, Zoey, and as-yet-unnamed baby boy Kent."

Stacy raised her glass. "Salute!"

Tori took a sip. "Good wine."

"It is good. I put Brody in charge of choosing the wine."

Tori arched a brow. "Really? I had no idea he even knew anything about wine."

"Well, you two are still learning about each other now that you're dating, aren't you?"

Uh-oh. "I…guess so."

Stacy patted her hand. "Relax. I'm not going to meddle. Much." She smiled behind the rim of the glass."

Tori didn't know what to say to that. "Stacy, I—"

"Is my mother giving you the third degree?"

Thank God for Brody's timely arrival, because she would have had no idea how to talk about Brody with his mother.

"I was not," Stacy said, giving Brody a hug and a kiss on the cheek.

He leaned against the counter. "Tell me again what I'm doing at a baby shower?"

"You were invited," Stacy said. "Riley wanted a couples shower. And since you and Tori are now a couple…"

"I'm sure I heard Wyatt calling me," Brody said, winking at Tori before he dashed out of the room.

"Coward," Stacy said. "I'll corner you yet today."

Tori laughed. "I don't think he's comfortable yet thinking about the two of us together."

"Well, the only thing I'm going to say about it is that it's about time."

"A lot of people seem to be saying that."

"And you aren't?"

She shrugged. "I'm just…taking it day by day."

"Look, Tori. I have no rose-colored glasses on when it comes to my son. I know all about his notorious reputation with women."

Good lord. She did not want to have this conversation. She prayed Calliope would come in soon. "Uh, reputation?"

"Don't play dumb with me. I know what a womanizer he's been in the past. But I also know he would never intentionally hurt you. There are too many people in this family who care about you. I think he's changed, Tori."

"He and I are getting along great." So far.

"Good. And I'm sure it'll stay that way. He might not have always been the best when it comes to relationships, but he's not stupid. He knows a great thing when he sees it. And you're the best thing to happen to him in a long time, Tori."

Her eyes stung as tears welled up. "Thank you, Stacy. I'm glad you think so."

"Aww, come here, honey. " Stacy folded her into her arms and hugged her tight. "I know you had a crappy family. You know no matter what happens, we'll always be here for you."

She squeezed Stacy and hoped what she said was true, because losing Brody would be devastating enough. Losing the whole Kent family would destroy her.

BABY SHOWERS WERE OKAY, if you liked blue shirts and blue outfits and blue hats and blue booties and blue everything and women oooh-ing and aaah-ing for an hour as every package was opened.

Thank God for beer or Brody would have never survived this. But Tori seemed to enjoy the present-opening part, and even his brothers had gotten into it, though he had no idea why Wyatt seemed so interested.

He smirked when Riley and Ethan opened his gift, a miniature construction bench with wooden hammer, wrench and the like.

"Oh, Brody, this is awesome," Riley said. She patted her belly. "My little construction worker, just like his daddy."

"Yeah, should be fun when he's bangin' on it while you're trying to sleep."

"Gee, thanks, Brody," Ethan said.

"You're welcome, bro."

Tori nudged him. "Such a cute gift."

"I did it to annoy my brother."

"It doesn't matter. It's adorable."

"You think every gift is adorable." But he grasped her hand and squeezed it, and she laid her head on his shoulder while the rest of the gifts were opened.

After that there was food, which he had to admit was his

favorite part. He stuffed himself, then went into the kitchen to toss his plate.

"Hey," his mom said, laying her head on his chest and wrapping her arms around him.

His family was demonstrative, and rampant huggers. He kind of liked that about them, so he held her close. "Good party, Mom."

"It was, wasn't it?" She tilted her head back. "Riley and Ethan seem to be having a great time and they received some lovely gifts."

"Yeah, if you like that baby stuff."

"Oh, you." She pushed at him and he let her go. "Maybe it's time you started thinking about that baby stuff."

"I don't have the right equipment, Mom."

She rolled her eyes and climbed up to sit on a stool at the center island to sip her wine while he grabbed another beer out of the fridge.

"You know what I'm talking about. A wife. A family of your own."

"Don't you have your hands full with the new grandson on the way?"

"I have enough love in my heart for a house full of grandchildren. And you're dodging the inevitable conversation."

He took a long swallow of beer. "What conversation is that?"

"You and Tori."

"What about me and Tori?"

"Are you serious about her?"

"I don't know. Things are progressing."

His mom took a sip of wine, then laid her glass down. "Brody, you know I love you like you're my own son."

"Ha, ha, Mom."

She winked at him. "Seriously, I love Tori like she's family, too. And I don't want her to get hurt."

"But it's okay if I do?"

She frowned. "You think she's going to hurt you?"

"I don't know." He looked around. They were alone in the kitchen. "I'm not used to relationships."

"Obviously, since you've been manwhoring your way through nearly every woman in town since you were seventeen."

"Jesus, Mom."

"It's the truth, isn't it? I don't live under a rock, you know. You've never had a steady relationship with a woman."

"I've been busy with the company."

"That's an excuse to avoid commitment."

"And you watch too much Dr. Phil."

"Actually, I'm into Dr. Oz now, but that's beside the point. You might want to blow me off as not knowing what I'm talking about, but I've been married to your father for thirty-seven years. And we've had our rough patches. He's hurt me and I've hurt him, but we have a strength in our love that's binded us."

Brody sucked in a breath. He knew the reason he and his brothers were solid was because of his parents, the upbringing they had. "I know love and marriage isn't easy. Except for you and Dad, of course."

His mom laughed. "Before your dad and I met and fell in love, I had my heart broken a few times by guys who couldn't commit, and despite me being deliriously happy with your father, I know the pain of having my heart broken. It's a pain you don't ever forget, so don't stand here and insult me by insinuating that I don't have personal experience in matters of love and heartbreak."

He'd never had this kind of conversation with his mother. "Okay. I'm sorry, Mom."

She scooted off the stool and came over to him and laid her hand in his. "I love you. Above all, I will always love you, no matter what. But I love Tori, too, and that girl has been through hell and back in her life. She looks at your father and I as family. She looks at Ethan and Wyatt as her brothers. But she has never once looked at you as family."

"No?"

"No. That girl has been in love with you since she was a teenager. Open your eyes, Brody, and be careful not to hurt her. Or if you realize she's not the one for you and you know you're going to hurt her, then let her down gently, and don't alienate her from the family she loves and who love her."

Fuck. "Yeah. Okay. I understand."

"Good. Then I'll butt out from now on. I love you, son." She reached up, grabbed his head and pulled him down for a kiss on his cheek. "I need to go ogle the cute baby gifts and take a few hundred more pictures."

After she left the kitchen, he downed the rest of his beer and grabbed another.

Talk about a Come to Jesus meeting. His mother had read him the riot act and had done it in her most gentle, sweetest voice, just like she always had done when they were kids. She'd never had to raise her voice to them. Calm reason had them dropping their chins to their chests and confessing their sins before they knew what was up.

Now he had to figure out what the hell he was going to do about what she'd told him.

It was one thing to have fun with Tori, to have a relationship with her because it wasn't complicated, and because it was what the two of them wanted.

It was another thing entirely to have the entire town and his family eagle-eyeing his every move.

"There you are."

He turned around as Tori entered the kitchen.

"I wondered where you'd disappeared to. Too much baby blue for you?" she asked with a grin.

"Yeah. Way heavy on baby land out there."

She laughed. "I think they're set for Baby Boy Kent's first couple years after that shower."

"It seems that way."

She tucked herself under his arm. "Things are wrapping up out there if you want to make your escape."

That was the nice thing about Tori. She always gave him an out and wasn't the clingy type. "Are you hanging here for a while?"

She nodded. "I'll help clean up the disaster after everyone leaves. I don't want to leave that for your mom or Calliope to deal with."

And she was generous, always thinking of others before herself. "Then I'll stay and help, too."

"Are you sure? We can handle it."

He bent and brushed his lips across hers, loving the way she yielded against him.

Maybe it was time he stopped thinking and worrying about what other people thought and focused only on what he felt. "If you can handle it, then so can I. Later, you and I can make our escape."

Her eyes sparkled with promise. "I love the sound of that."

EXHAUSTED AND GIDDY from the baby shower, Tori was more than a little thrilled when Brody had asked her to follow him to his place after.

He'd spent the evening looking like a miserable cornered

deer. She knew it wouldn't be his kind of venue, but he'd been a trooper about it. She supposed that's what family did for each other, at least family that cared about each other, another reason she loved all the Kents. They stood up for each other and by each other, even during the uncomfortable events. Even Brody's dad had showed up and dutifully showed enthusiasm over every baby item that had been unveiled.

Now she was exhausted and more than ready to kick off her uncomfortable shoes, so when she pulled into Brody's driveway, he came to meet her at her car.

"Pull into the garage. It looks like rain tonight."

She laughed. "My car has more golf-ball-sized hail dings on it than I can count. I don't think a little rain will hurt it."

"Pull it into the garage, Tori."

She shrugged. "Okay."

It seemed weird to park her car next to his truck. Silly perhaps, but it made them look like a couple and she hadn't yet reconciled them to that place yet.

He waited for her to get out, then held the door for her as she walked in from the garage.

"Tired?" he asked.

"Very. But it was a nice baby shower, and I'm glad it went well, both for Riley and for your mom, who was stressed about the details."

"And now it's over."

She kicked off her shoes inside the door. "Yes. Thank God. Now it's over."

"Would you like something to drink?"

"A giant glass of ice water would be great." She'd had a couple glasses of wine and a few beers throughout the night but plenty of food, so fortunately she wasn't buzzed, just tired. When Brody handed her the water, she took several swallows.

Brody swept his hand over her hair. "You look tired."

She lifted her gaze to his. "That's a euphemism for I look like hell, right?"

He laughed. "No, it means there are dark circles under your eyes like you need some sleep. Let's go to bed."

She couldn't argue with him. "That sounds good. I am tired."

They went upstairs and she realized how comfortable she'd grown undressing and climbing into bed with him. He pulled her close and wrapped his arms around her, then kissed the top of her head.

She closed her eyes, relaxing into his body, smoothing her hand over his chest, drifting across his abs, then even lower. She could never get enough of touching him. Every moment they had together was precious to her, because she never knew when it would end.

"You keep touching me like that you're not going to get to sleep."

She lifted her head, searching his face in the darkness as she wrapped her hand around the hot, thick, oh-so-hard part of him. "I'm not *that* tired, you know."

He shifted her underneath him. "Is that right?"

"Yes."

"I have ways of exhausting you."

"Yeah? Show me."

His mouth met hers in a tangle of lips and tongues. She sensed a desperate passion in Brody tonight, and she met it with wild abandon. He smoothed his hand over her hip and down her thigh, lifting her leg as he put a condom on in record time and entered her with a quick thrust. She gasped as he moved within her, teasing her with slow, deliberate movements that made her climax so quickly it shocked her into a surprised cry.

But he wasn't finished with her yet, because he rolled her

onto her knees and took her from behind, teasing her nipples and breasts and reaching between her legs as he rocked hard and fast into her. He was relentless and ever patient, and when she came again, he stayed with her, giving her the strokes she needed to catapult her into oblivion.

And still, he only shifted her over onto her side, letting her catch her breath by kissing her, stroking her hip and raising her leg over his so he could thrust slow and easy.

"Brody," she whispered, staring up into a face she'd grown to love so deeply it hurt. "What are you doing to me?"

"We have all night," he said, brushing her bottom lip with the pad of his thumb. She grabbed his thumb and sucked it between her lips, rewarded with his harsh groan of pleasure. He replaced his thumb with his mouth, shattering her with the intimacy of the gesture. She fought for breath as he took her right to the edge again, refusing to let go until she did.

She didn't think she could, until he rolled her on top of him, giving her the control. He grasped her hips and held her while she rolled back and forth and he lifted up into her, burying himself deep. He cupped her breasts and brushed his thumbs over her nipples, searing her with the deepest pleasure until she arched against him, giving him everything he'd asked for, baring herself to him down to her soul. And when she came, this time he thrust, then groaned, his fingers digging into her hips as he roared out his climax and fell with her.

She collapsed on top of him, utterly spent. She vaguely registered Brody moving her off him, leaving her for a few minutes and coming back to the bed to cuddle up behind her. She only recalled his strong arms wrapping around her as he pulled the covers over them both.

Then she let sleep take her.

ELEVEN

THE OUT-OF-TOWN job had been going smoothly, and plans for the new supermarket were well underway. Brody had a handle on everything, and even his personal life seemed to be going well for a change.

He and Tori had settled into seeing each other fairly regularly, which he liked. It was new territory for him, this whole relationship thing, but it sure beat the hell out of coming home to an empty house every night.

He wasn't even freaked out that, little by little, her things were starting to take up residence at his place.

First it was a toothbrush, because she spent the night frequently. Then it was shower things and a few clothes for overnight stays. And he had to make closet and drawer space for her to put her things. He had plenty of room, so no big deal, right?

She was even cooking for him, and what guy would mind that? She sure as hell was a better cook than he was.

He had to admit he liked having her at his place rather than that hellhole of an apartment she lived in.

Which begged the question of why he didn't just ask her to move in with him. It wasn't like they were strangers to each other. He'd known her for years. They got along great. The sex was fantastic and they enjoyed each other's company.

It was that next step dilemma that kept him from pulling the trigger. They were having fun. It was light and simple and easy between them. She didn't ask for anything or tie any strings to him. He could pretend he was still the carefree bachelor he'd always been, because, technically, Tori wasn't living there.

But she *was* a part of his life, and he didn't like to think about her going back to her place and the two of them living separate lives. He didn't want to think about his life without her in it. He didn't want to think about her possibly finding someone else and leaving him.

Was that love? Did he love her? That was his problem. He had no idea what love was. He'd seen it, been surrounded by it with his parents and Wyatt and Calliope and Ethan and Riley. He knew it from the outside, but he'd never been in love with a woman before, so he didn't have a freakin' clue.

All he knew was he liked the way things were. Wasn't that enough for now? Did it have to be defined?

He didn't want to think about the deep shit anymore. All he knew was having her at the house made it easier for her to plan the company Christmas party, which she'd done a fantastic job of putting together. She'd made arrangements for caterers and the band and the booze and those outside heater things, and there was even someone coming to move furniture and bring in tables and a dance floor.

Whatever. He was kind of oblivious to it all because he had his work to do, but on the nights they were together she'd discuss it with him. He had to admit he liked the end of the day rehash they always did when she stayed over.

He was toying with the idea of asking her to stay at his place when he had to be out of town, though he couldn't yet figure out how to make that work.

Why would she need to be at his place when he wasn't there? It wasn't like he had a dog that needed watching or anything.

Maybe he should get a dog.

"Brody. Brody!"

He snapped to attention at Wyatt's sharp tone, realizing he'd been so deep in thought he hadn't even realized his brother had been talking. "What?"

Wyatt rolled his eyes. "Were you even listening?"

"Uh…no. What were you saying?"

"I've just spent the better part of ten minutes going over inventory for the jobsites. Where were you?"

Brody dragged his fingers through his hair and stood, pacing the office conference room. "I don't know. Somewhere else. Sorry."

"Is it a job, or is it something else on your mind?"

"Oh. A job."

"Okay." Wyatt closed his laptop. "Let's talk about it. Which job is giving you hell? We'll talk about it and fix it."

Shit. Every single job he managed was going smoothly right now. He couldn't manufacture a problem if he tried. "Okay, it's not a job."

"Then it's Tori. Did you fuck something up?"

He rolled his eyes. "No, I didn't fuck anything up. Things are fine."

"Then what's got your head so far up your ass that you daydreamed away ten minutes of our conversation?"

He shot Wyatt a smirk. "Maybe you're boring."

"Screw you. Inventory might be boring, but I am never boring. Just ask my wife."

"No, thanks. I'd rather not hear the gory details of your sex life."

"Man, you're missing out. They're epic. Okay, then tell me about yours."

"Perv. I'm not telling you anything about mine."

"Not your sex life. Tell me what's going on with you and Tori."

"Nothing. We're dating. Things are going fine."

Wyatt cocked a brow. "Now that's boring. Calliope and I are more exciting than that, and we're married."

"Correction. You're newly married. You should still be

exciting. If you're not still rocking her world every night, then she should trade you in for a newer model."

"Again...screw you. And you're changing the subject so you don't have to talk about you and Tori."

"Noticed that, did you? And still, you're not grabbing a clue. See, I always knew you were a moron."

"So is it getting serious?"

"What is it with my family and Tori? If I was having a relationship with Rita Melner of Hair Raising's salon, no one would say boo to me about it. But since it's Tori, everyone has to be all up in my business about it."

"That's true," Ethan said as he walked into the conference room and shut the door. "But you're not dating Rita Melner. Zack Dorman is."

"Our foreman on the upcoming supermarket job?" Brody asked.

"Yeah." Ethan set his laptop down. "Riley told me when she went to get a pedicure yesterday that Rita's been seeing Zack for about a month now."

"Huh," Wyatt said. "Interesting. But not as interesting as Brody and Tori."

Dammit. He was so sure they'd start gossiping about Rita and Zack and he'd be off the hook.

"There's nothing interesting going on with the two of us. We're dating. Subject's closed."

"And things are going well I assume?" Ethan asked.

"Why? Did Mom ask for a report?"

Ethan snorted. "No. I just care about Tori."

Brody rolled his eyes. "I'm not going to talk to the two of you about Tori. Not now, not ever. Not again."

"You know, I do like to give you shit about this," Wyatt said. "But we care about you, too. This is a good relationship for you, Brody. For God's sake, it's the first one you've been in since high school. She's good for you."

"Wyatt's right, man. Make this one stick," Ethan said.

Brody had nothing to say to that. He just wanted to be able to see Tori on his own terms without his damn family interfering every step of the way.

What would be with the two of them would be. And no amount of family interference would alter the outcome.

He looked outside the conference room where Tori sat at her desk, busy on the phone. Her gorgeous hair was piled up on top of her head, two pencils stuck in it to hold it up. Pieces of it rained down her long neck and all he could think about was sneaking up behind her and taking a nibble.

He was getting hard just thinking about it.

"Do you think he's even aware we're talking about him?" Ethan asked.

"I spent ten minutes going over inventory and he was daydreaming."

"I hear the both of you," he said, focusing his attention away from Tori, but only briefly, because she came to the door, her eyes wide with worry.

"Ethan. Is your phone off?"

"Uh...no. It's never off." He pulled it out of his pocket. "Shit. I must have hit the button."

"Riley called. Her water broke and contractions have started."

Ethan paled. "Oh, shit." He stood, and started shuffling papers into his bag.

"Just go, man," Wyatt said. "Leave that stuff here. And call us."

"Yeah. You're right." He looked at all of them and grinned. "I'm going to have another baby."

"And you're going to miss it if you keep standing here talking to us," Tori said. "Move it. Your wife is waiting for you."

Ethan made a mad dash out of the conference room while Brody, Wyatt and Tori grinned at each other.

Fourteen hours later, Brody and Tori made their way into Riley's hospital room to get their first glimpse at the baby.

Tori had worried all day and into the night. Brody distracted her by taking her out to dinner after work and then they went to the hospital to hold vigil with the rest of the family until the baby was born. Zoey was hyper excited, so Tori and Calliope kept her amused with electronic games until Ethan, grinning like crazy, came out and told them that Gideon Roger Kent had made his arrival, screaming like a banshee as he came out.

Tori unabashedly sobbed with joy on Brody's shoulder. Brody's parents went in first while they all waited. They didn't want to crowd the room too much. After a while, they got to go in. Riley, who looked gorgeous as usual but tired, smiled as they walked in.

"Come see our baby," she said. Ethan took him from her and deposited him in Brody's surprised arms.

"Eight pounds, two ounces," Ethan said with a smile.

"Wow," Tori said, looking at his red, scrunched-up face. She smiled over at Riley and Ethan. "He's gorgeous."

"Daddy says he looks a lot like I did when I was born," Zoey said.

"He does, doesn't he?" Brody said, and Tori was awed at the shine of unshed tears in Brody's eyes.

"Do you want to hold him?" Brody asked.

"I'd love to." She washed her hands and held out her arms, a feeling of instant love and protectiveness washing over her as soon as Gideon was placed in her arms.

She took a seat in one of the vacant chairs and made room

for Zoey, who couldn't seem to get enough of her new baby brother. But after such an exciting day, it was obvious she was wearing down, and she soon fell asleep on Tori's shoulder.

This was what she wanted, Tori thought. This life, with children in her arms. She shifted her gaze to Brody and found him watching her, an expression on his face she couldn't fathom. She didn't know if it was discomfort, the same kind of wonder she felt tonight, or something else entirely.

But she'd never seen that look on his face before, and she didn't know what to make of it.

She wasn't even going to try and figure it out, because today wasn't about her and Brody's relationship. Today had been about small miracles.

BRODY WATCHED THE wonder on Tori's face as she held baby Gideon in her arms, the way she cradled him close as if she was born to hold a child.

He'd always pushed the idea of marriage and children to the back of his mind, figuring that would come later in life, when he was ready for it. Though he didn't really know when that "ready" time would be.

Maybe when he found the right woman.

But as he stole glances at Tori, as she carefully stood and handed Gideon off to Riley, almost with a sense of regret at letting go of the baby, he realized that it was time to start thinking about those things.

Holding the baby had seemed natural to him. He knew that feeling of not wanting to let him go.

It was time to start reevaluating what was important to him, and what he wanted.

And when.

But on his terms, and Tori's terms.

Not his family's.

TWELVE

STAYING MORE OFTEN at Brody's house had definite advantages, the biggest one being the Christmas party. Now that she was intimately familiar with his house, she knew exactly where everything—and everyone—would fit.

Plus, her clothes were already here for the party tonight. She had taken the day off work so she could meet the caterers and the party planner who was helping her put this event together.

She was trying not to stress. Sex with Brody in the shower this morning had certainly helped. He'd called it medicinal, and for stress release. She'd called it rockin' hot, but she was a lot calmer now.

Calliope had already called her three times and texted her twice asking if there was anything she could do to help. She'd offered to take the day off, too, but Tori had refused. She had a handle on this.

When the doorbell rang at noon, she was in a panic. The caterers weren't due for hours and the party planner wasn't coming until two, so she was shocked to see Brody's mom at the door.

"Hi, Stacy. I didn't expect you to show up until the party tonight."

Stacy waved her hand. "Oh, please. Did you think I'd let you handle all this by yourself?"

Tori laughed and made room for Stacy to come in. "It's no problem. It is my job, after all."

"Maybe, but that doesn't mean you couldn't use some help."

Grateful for the assistance, they talked about table placement and food and drink as well as door prizes and who had RSVP'd. Stacy helped her wrap some gifts and put the finishing touches on the enormous Christmas tree she'd coerced Brody into buying.

"I brought over some of Brody's childhood ornaments," Stacy said, bringing out a box. "I thought those would make a nice touch."

"Oh, that's so sweet. Thank you. I know those will mean a lot to him, this being the first tree he's put up in here."

Stacy shook her head. "You'd think with this being the perfect spot for one, he'd have put one up before now."

"That's what I told him." She hung the ornaments, loving the Baby's First Christmas and the sports-related ones, especially the one with the gap-toothed photo of an eight-year-old Brody in his baseball uniform.

"It's going to be a great party tonight," Stacy told her after they'd finalized everything. "You've done a remarkable job."

"Thanks. I hope so. I'm so nervous, since this was my idea. If it bombs, the buck stops here."

"It's not going to bomb. Everyone's going to have a great time."

She hoped so. They'd never let her plan another Christmas party again if this one failed.

Stacy stayed until the setup crew arrived and put all the tables and decorations in order. Tori grabbed a jacket and went outside to supervise the placement of the heaters and fire pit. As she scanned the sky, she noted the gray clouds overhead.

As cold as it was getting, it could possibly snow. She hoped it would hold out until after the party. She'd really love people to be able to use the heaters and pit out here. They'd brought in some lovely, comfortable furniture and it was going to be toasty warm for folks who wanted to step out for some fresh air tonight.

Stacy left after everything was set up, saying she'd be back before the guests arrived. Once everything was in place, Tori dashed off and showered, did her hair and makeup and threw on a robe. She'd put on her dress right before the caterers came. The caterers were going to bring the food and set up the bar an hour before the guests were due to arrive, so she had the timing all planned out.

Brody came home early to help—she was so grateful for that. She directed him to the shower first.

She was in the bedroom ready to put on her dress when he came out of the bathroom smelling fresh and clean, a towel slung over his hips.

She took one look and pure lust took over.

"If I hadn't already done my hair and makeup, you'd be in trouble right now."

He gave her a look that made her swell with arousal. "You'd better get that dress on, or your hair is gonna get mussed up and then you'll be mad at me."

She grabbed her dress and shoes and dashed into the spare bedroom to dress. Much as she'd like to spend the next hour naked and in his arms, that would spell disaster. The last thing she'd need was to be lying in bed with Brody and have the caterers ring the doorbell.

But it was something fun to think about as she climbed into her dress.

She couldn't do the back zipper, so she slid into her heels and went back into the bedroom. She stalled at the doorway. Brody was slipping into his jacket.

He very rarely wore a suit, typically reserved only for important business meetings and the company Christmas party.

Usually he was a jeans and T-shirt or Henley kind of guy, or shorts in the summer.

Lord, the man cleaned up well. Though honestly whether he was naked, dressed up, or anything in between, she loved him. It didn't matter what he wore—or didn't wear.

"You look amazing," she said. "And I need help with this zipper."

He turned with a smile, but his smile disappeared when he saw her.

He came toward her and she turned her back to him, shocked when she felt his lips against the side of her neck.

"You are the most beautiful woman I've ever laid eyes on. How did I ever get so lucky?"

She shuddered, then his fingers brushed her bare back as he pulled the zipper up.

"Later, I'll be dragging this zipper down when I get you out of this dress."

Her body in flames, she turned to face him, laid her palms on his chest. "I'll be thinking about that all night."

"You know, I could make love to you without messing up your hair."

He leaned in and her heart stuttered, every female hormone in her body gravitating toward him. "Is that right?"

The doorbell rang.

"Dammit."

She laughed and gave him a quick kiss. "Something to think about all night."

She dashed around him and went to the door, grateful the caterers were on time, even if they did put a crimp in her love life.

Brody's gaze tracked Tori like a hungry animal. He couldn't help himself. One look at her in that shiny black dress that hugged her body, and he was a goner. She'd left her hair down tonight, the waves spilling over her bare shoulders like a shiny red waterfall. He wanted to be close to her, to inhale the scent of that shampoo she used that smelled like strawberries, to lick that spot on her neck that never failed to raise goosebumps on her skin. He wanted to hold her in his arms and never let her go.

He couldn't wait to get her alone. And out of that damn dress that had been haunting him since he'd first seen it.

Mainly, he just wanted to touch her, to have a minute alone with her. But since the caterers arrived, it hadn't happened. Because then his mom and dad showed up, then Wyatt and Calliope, then Ethan, minus Riley, of course, who was home with the kids. After that, people started spilling in and he had to play host. So did Tori, who smiled and greeted people and showed them where the food and bar was.

She'd spent the past several hours flitting around like a hummingbird, and his house was packed with people he had to talk to, be nice to, visit with and welcome into his home.

Bleh. He knew it was a part of business, that he and his brothers put on this party every year not only for business partners and customers, but for the community. It fostered goodwill and brought in even more business. It was a necessity. Usually he enjoyed the Christmas party.

But tonight, he had more important things on his mind—his woman. He wanted alone time with her, to touch her, taste her, and eventually have a very important conversation with her.

"Brody. I hear you're going to be spearheading the building of the new supermarket."

The mayor. Time to put his work face on. He shook Stanley Shims's hand. "Mayor Shims. Yes, I am. We're very excited about this project."

"So are the citizens of Deer Lake. We'll be watching its progress closely. When do you think you'll break ground?"

He spent several minutes tied up with the mayor discussing the supermarket project. Members of the city council stuck their noses in, too, so he was cornered, and lost sight of Tori. When he finally extricated himself, he went to the bar to grab a much-needed beer. Wyatt met him there.

"Having fun?"

Brody rolled his eyes at his brother. "Tons. You?"

"About as much as we can given the circumstances. But it's a good turnout."

"Yeah. Whiskey?"

"Hell yes."

Brody ordered two shots of whiskey. "To another good year."

"I'll definitely drink to that."

"Hang on." Ethan showed up, ordered another shot. "You can't toast without me."

"In that case, to another good year, and another Kent in the family."

Ethan grinned, and they drank, then laid their glasses down on the bar. Brody followed up his shot with a long swallow of beer, turning to face the crowd. "We're very lucky."

"We are," Ethan said. "Business has been steadily picking up the past two years. We're adding people. Wyatt and I have gotten married and I just had a baby."

Wyatt turned to Brody. "Now it's your turn. So when are you going to ask Tori to marry you?"

Brody frowned. "I don't want to talk about Tori."

"Why?" Ethan asked. "You two have a fight?"

"No." He finished his beer, pushed the empty bottle toward the bartender, then grabbed a fresh one. "What's between us is our business. Not family business."

Ethan arched a brow. "Ooh. Touchy."

Wyatt leaned against the bar. "Agreed. Why is that, Brody?

You know we only want the best for you. And for Tori. So why do you act like such a dick whenever we bring up her name?"

"I'm gonna go mingle." Brody wandered off and visited with some of his clients, trying to put the conversation with his brothers out of his head. He found his parents sitting in the living room.

"Are you having a good time?" he asked.

His dad grinned. "I'm so proud of what you and your brothers have done with the company, Brody. You've really built the business well. I couldn't have left it in better hands."

"Thanks, Dad."

"Where's Tori?" his mom asked.

"I have no idea. Doing her job and making sure our clients are happy, I would imagine."

"How are things going with you two?"

His jaw tightened. "Fine."

His mom smiled. "Will we be hearing wedding bells in the future? Maybe an engagement at Christmas?"

What. The. Hell. What was it with his family trying to push him into something he wasn't ready for? Or maybe he was ready for it, but why couldn't he do it himself and not feel like his entire family was behind him, prodding him.

It was pissing him the fuck off. "I see someone I need to talk to, Mom. Excuse me."

He wandered off, beer in hand, heading outside for some fresh air. Maybe there was someone out there who didn't know he was dating Tori and wouldn't give him the third degree about his intentions.

He found Lee Alison and Tim Dyson, two building contractors they often worked with.

"Great party, Brody."

"Thanks." It was cold outside, but Tori had been right.

The heaters made it comfortable enough to sit outside and enjoy the night. He took a seat next to the guys and finished off his beer. He visited with Lee and Tim, talked shop for a while.

"I hear you've been dating that hot little number in your office," Lee said.

"Tori, I think her name is," Tim said. "Is she off the market now? Heard you two have been exclusive for a while."

So far tonight he was getting engaged, picking out rings and proposing. He was so tired of having his goddamned life with Tori planned out for him. Why couldn't he do this at his own pace? Why couldn't his relationship with Tori be what he wanted it to be?

He wanted everyone off his back about it. "We've gone out. It's no big deal or anything."

"So, your reputation is still intact, huh?" Tim asked with a laugh. "I'd hate to see the notorious Brody Kent off the market. I mean I've been married for twelve years now. Who will I live vicariously through if you're not with a different girl every week?"

Brody laughed and slapped Tim on the back. "No problem there, Tim. I'm still a free agent."

"So your fling with Tori is nothing special?"

He looked over at Lee, wanting to tell him exactly how he felt about Tori, how special she really was to him. But at the same time he was so damn tired of everybody knowing his personal business, and the corresponding advice he'd get about love and marriage, the only reply that spilled from his lips was, "Yup. Nothing special."

TORI STOPPED AT the doorway, her forward motion halted at Brody's words.

She was nothing special to him. He was still a "free agent."

All this time she'd thought they'd been headed toward something. She didn't know what, and frankly hadn't cared, because they'd had a connection. She knew what it was—or she thought she knew. He had made her feel special, like she was the only one in his life, that this time it was different, that his playboy days were over.

God, she was so stupid. He'd played her, and she'd fallen for it.

Maybe all this time he'd been seeing other women, and she'd been so myopic about seeing only him, falling for only him, she hadn't even noticed.

She turned around and headed inside, her face flaming. She headed straight for the master bedroom, one of the rooms off limits to the guests tonight. She went into the bathroom and locked the door, staring at her flushed face in the mirror.

"Idiot," she said to her reflection, forcing the anger instead of the heartbreak.

She'd known who he was all along, yet she fell for it—for him—anyway.

His conversation with Lee and Tim outside still hurt, the raw pain tearing through her almost unbearable. She wanted to grab her keys, get into her car and go back to her apartment so she could crawl into her bed and cry until there were no tears left.

But she couldn't—wouldn't do that. Because she refused to lose her job over that asshole. She took pride in the work she did, and she'd fight him to the death over keeping her job.

She paced back and forth, taking deep breaths until she'd calmed herself enough to walk out of the bathroom. Then she grabbed a bag and packed up all her things, sliding the bag into the closet before heading back out to the party.

Thankfully things had started to wind down, because if

she had four hours of this to put up with she didn't think she could take it.

Avoiding Brody would be easy. She'd wanted to be with him tonight, but she'd been so busy—and so had he. Now she was grateful for it.

"Hey, honey. Roger is tiring, so we're heading out."

At the tap on her shoulder from Stacy, she squeezed her eyes shut, mentally preparing herself. She put on a smile and turned around. "I hope you had a good time, Stacy."

"We had a great time, and everyone I spoke to tonight loved the fact the party was held here. It was so much fun, and the dance floor you had put over the floor in the dining room was perfect."

"I'm so glad."

"It was a good idea, kiddo," Roger said, pulling her in for a hug. "I always knew you had smarts."

She hugged him and Stacy and saw them to the door, then said goodbye to several other guests who were making their way out. She saw Brody try to ease his way to her, but she ducked out through the kitchen and went out back to pick up a few discarded bottles, then headed around the side toward the garage, adeptly avoiding him.

By the time the party closed down, it was just Brody and her and Wyatt and Calliope. Ethan had left early to be with Riley, Zoey and the baby. The crew came in to remove the tables and all the equipment, and they helped the caterers remove the rest of the food.

Calliope turned to her at the door when she and Wyatt walked out. "Call me tomorrow?"

She nodded. "You bet. You all be careful going home."

"I'll walk them out and I'll be right back," Brody said.

She nodded, but as soon as he headed out the front door, she hurried into the bedroom, grabbed her bag and her keys and threw her bag in the car. She was standing in the kitchen, keys in hand, when he came back.

He frowned. "Going somewhere?"

"Home."

"Why?"

"Because I'm nothing to you."

"What? That's not true."

"It is. I heard you say it tonight."

"Wait. Tonight? What are you talking about?"

"I walked outside when you were talking to Lee and Tim, assuring them that manwhore Brody Kent was still alive and well, that I was nothing special to you and they had nothing to worry about. You were still a free agent."

He had the decency to look away. "Oh. That. Let me explain, Tori."

"No, thanks, Brody. I fell for your lines once. I won't fall again." She turned and went into the garage, the gust of cold wind making her shiver. She needed it, needed that reality to slap her across the face.

Because she'd been living in a fantasy for far too long.

Brody followed her to her car. "Tori, if you'll just let me explain…"

She slid into the car and started it up, closed the door and locked it, not even bothering to look at him as she backed the car out of the garage, down the driveway and headed out onto the street.

He could explain all he wanted, but there would never be anything he could say again that she'd ever believe.

Her phone vibrated in the seat next to her. She didn't bother to look or to answer. It was Brody, no doubt ready with a pack of lies that she'd never believe again.

As she headed toward home, the first snowflakes started to fall.

And so did the tears sliding down her cheeks.

Hopefully she'd make it all the way home before she completely fell apart.

BRODY LISTENED AS the tenth call he'd made to Tori went to voice mail.

He got in his truck and, despite the snow coming down harder, drove to her apartment.

He breathed out a sigh of relief to see her car parked in the lot. He went up and knocked on her door, not surprised when she didn't answer. He knocked again, harder this time. And again, when she didn't answer.

"Tori. Open the door. I know you're in there."

She didn't. He leaned against the wall, still in his suit, and watched the snow come down. It was getting colder and he hadn't grabbed a coat, hadn't thought about anything other than getting to Tori so he could explain what he'd said.

Not that there was a reasonable explanation.

He'd been a total dick, so tired of people pushing him toward something he wanted anyway.

What the hell was wrong with him?

He turned and banged on the door. "Tori. Please let me explain."

But he already knew she wasn't ready to listen. If it were him, he wouldn't listen either.

He pulled his suit coat around him and walked down the stairs, the snow coming down so heavy he was soaked by the time he got into the truck.

He climbed in, shut the door and turned on the ignition, firing up the heater. He looked up at her apartment window, waiting for her to turn on the light.

No light came on.

He finally put the truck into gear and pulled out.

THIRTEEN

"WHAT THE HELL did you do to Tori?"

Brody ignored Wyatt's question as they drove together to inspect a jobsite.

"I'm asking you a question."

"And I'm not answering it."

"It's been two weeks since the Christmas party, and it's like someone died, Brody. She won't talk to us."

"Maybe it's you who pissed her off."

Wyatt gave him a look. "I don't fucking think so. It's like she's broken, man. You can see it on her face. It's not even anger. It's...sadness. Christ, what happened between the two of you?"

Brody pulled into the parking lot of the site and turned off the ignition. "You want to know what happened? Everybody happened. You. Ethan. Mom and Dad. Hell, even other contractors. Everybody got into my business about Tori. When are you going to get engaged? When are you going to marry her? What's going on with your relationship? What's the next step? Fuck. How was I supposed to react to that?"

Wyatt arched a brow. "What did you do?"

He shrugged. "I told Lee and Tim that Tori didn't mean anything to me, that I was still the carefree bachelor that I always was, notching my bedpost with the latest conquest. Tori overheard me say that."

Wyatt slouched in the seat. "Shit. You really fucked that one up. What were you thinking?"

"I was thinking I wanted people to leave me alone about Tori so I could make my own decisions on my own time."

"So you were afraid to pull the trigger."

Now it was Brody's turn to frown. "What?"

"You got cold feet. You couldn't admit to anyone you were in love with her, which you obviously are because you're just as miserable and unpleasant to be around as she is. So instead of coming clean and telling the world how you felt about her, you pretended not to care."

"That's bullshit."

"It's not bullshit. It's exactly what you did when you told Lee and Tim you were still cock of the block."

"Well I didn't goddamn know how to handle it." He punched the steering wheel with the palm of his hand.

Wyatt laughed. "No shit. The big question now is, what are you going to do to fix things?"

Brody stared out the windshield of the truck. "I don't know. She won't talk to me at work and she won't answer my calls. I go to her apartment and she won't answer the door."

"You already know she's one stubborn woman. I guess you'll have to keep trying. If you think she's worth it. Do you think she's worth it?"

"Hell yes I do. I'm in love with her."

"Now, was that so hard to admit?"

Brody glared at his brother. "You're an asshole, Wyatt."

"Yeah, I know," Wyatt said with a grin. "Now let's go to work."

NO AMOUNT OF cajoling from Calliope or Riley or even Brody's parents was going to force Tori to talk to Brody.

It was over, and as soon as everyone adjusted to that, things could go back to the way they used to be. Eventually—maybe—she and Brody could get back to that place where they could work together.

Or she'd just find another job. She'd hate it, but she'd do it if she had to.

The past two weeks had been awful. Seeing him at work every day had been the most painful. She thought it would be better after work and on the weekends, but it wasn't. She missed him, missed being with him, missed being able to talk to him about anything and everything. She missed touching him and kissing him and sleeping with him.

She was so tired of crying, and so tired of hating that he hadn't been the man she thought he'd been.

He'd tried to talk to her. He'd pulled up his chair next to her desk several times and had tried to launch into an explanation. Each time, she'd gotten up and left the office. She'd told Wyatt and Ethan to have Brody leave her alone or she'd keep leaving. And if that kept happening, the work they needed her to accomplish wouldn't get done.

Eventually, he stopped trying to talk to her at work. But he called her, texted her and came by her apartment. She told him to stop coming by or she'd call the police and tell them he was harassing her.

It hurt her to tell him that when all she really wanted was to let him in, to throw her arms around him and have him be the man she wanted him to be.

But no amount of explanation would change a person who couldn't be changed.

Brody was who he always had been, and she'd been stupid to think otherwise.

She'd never be stupid again.

Shuddering out a sigh, she blinked and tried to concentrate on the spreadsheet in front of her. It was two days before Christmas and she had to finish this report before the holiday break. It was quiet in the office—for a change. The guys were all out on jobs, so at least today she'd have some peace and quiet to get caught up.

She heard the sirens outside and her head shot up. A lot of sirens. First from a distance, then growing closer. She hoped nothing was on fire. There was nothing worse than a fire right before Christmas.

The sirens were getting closer. And closer. But it wasn't fast-moving like they were rushing to a location. It was slow. And growing ever louder, heading in the direction of the office. And she heard a voice, like on a loudspeaker.

What the hell was going on out there?

Grabbing her coat, she put it on and headed out the front door, her eyes widening as she saw the sheriff's car, the two town fire engines and a parade of people marching behind them.

And Brody's voice on the sheriff's loudspeaker.

"Tori Lewis. Please come outside and hear me out."

Oh. My. God. What was he doing?

She shook her head and started to back away.

"Can't run this time, honey. Might as well hear him out and get this over with."

It was Wyatt. He'd come around from the back.

"I don't want to hear him."

Wyatt laughed. "I don't think you have much choice, considering the commotion he's causing."

She watched as the parade of sheriff's cars and fire engines, horns blowing and sirens blaring, stopped in front of the gate to the construction offices. Brody got out and climbed on the roof of the sheriff's car.

"Is he insane?" she asked.

"Probably," Ethan said, coming around the other side of

her. He laid his hand on the small of her back and propelled her forward. "Go on and hear him out, Tori."

She took a tentative step forward.

Brody wasn't smiling. He stood there looking as gorgeous as ever, the biting wind blowing his dark hair, his boots firmly planted on the sheriff's roof as he held the mic in his hand.

"Tori. I hurt you because I was afraid to tell you—hell, to admit to anyone and everyone how I felt about you. So instead, I downplayed it. I told people that you meant nothing to me, when in fact, you mean everything to me and you always have.

"From the first moment you stepped foot in our offices, you caught my eye. We sparred and traded barbs and it was fun, but I wasn't ready yet.

"But then at the Christmas party last year we kissed—"

The crowd went aww and Tori heated as she blushed.

"And it all came so fast for me I didn't know what to do about it, or how I felt about this feisty redhead who called me on all my—bs."

The crowd laughed.

"I've always shied away from commitment. Everyone in this town knows my reputation. I liked my freedom and I figured someday I'd settle down, but I never knew when that would be. I always figured when the right woman came along.

"Well, the right woman came along, only I didn't know it, until you came into my life. That was you, and I knew it for certain that night a year ago at the Christmas party. There's been no one but you since that night, and there will never be anyone but you."

Tori's heart squeezed, and the dark part of her that had given up hope began to let a tiny sliver of light shine in.

He met her gaze straight on, and she saw the truth in his eyes.

"Tori, you've always been the best part of me, and the best thing that's ever happened to me. You asked me once who I confided in when I needed someone to talk to about the bad things. I realized that person has always been you. Those months when you weren't talking to me were pure hell, because I realize you've always been my confidant, the one I go to when I have a bad day.

"You soothe me, make me feel better. You're my best friend, my lover, and the woman I want in my life, always and forever.

"I love you, Tori."

She gasped out a sob and ran to him. He hopped off the car and grabbed her in his arms, his mouth coming down on hers in a searing kiss that told her so much more than words ever could, because she tasted his tears in that kiss, too.

"I love you, Brody," she said. "I love you."

"Forgive me," he said, his words barely audible amidst the horns hooking and the sirens and the clapping of the crowd.

She laughed at the sounds. "You're forgiven."

He turned to the crowd and grinned. "Go away. I need some privacy with my woman."

They all cheered again, then Brody embraced Tori in his arms and sealed the deal with one hell of a public display of affection.

FOURTEEN

At Brody's insistence, Tori moved out of her horrible apartment and into his house the day after his very public announcement of his love for her, something she would likely remember until her dying day.

They spent Christmas at his family's house, something she'd missed last year. This year, she wasn't alone. She had his family—her family—at her side. And she had Brody. She was Brody's girlfriend, and as the gifts were handed out, the very last gift was Brody, on bended knee, very publicly in front of his entire family proposing marriage to her.

She hadn't expected it. Brody did things on his own terms, and on his own timeline. He'd explained to her his issues with his family pushing and prodding him about his relationship with her, which had caused him to act like a dumbass. She'd understood his issues, and she'd forgiven him—again.

She'd expected they'd live together for a while. Possibly a long while, knowing Brody's issues with commitment. And God, she'd have been so content to do just that, to just be with him.

So his proposal had been very unexpected, causing tears to flow down her cheeks. But she'd very enthusiastically nodded and accepted on the spot, because she loved him with all her heart, and not once would she ever doubt his love and commitment to her.

Because he was the best thing in her life, and always would be.

"Surprised?" he asked her sometime later Christmas night

after all the gifts had been opened and all the food had been consumed. They sat in his parents' kitchen, having a quiet moment of alone time together after a day of madness and family.

She laced her fingers with his. "Understatement. I didn't think you were ready for this."

"For what? This?" he asked, tracing her ring. "I'm more than ready for it. I've been ready for it. It took almost losing you to realize it." He pulled her off the kitchen bar stool and onto his lap.

"I don't want to be without you anymore, Tori. You belong with me. In my house—in our house—our lives entwined, forever. I've wasted enough time not making the commitment I should have made to you a long time ago."

Her heart squeezed, so filled with love for him. "This doesn't seem real."

He brushed his lips across hers. "It's real. For both of us."

She kissed him back. "I'm sorry I wasted so much time with my insecurities. A whole year."

"So it's your fault."

She laughed and pressed into him. "I needed you to really want me."

"Babe. I've really wanted you for a long time."

"But you weren't ready until now."

"You might be right about that. I think the timing was perfect. You needed to get past your trust issues, and I needed to grow up a bit. Now, we're right where we need to be."

She batted back the tears that overwhelming happiness brought. He swiped one away that drifted down her cheek.

"Happy ones, I hope?"

She smiled and nodded. "The happiest ones."

"You're not going to go all sweet and nice on me now,

are you? My brothers will kill me if you undergo some personality change. They won't know how to deal with you."

She laughed. "No fear of that. I'm still the same old me, Brody. Bossy, opinionated, and sometimes downright mean, especially at the office, where I'll run roughshod on you three like I always have."

"Good, because that's the you I fell in love with." He stood, placed her on her feet and kissed her soundly. "Let's go watch Christmas movies with our family."

Our family. She had a true family now. Beginning with this man she loved. And it would only grow from there.

The best was yet to come.

★ ★ ★ ★ ★

Made in the USA
Middletown, DE
21 November 2014